A TELEGRAM FROM LE TOUQUET

A TELEGRAM FROM LE TOUQUET

JOHN BUDE

With an Introduction by
Martin Edwards

Published by Poisoned Pen Press, an imprint of Sourcebooks,
in association with the British Library
P.O. Box 4410, Naperville, Illinois 60567-4410
(630) 961-3900
sourcebooks.com

A Telegram from Le Touquet was first published in
1956 by MacDonald & Co., London.

Cataloging-in-Publication Data is on file with the Library of Congress.

Printed and bound in the United States of America.
VP 10 9 8 7 6 5 4 3 2 1

To my good friend and neighbour
Philip Lindsay

CONTENTS

INTRODUCTION

John Bude was at the height of his career when, in 1956, he published *A Telegram from Le Touquet*. He was an experienced full-time writer who had focused increasingly on the crime genre and become a leading light in the recently established Crime Writers' Association. His regular series character was Superintendent (formerly Inspector) Meredith, but in this novel, he tried something different. The structure of the story is unorthodox, and although there is a cameo appearance for Meredith towards the end of the book, centre stage is taken by Inspector Blampignon of the *Sûreté Nationale*, who had previously appeared in *Death on the Riviera*, also published in the Crime Classics series.

The story is divided into two distinct parts. The first, "Prelude to Violence," is narrated by young Nigel Derry and sets the scene. He arrives to spend Easter at Cockfosters, the country house owned by his charming, attractive, and wealthy godmother Gwenny Marrable. Unfortunately, Gwenny is also impulsive, amoral, and unpredictable. She is the guardian of

Sheila, whom Nigel wants to marry, and at first the young couple are optimistic that Gwenny will give them her blessing. Before long, however, their hopes are dashed. Gwenny objects to the relationship, for reasons that seem inexplicable, and makes it clear that she is determined to put an end to it.

Among those staying at Cockfosters are Gwenny's sister Deborah and two mysterious individuals, George Gammon and Harry Skeet. Tensions mount, and when a man called André Duconte arrives, Harry immediately lunges at him and is attacked with a knife. He isn't seriously hurt, but as the house party disintegrates, Nigel is baffled by this latest turn of events, as well as by Gwenny's enigmatic behaviour, which seems to be alienating one person after another.

At this point, there is an abrupt break as Nigel's narrative ends and is followed by the second—and much longer—part of the story, "Post Mortem at the Villa," which is set in France and told in the third person. A body is discovered and Nigel, who has so far appeared to be a sympathetic character, is among the suspects. He was, he claimed, summoned to the Villa Paradou by a telegram that Gwenny sent from Le Touquet. Is he lying? And if he is telling the truth, who has tried to frame him, and why?

Blampignon is called in to investigate. He is introduced as "the most experienced and successful detective along the Côte d'Azur. He was a personality in the police world... Hardly a month went by without his name cropping up in the papers." At the outset he opines that: "In nine cases out of ten, the solution to the problem posed by a murder case is to be found in the character of the victim." This theory is ultimately vindicated when he uncovers the truth.

As Blampignon soon discovers, the case is "fantastic... At 11.45 a.m. on Friday, April 22nd, a woman drives out of the Customs sheds at Boulogne Maritime. Four days later...the dead body of this woman is discovered in a trunk some eight hundred miles away...not a word of her, not a sign. It was as if the car had sprouted wings... But wait!—that wasn't exactly true. Somebody had seen her after she left Boulogne. What about the assistant in the post-office at Le Touquet who had handled her telegram... But why Le Touquet? Why did she take the coast road to Abbeville, when the fastest and most direct route would have been through Montreuil?"

The plot is intricate, but after an investigation that Nigel Derry describes as "tireless and brilliant," Blampignon finally makes sense of everything that has happened, while emphasising in the closing words that the vital lead was indeed the "telegram from Le Touquet."

Bude's experiment in storytelling earned the approbation of that famously acerbic critic Julian Symons. Reviewing the novel for the *Manchester Evening News*, he described it as "a racy drama" and commended the author: "what a finely drawn character he has in the prodding, probing, portly Inspector Blampignon...one of the many characterisations which make this book a delight to read." Anthony Shaffer, however, reviewing the book for the *London Mystery Magazine*, felt that Bude was rather cynical when it came to playing entirely fair with his readers.

Before the war, Bude had employed a variety of English locations (Cornwall, the Lakes, the Sussex Downs, Cheltenham, and so on) for his fiction and in the post-war years of austerity, he sought to offer his readers a little escapist glamour by utilising settings on the Continent, starting with the 1949 novella "Murder in Montparnasse." Blampignon was a manifestation of this increasingly cosmopolitan approach. He was also the latest in a line of interesting French detectives created by British writers. Jules Poiret and Hercules Popeau, created by Frank Howel Evans and Marie Belloc Lowndes respectively, might be seen as precursors to a rather better-known Belgian detective, but the pre-eminent character in this vein was Inspector Gabriel Hanaud, who was introduced by A. E. W. Mason in *At the Villa Rose* in 1910 and reappeared intermittently over the next three and a half decades.

Sadly, John Bude died shortly after celebrating his 57th birthday, just a couple of years (and three books) after publishing this novel. His real name was Ernest Carpenter Elmore, and he adopted the Bude name when he turned to detective fiction with *The Cornish Coast Murder*, which was swiftly followed by *The Lake District Murder*. Both books first appeared in 1935, but then faded into obscurity for about three-quarters of a century. Indeed, Bude himself was largely forgotten.

Those two mysteries were the first which I was asked to introduce for the British Library Crime Classics, ten years ago. At that time, the series was in its infancy (the first titles from the twentieth century were three books written by Mavis Doriel Hay) and Rob Davies of the British Library had the inspired idea of using vintage railway poster artwork for the paperback covers. The pleasing appearance and high production values of the books soon attracted bookshops and book-buyers, and since then the Crime Classics have gone from strength to strength. Several further Bude novels have featured in the series, and readers have continued to ask me when the next mystery from this prolific entertainer is likely to hit the shelves. I'm optimistic that they will enjoy *A Telegram from Le Touquet*.

Martin Edwards
www.martinedwardsbooks.com

was originally published with two edits to the text and with minor edits made for consistency of style and sense. We welcome feedback from our readers.

PART I

PRELUDE TO VIOLENCE

I

As I swung the car off the London–Canterbury road into the sunken lane that led to Wendhurst my thoughts turned naturally to Aunt Gwenny. She wasn't really my aunt but my godmother and an old friend of my mother, and although I still thought of her as Aunt Gwenny—a hangover, I suppose, from my boyhood—I'd long ago given up calling her "Aunty." It was six months or more since I'd last stayed at Cockfosters. That had been in the first fortnight of September. Now it was early April, a few days before Easter.

The weather, after a long and bitter winter, had suddenly turned springlike. The air was soft and warm. There were lambs frisking in the orchards and the white cowls of the oasts looked dazzling in the clear sunshine. Even above the noise of the car I could hear the full-throated singing of the birds.

I recalled my last sight of Aunt Gwenny, standing, one golden September afternoon, on the broad steps of the old ragstone house, her warm contralto voice calling after me as I slipped the car into gear:

"You know the arrangement, Nig. Come when you like and stay as long as you can. I shan't trouble to invite you. Just give me a ring."

Speaking of her as Aunt Gwenny it's easy to give the wrong impression. The name conjures up, perhaps, a dowdy, passé creature with impossible clothes and a Victorian sense of morality. Nothing could be further from the truth.

I like Gwenny and I've no wish to malign her, but there's no doubt that she was a nympho, a man-eater. She was somewhere in her middle forties, good-looking, and always beautifully turned out. Her figure was superb. A little opulent, perhaps, but none the less striking on that account. She was impulsive, amoral, and utterly unpredictable. With Gwenny around, life was never dull. Men were her hobby. She collected them as other women might collect rare china or Jacobean furniture. Ever since old Humphrey Marrable had collapsed on the steps of the Parthenon Club and died of heart failure, leaving her a fortune, Gwenny had been passionately involved with one man after another. These affairs never lasted long, because in the end she always suspected that her paramours were less interested in her than in her money. Having met several of the plausible types to whom she seemed fatally attracted, I think her judgment was probably sound.

Last September there'd been a fellow called George Gammon staying at Cockfosters. I wondered if he were still there. And Harry Skeet? I'd never quite got to the bottom of the relationship between Harry and Gwenny. He'd been *persona grata* at the house for as long as I could remember. That in itself set him apart from the others. Why he'd lasted so long I can't say, because Gwenny didn't really seem to like him. He was a painter, living in a converted windmill down in the village. A shrewd cynical sort of chap, but good company if you didn't have too much of him.

I'd had several letters from Sheila addressed to me at Bellwood Preparatory School near Farnham, where I'd recently taken up a post as junior English master. She hadn't mentioned either Gammon or Skeet, but that didn't mean a thing. At the moment there were only three people in whom she was really interested—herself, myself, and Aunt Gwenny. We were, in fact, caught up in a situation, or, better still, a tug-of-war—with Aunt Gwenny at one end of the rope, Sheila and I at the other.

Sheila lived at Cockfosters because Gwenny was her guardian. When she was only two Sheila's parents had been killed in a car crash near Johannesburg, where her father, John Tallent, was a mining engineer. Mrs. Tallent and Gwenny were second cousins or something of the kind, and evidently there'd always been a tacit understanding between them that if Sheila were ever left an orphan Gwenny would look after her. So after the accident the Tallents' nurse brought Sheila over to England, left her at Cockfosters, and a year later Gwenny legally adopted her.

I'd been seeing Sheila on and off for years. First a mere kid, then a schoolgirl, now a young woman of nineteen with whom I'd recently and violently fallen in love. Luckily, too, because Sheila confessed that she'd felt the same way about me for the last eighteen months and was surprised that I hadn't noticed it. Gwenny had. There was no doubt about that. She missed nothing and said nothing. Even when we started pairing up for the local dances, driving over to the cinema in Canterbury, taking long walks together, she still kept silent. But something warned me that she was rattled. Outwardly she was still the same difficult, demanding, good-natured Gwenny, but I sensed that if it came to a showdown, if I told her I wanted to marry Sheila, I'd be running my head against a brick wall.

In her last few letters Sheila had been urging me to tackle Gwenny when I came down at Easter. She felt we couldn't just drift on as we were. I was twenty-six and she wasn't a kid any longer. I was in a safe job even if it wasn't too well paid. Gwenny had known me for years and obviously approved of me. She couldn't possibly put up any objection to our engagement. Sheila's optimism was encouraging.

But as I cleared the last cottages in the village and caught my first glimpse of the roofs and chimneys of Cockfosters above the trees of the park, I had a sudden premonition that I was heading for trouble. I felt uneasy and apprehensive. Even the thought that in a few minutes I should be seeing Sheila didn't really counterbalance this curious mood of depression.

II

Cockfosters stands on a knoll in the middle of a thirty-acre park. It is approached by a drive up a magnificent lime avenue. It's an ugly, rather forbidding house, with its grey ragstone walls and Cornish slate roofs. Clematis and climbing roses do something to relieve its severity, but taken out of its setting it might easily have been mistaken for a barracks. True, the front of the house faces north, and its south aspect is markedly more congenial. But its general atmosphere is rather stark.

As I dropped into bottom gear and urged my ancient car up the last steep rise, a figure appeared on the curving steps that led up to the front-door. It was Sheila.

A moment or so later, taking me by surprise, her arms were round my neck and she was kissing me with an abandonment that was more flattering than discreet.

"I say, isn't this a bit risky? After all, if Gwenny happened to—"

Sheila said mockingly: "Still terrified of upsetting her wretched susceptibilities. Well, you needn't worry, darling. They're all out on the loggia having tea. I've been watching from the window of the music room."

At that I relaxed and kissed Sheila in turn. We were bubbling over with delight and excitement. After all, apart from a brief meeting or two in London during the Christmas holidays, we hadn't really seen each other for six months.

I got my suitcase out of the boot, linked my arm through Sheila's, and went into the cool and shadowy interior of the house. She said: "You're in the chintz room. If you like to take your case up and have a wash, I'll let Aunty know you've arrived."

At the foot of the curving staircase, I asked: "By the way, who's here?"

Sheila pulled a derogatory grimace.

"George Gammon for one."

I whistled softly.

"So he's still in favour. I had an idea that—"

"Hanging on by the skin of his teeth, darling. Of course, George is far too conceited to realise it. He thinks he's dug in here for life. But to judge by one or two hints that Aunty's let fall lately…"

"Anybody else?"

"André Duconte. Dark, dapper, and French. I don't think you're going to like him any more than I do."

"Duconte? He's a new one on me. He hasn't been here before, has he?"

"No. Aunty met him in January, when she was staying at the villa. He lives in Menton. Like most of Gwenny's fancies, he doesn't seem to have any settled kind of job. I rather suspect that he's earmarked to fill the gap when George gets his marching orders."

"And that's the lot?"

"Except for Aunt Deborah. She turned up about ten days ago."

I smiled.

"Just the same, eh?"

Sheila smiled in turn.

"Just the same...only more so!"

As I went up to my room I wondered why one always smiled when one thought of Deborah Gaye. I suppose it was due, in part, to the startling discrepancy between the actual woman and the personality conjured up by her name. She sounded glamorous. One expected a film star. And what one actually got was a naïve, self-effacing, rather mousy creature of forty. Although she was five years younger than her sister she looked older. Physically they resembled each other. The same well-rounded features, big brown eyes, warm colouring, and bright auburn hair. The same opulent figures—neither of them very tall, but carrying themselves with a natural grace and dignity that made them appear taller. But there all further resemblance ended. Gwenny was everything that Deborah

was not—tempestuous, impulsive, positive, assertive, amorous. Like many wealthy people, Gwenny could be damned
mean at one moment and wildly extravagant at the next.
Deborah couldn't afford to be either. She was one of those
unhappy creatures who have an almost fanatical regard for
other people's opinions, who dissipate half their energies in
keeping up appearances.

The other half she put into the writing of novels. Light
romantic novels that had a small but loyal public at the lend-
ing libraries. I don't think she made more than a bare living
out of her writing. In fact, Sheila and I suspected that she was
subsidised by Aunt Gwenny. Not in a big way. Just enough
monetary assistance to make Deborah feel under a perpetual
obligation to her sister, without ever enjoying the luxury of
real independence.

III

When I entered the sun-loggia, I sensed at once that something was wrong. Silence had fallen on the little group sitting about the wicker table. Everybody was staring at George
Gammon, who was leaning back in his chair with a sulky,
rather defiant expression on his florid face. Gwenny was
scarlet with repressed anger. Deborah was nervously picking
crumbs off her lap and dropping them on her plate. André
Duconte was fiddling with the polka-dot handkerchief that
jutted from his breast pocket. Sheila was stirring her tea.

On seeing me Gwenny gave an unnaturally loud bleat of
welcome and held out an impulsive hand.

"Well, thank God you've turned up! George has just been

damned insulting. Had a good journey, darling? You're in the chintz room. You know everybody, don't you?"

I greeted Deborah and George, and turned to André Duconte, who had risen and given me a little bow.

"I don't think…"

Gwenny's voice took on a sudden warmth.

"André, this is my godson, Nigel—Nigel Derry. André Duconte. A near neighbour of mine at the Villa Paradou."

I shook hands with Duconte, gave him a friendly smile, and noticed at once that his eyes avoided mine. His hand felt clammy, boneless, like a lukewarm shellfish. A thin, dark moustache curved over his upper lip. A faint whiff of perfume was distilled from his person. Gwenny's perfume. I decided on the spot that I didn't like the fellow any more than I liked George Gammon. It was curious how my godmother seemed to pick on these smooth, unreliable types, instead of fitting herself up with an honest-to-God sort of chap and marrying him. Like all egocentric women with superabundant vitality, she needed the steadying influence of a husband. That was my private thought. I'd have sooner gone into a cage with a man-eating tigress than have aired this opinion in Gwenny's hearing.

I sat down in a vacant chair next to Deborah, accepted a cup of tea and an anchovy sandwich, and asked how her work was going. As usual she was very diffident about her "scribbling" as she called it, but more than ready to talk earnestly and at great length about the tribulations of authorship. After the first five minutes my mind became a blank, my eye glassy. I gave up trying to concentrate and glanced stealthily at the others seated round the table. The atmosphere was still rather strained. Gwenny was talking to Duconte about a certain Mam'selle Fabre, who owned the villa next to her own at Cap Martin. Sheila and Duconte had both evidently met the young woman. George Gammon had not—which cut George out of the conversation, which was just what Gwenny had intended. Not that he seemed unduly piqued. He'd pulled out a big drooping pipe and was slowly filling it, staring up through the glass roof of the loggia, humming softly to himself. I was surprised by his docility. His usual reaction when slighted by Gwenny was to turn silent and sulky, or stamp off in a huff. I noticed an odd little smile playing about his mouth, as if he were enjoying some private joke. He'd coarsened considerably since I'd last seen him. His cheeks were webbed with a network of tiny red veins and his eyes had a bleary look. He kept sucking at his sandy moustache with his lower lip, then suddenly baring his teeth. Once I saw him throw a quick sidelong glance at Deborah, who, happening to catch his eye, flushed scarlet. To my amazement George gave her a little nod and then, unmistakably, winked!

Afterwards, in thinking about it, I tried to persuade myself that it had been an optical illusion, some trick of the light as it flooded with such dazzling brilliance through the glass walls of the loggia. That a man should wink at Deborah was something approaching sacrilege. Even at forty she was so innocent, so virginal. I doubt if any man had ever made love to her. Not that she was unattractive in a soft and negative way, but obviously "that sort of thing" had never held any fascination for her. I'd once steeled myself to read one of her novels. It was called—as far as I remember—*Love Comes to Katie*. And it came to her so discreetly, so tentatively, that the poor wretch had to wait until the last chapter before she was even kissed. When—again if I remember rightly—"William cupped the pale oval of her face between his sensitive hands and pressed his lips lightly to hers." All the love affairs in Deborah's books, I imagine, inched forward with the inevitability of a Greek tragedy to a white wedding, a honeymoon at Torquay and a row of asterisks.

So that wink, if it had really happened, was something beyond my comprehension. It didn't fit in. It puzzled me and roused my curiosity.

IV

Tea over, I exchanged a meaning glance with Sheila and we edged towards the glass-paned door that led into the garden. But Gwenny forestalled us. Whether she was deliberately trying to keep us apart I can't say, but I know I felt pretty murderous. After all, Sheila and I had been six months apart and we had a lot of leeway to make up.

"Oh, Sheila darling—M'sieur Duconte wants to send a cablegram. An urgent business cablegram. You might take the Panther and run him down to the post-office."

Duconte broke in apologetically: "But please… I have no wish to…"

Gwenny silenced him with a look.

"My dear André… Sheila will be delighted. Run along and do as I say. I want to have a nice long talk with Nig." Deborah had already slipped away into the house. But George was still lounging in his chair, puffing away stolidly at his pipe. Gwenny fixed him with a basilisk stare and added pointedly: "A *private* talk!"

At first I thought George wasn't going to take the hint. Then he threw Gwenny a sullen glance, shrugged, got slowly to his feet, and staggered off sleepily into the garden. Gwenny gave an exasperated sigh, lit a cigarette, and sank back against the cushions of her chaise-longue.

"Well, having cleared the decks... Now tell me all about yourself, darling. How are all those little ruffians at Bellwood? Had a good term? And your mother? Still living at Harrogate, of course. It's months since I heard from her. How's her wretched arthritis? Did she go to that man I recommended?"

For a time she let me ramble on about this and that, but I couldn't dismiss the impression that she wasn't really listening, that she was impatient to have done with the small-talk so that we could get down to more serious matters. And, suddenly, I felt apprehensive. Something told me that she was going to discuss my relationship with Sheila. She wasn't going to wait until I'd marshalled my arguments and keyed myself up to have it out with her. She was going to get in first while I was still, so to speak, off balance.

I didn't have to wait long to know that my guess was a good one. Suddenly Gwenny came upright in her chair, stubbed out her half-smoked cigarette and said with a shrewd expression:

"Look here, Nig... are you seriously in love with Sheila?"

Although I'd anticipated the question, Gwenny had jumped it on me so unexpectedly that my stammer, which always affects me when I'm nervous, was painful. I said:

"Well, yes... I—I suppose I am. B-but I'd no idea that..."

"I'd tumbled to the fact?"

"Well...yes."

Gwenny's laugh was edged with sarcasm. Her eyes were

no longer warm and friendly. They were curiously hard and hostile. It was the way I'd seen her look at George when he'd done or said something of which she disapproved.

"My dear boy—I've got eyes in my head! And Sheila's far too ingenuous to dissimulate with any success. We've known each other for a long time, Nig, and I hope we can be frank with each other." Then with an abrupt return to her usual genial, rather gushing manner, she added: "You *will* be frank with me, won't you, darling?"

I said dutifully: "Of course." Then asked: "But frank about what?"

Gwenny said: "Your intentions towards her."

I said facetiously, "Oh, they're strictly honourable and all that," but it didn't go down too well. Gwenny was in no mood for joking. She'd pitched the conversation on a serious note and she wasn't going to let me unsettle her mood by being flippant.

"You want to marry Sheila?"

"Yes"

"When?"

"As soon as I…as we have your permission."

"I see."

Gwenny had risen and moved away to gaze out into the garden. I waited, almost holding my breath. I still wasn't sure which way the cat was going to jump. That was the trouble in dealing with Gwenny. Her mind was like broken water. You could never get a clear picture of what she was thinking. She had no pattern of behaviour on which, with the help of past experience, to forecast her reactions. For an instant I thought it was going to be all right. Then the blow fell.

"It's out of the question."

Just that, and I knew that the old easy relationship between Aunt Gwenny and me was over and done with.

I said hotly: "But why? I can't see that you've any possible objection. You know all about me...my family and background and all the rest of it. I'm twenty-six and in a steady job. I admit we'd have to live pretty simply at first, but Sheila's quite prepared to do that. She's not yet of age, of course, but I can't see—"

"No—it's out of the question."

It was like having a series of heavy stones dropped on one's head. Again I asked Gwenny for her reasons. She didn't answer me at once. Then she turned in from the window and said bluntly: "Sheila's no more than a child. I'm not going to have her make a fool of herself."

"But if we agreed to a long engagement?"

She shook her head.

"I've seen so many girls who've rushed into early marriages and then regretted it. Then, of course, there's the money."

I looked at Gwenny blankly.

"Money? What money?"

"I'll explain."

It was simple enough. If anything happened to Gwenny her estate was to be divided equally between Sheila and Deborah. They were the sole legatees named in her will. But Sheila's inheritance was conditional. If she married before the age of thirty, then Deborah would automatically come into the whole of her sister's estate.

Gwenny concluded: "So if you want to cut the child out of my will you've only got to clear off with her to Gretna

Green. So far I haven't told her of these conditions. But now I intend to. And frankly, Nig, when she realises what's at stake I wouldn't be surprised if her present infatuation for you suddenly cools off." Gwenny gave a hard little laugh. "Does that sound cynical? But when you've learnt as much about human nature as I have…" She broke off and pointed to one of the wicker tables. "Now hand me a cigarette and forget all the murderous thoughts you've got about me. In the long run you'll see just how sensible I am!"

I held a lighter to her cigarette, then, with another little laugh, she tweaked my ear and went into the house.

2

I DIDN'T GET A CHANCE TO SEE SHEILA ALONE UNTIL
after breakfast the following morning. Gwenny hadn't come
down. Nor had George Gammon. The previous evening
after dinner there'd been more unpleasantness between
them. She'd accused George—not in private but in front of
us all—of drinking too much. She'd called him "a disgusting
old soak." With an insolent air, George had crossed to the
whisky decanter, slopped himself about half a small tumbler-
ful, tossed it down neat and stalked out of the room. At this
show of defiance Gwenny at first had been almost speechless
with rage. We'd spent the next half hour trying to calm her
down and trailed up to bed early. But as I was coming out of
the bathroom, I'd seen Gwenny at the far end of the corridor
slipping into Sheila's bedroom. I knew she'd gone in to tell
Sheila about her talk with me.

As I was short of cigarettes, I suggested to Sheila that we
took the field path to the village. It was still pleasantly warm
and springlike. Just a few fleecy clouds rolling great shadows

over the countryside, and a little breeze stirring the high branches of the trees in the park. We hadn't gone a dozen yards before Sheila burst out:

"I can't understand what's come over her! She's out of her mind."

"Gwenny?"

"Of course. She came into my room last night and said you'd spoken to her about our marriage. All very sweet and reasonable at first. Was I quite sure I was doing the right thing? Wouldn't it be better to wait a couple of years and see how we felt about each other then? Had I really thought what it would mean to make do in a two-room flatlet? Wasn't I too young to know my own mind? Then she told me about a settlement she'd made on me that I'd forfeit if I married before I was thirty. When I told her I didn't care a hoot about the money, and that we could manage to rub along perfectly well without it, she nearly threw a fit." Sheila laughed tonelessly. "She doesn't seem to think you're worth seventy thousand pounds, darling."

I whistled softly.

"Seventy thousand! I'd no idea it was as much as that. Are you sure—?"

Sheila flashed up.

"Now don't *you* start on me, Nig. If you think it's worth while hanging back for another ten years or so for the sake of Gwenny's wretched money. . . well, I don't. Gwenny's going to live for a good many years yet. We'd probably be middle-aged before we came into a penny of her blessed money."

"Don't be ridiculous. If you don't care about the money I'm damned if I do! But the point is, until you're twenty-one we can't marry without Gwenny's consent. How are we going to get round that one? Do you think she'll weaken?"

Sheila said emphatically: "Not a hope. I know her only too well when she's really dug her toes in. She's absolutely dead set against us marrying."

"Just because she thinks you're too young to know your own mind?"

"That's what she says. But if you ask me..."

Sheila tailed off. I waited for her to go on, but when she didn't, I said:

"Well? If I ask you...what?"

She seemed to be groping for words to express what she felt. Even when she came forward with an explanation it was vague and diffident.

"I don't know exactly. It's a feeling I've got that there's something more to this than we imagine. Gwenny's not really telling the truth. She's got another reason for refusing her consent."

"What makes you think that?"

Sheila was more vague than ever.

"I don't know. Just an impression I got... something about her manner... the way she nearly bit my head off when I tried to argue. After all, Nig, she's known both of us for years. You're in a steady job, and it isn't as if we'd just met. From a rational point of view I can't see how Gwenny could possibly object. But she won't even hear of us becoming engaged. She's made up her mind from the start to say 'No,' and nothing we say is going to shift her. It's a pretty hopeless outlook for our future, darling."

We went on discussing the matter all across the fields to

Wendhurst, but when we arrived at the village we hadn't really got any further. The only conclusion we arrived at was that Gwenny, for some reason known only to herself, was behaving like a bitch!

II

After I'd bought half a dozen packets of cigarettes and some notepaper at the general store, Sheila said:

"Now we're in the village let's go and have a word with Harry. I haven't seen him for weeks."

The converted windmill stood on a little rise at the north end of the village street. A rutted track led up to it through a rough patch of whin and bramble. Its lower storey was little more than a glorified shed with a couple of lopsided doors, behind which Harry Skeet garaged his decrepit car. A rickety outside staircase mounted to the studio door, which was painted, in keeping with the casements, a vivid butcher blue. A cowbell was fixed to one side of the door, actuated by a lavatory chain that bore on its porcelain handle the name of a well-known firm of sanitary engineers. A pair of khaki shorts and a grey singlet had been flung over the stair-rail to dry. On a string attached to the tarred weatherboards above the door were several pairs of socks and one or two paint-stained handkerchiefs. Sheila gave the chain a few sharp tugs and the bell tinkled melodiously.

A long silence at first, then a surly voice growled, "Who the hell's that?"

Sheila said brightly, "It's Nigel and me. Can we come in, or are you still in bed?"

"Of course I'm still in bed. Where else would I be at this ungodly hour? But that's no reason why you shouldn't come in. I never lock the door."

We went in. Harry was lying flat on his back on a camp-bed, arms raised, his hands cupping the back of his head, his pyjama jacket unbuttoned. A stubble of white hairs gleamed against his brick-red skin. He looked comfortable, unconcerned and slightly scruffy. The room itself was as I'd always remembered it—a jumble of unrelated objects set down in all the wrong places, yet in some curious way combining to suggest an air of cosiness and domesticity. I knew well enough that Harry could easily have afforded a daily woman to cook his meals and keep the place tidy, but this was the way he liked to live—unbothered, unbuttoned, anyhow, his own master. Every now and then he packed his painting gear and went off for weeks at a time to Italy or Greece or Yugoslavia. One day he was down at the butcher's buying a couple of chops, the next day he was gone, nobody knew where, to return with the skin peeling from his nose and his bald head the colour of a ripe nut.

Sheila sat on the foot of the bed. After I'd removed a couple of empty beer bottles, a tube of Flake White, and an old panama hat from a Victorian sewing-chair, I sat down in turn. Harry reached out for a tin of cigarettes and a box of matches, and began to smoke like a chimney. Sheila said:

"What are you working on now, Harry darling?"

"I'm not. A period of gestation, my dear. It's no good working without enthusiasm, and at the moment I'm as full of enthusiasm as a gutted herring. Why haven't you been to see me?"

"Oh, this and that. You know how it is with Aunt Gwenny around. She keeps one moving."

Harry grinned sardonically.

"How is the old so-and-so? Time I looked in on her and had a square meal and a good bottle of wine. What's to-day?"

"Thursday."

"Fine. I'll come up to-day. I'll come to lunch." Harry's quick fierce gaze swivelled to me. "When did you turn up?"

"Yesterday."

"Is that bolt-eyed old toss-pot still shoving his legs under Gwenny's table?"

"Gammon?"

"That's the bloke. Gwenny's a bad picker, but how she hit on that one, God knows. You mark what I say—he's out to get his forks on her money. They all are, but that old so-an-so's too conceited to see it." He coughed gustily and blew a scattering of burning ash over his naked chest. Slapping himself violently, he went on, "Gwenny may look an easy catch but she's a sly old trout. She needs careful playing. That's where all these toady-boys go wrong. She gives them a come-hither look, butters 'em up a bit, flashes her diamonds under their greedy snouts and they come sniffing to heel, thinking they're going to be on easy street for the rest of their lives. But does it work out that way? Like hell it does! Just when they think they've hooked the old trout, she flicks her tail in their faces and fills 'em with fury and frustration. I've seen them come and go, one after another—in, out, like a queue at a shilling dentist's. And for why? Because an old war horse like Gwenny needs a short curb and a strong hand. Treat the old so-and-so rough and rude and you're in for life!"

Sheila said laughingly, "Like you, Harry?"

He was quite unabashed.

"And why not? Do I wait for the crumbs that fall from Gwenny's table? I do not. I barge in, make myself generally unbearable, order the old girl about, and hey presto!... I've got the old war horse eating out of my hand."

Which, of course, was true. Harry walked into Cockfosters as if he owned the place. If he asked at lunch for the Chambertin' 49 he got it. A cigar? Then Gwenny unlocked the Chinese cabinet and found him a box of Henry Clay's. And all this with an insufferable disregard for Gwenny's susceptibilities. At table there was nothing Harry enjoyed more than to dissect Gwenny's character in front of her guests—never in such a way as to be insulting or offensive, but with a bawdy gusto, a sly shrewdness that had everybody round the table laughing at Gwenny's efforts to shut him up. Yet curiously enough, even at his worst moments, she never lost her temper with him. Sheila and I had often speculated on the reason for Gwenny's toleration of Harry's deliberate coarseness. Perhaps he was a refreshing change from the spineless fellows to whom Gwenny was always attaching herself—a boisterous wind blowing through a hot-house.

For myself, I liked Harry Skeet. He may have been an old reprobate, but there was a warmth, a simplicity, a total lack of self-consciousness about him that was as stimulating as a glass of schnapps. Sheila liked him too. And Harry liked her. At one time she'd often accompanied him in his little open car to the places he'd earmarked as suitable subjects for a new canvas. He was always gentle and patient with her. While he painted, he talked to Sheila about all manner of things—about painting and the places he'd visited, about himself and his philosophy of life. Sheila claimed that Harry had taught her more than she ever learned at school. He never talked down to her as Gwenny did. He treated her as an adult—an intelligent adult.

Then, suddenly, Gwenny put her foot down. Harry's reputation around Wendhurst, she said, was far from savoury, and she wasn't going to have Sheila talked about. These outings to lonely spots around the countryside had got to stop. Sheila was furious, but she couldn't flatly disobey. So she had to fob Harry off with some excuse, not wanting to hurt his feelings, and her meetings with him had grown more and more infrequent.

III

About twelve o'clock we ambled back across the fields to Cockfosters—Sheila in the middle, her arms linked through ours. Before leaving the studio Harry had slopped about in a basin of water, turned his back on Sheila and put on a pair of faded blue shorts and a bush-shirt. The white stubble of his unshaven jowl was even more apparent in the bright sunshine. I wondered what the immaculate André would make of Harry. Some such thought must have occurred to Sheila because she said:

"By the way, Gwenny's got a new one in tow. A Frenchman she met at Menton. He's been staying at Cockfosters for a week. I thought I should warn you. And Aunt Deborah's there. So we're quite a party."

Harry gave one of his infectious grins, displaying the blackened stumps of the few teeth he still possessed.

"The pale lilac passion flower! Still as virginal as ever? If Gwenny were less rapacious she'd have a share-out of her toady-boys. Poor old Deborah could do with a bit of fun. She's got the figure for it, too. Has it ever struck you, kiddie, that the old war horse has got nothing on Deborah except her money and her cussed temperament? And she'd be a nicer woman without either."

At that moment we were climbing over a stile on the edge of the park. Ahead of us a curving path led through a small glade of silver birch. Harry had gone into the lead, when suddenly, rounding a bend, he stopped dead and let out a muffled exclamation.

"My God!"

Sheila asked, "What is it?"

"Take a look at that."

He edged aside to give us a clear view of the path ahead. We stared in astonishment. A man and a woman were strolling at a leisurely pace away from us. Their arms were about each other's waists, and the woman's head rested, somewhat awkwardly, on the man's shoulder. Although I couldn't see their faces, I recognised at once the shapeless floral dress and ginger sports jacket.

It was Deborah and George Gammon.

Harry said, "The old sly-boots! I spoke too soon. She's off at last. I wonder what the hell Gwenny would say if she ever found out."

We stayed discussing the phenomenon until the couple were out of sight, then strolled on again. We hadn't gone far, however, when we heard a sharp little feminine neigh of protest, followed by a repressed giggle and the rumble of

George's voice coming from behind some thick bushes to the left of the path. Harry shied like a startled horse, held up a warning finger, and hurried us forward—away, as it were, from the danger zone.

Then he said with a broad wink: "Discretion, *mes enfants*... discretion..." and began to shake with silent laughter.

But I couldn't help feeling sorry for Deborah, because it was pretty obvious that George was doing this to get his own back on Gwenny. He'd deliberately make it clear to Gwenny just what was happening, hoping, no doubt, to rouse her jealousy and crawl back into favour before André Duconte got too firmly in the saddle. I don't think George had got much hope. This affair with Deborah was the last desperate gesture of a condemned man. The old war horse—as Harry always called her—had already made arrangements for his execution. I gave George another week at the most.

IV

Before lunch everybody drifted into the sun-loggia at the back of the house for drinks. When we turned up nobody as yet had put in an appearance. Normally Sheila and I would have waited for Gwenny before pouring our drinks, but Harry made a bee-line for the cocktail cabinet, set himself up a large pink gin and dropped into one of the wicker chairs. Then he helped himself to a cigarette from the silver box, undid the three top buttons of his shirt, and flopped back with a sigh of contentment that ended in a sudden resounding belch.

Then Gwenny came in. She stopped dead, took a long acid look at Harry, sniffed and said shortly, "So it's you!"

The Poisoned Pen
A Mystery Bookstore... And More
4014 N. Goldwater Blvd., #101
Scottsdale AZ 85251
(480)947-2974 Fax (480)945-1023
Visit us at: www.poisonedpen.com
We regret we can issue no refunds

Tue May20-25 11:56am
Inv: B79621 IS 00

	Qty	Price	Disc	Total	Tax
Coffin Island	1	28.99		28.99	
Telegram from Le Touquet,A	1	15.99		15.99	
GC*****9886 Gift Card Redeemed		-48.60			
Gift Card balance: 52.08					

Subtotal		-3.62	
a TAX 8.05%		3.62	

Items   3   Total   0.00

5/14 DAVE BARRY
5/15 LUCINDA BERRY
5/17 ELIZA RIED & CHRISINA ESTES
5/18 TORI ELDRIDGE
5/19 MICHAEL MCGARRITY
5/12 ARVIND ETHAN DAVID

Harry gazed at her innocently over the top of his tilted glass and flapped a vague greeting with the hand holding his cigarette. I noticed a fly exploring the grey pelt of hair that frothed in the opening of his shirt. Suddenly, tickled by the fly, he set down his glass and began assiduously to scratch.

I asked Gwenny if I could pour her a drink. She said meaningly, "A gin and Lillet, darling...a big one." Then, turning to Sheila, she added: "You'd better slip inside and tell Daisy to lay another place for lunch." When Sheila had gone, she asked Harry sweetly, "You *are* staying to lunch, I take it?"

Harry said irrelevantly, "By God, old girl, you're putting on weight a bit, aren't you? That dress of yours is damn near bursting at the seams. You ought to take more exercise." Then the old devil tried to involve me in the conversation. "Don't *you* think she's putting it on a bit round the hips? Not that I'm allergic to opulence. Far from it. But, frankly, young fellow—"

Luckily at that moment George and Deborah came in through the garden door, and Harry, stealing a quick sly glance at them, began to quiver with silent laughter.

Gwenny said at once, "Where have you two been? I've been hunting all over the place for you. I've never known such selfishness. A dozen things to be done about the place—the flowers to arrange in the sitting-room, the cacti to water, the goldfish to feed—and you rush off and make yourselves scarce. I won't have the staff overworked. This isn't an hotel. What about that lawn you were going to mow, George? Have you done it?" She flashed round on Harry and snapped out viciously, "And what the hell are you laughing at?"

"I'm happy," said Harry.

"You look sozzled."

"Don't you believe it. When I'm in my cups I grow melancholic and cry like a kid." As Sheila came out from the house, he turned to Gammon. "You ought to have done as Gwenny told you and mown that blasted lawn. Now she's in a bad temper and we're all going to suffer for it. As for you, Deborah…you ought to be slapped. Have you no respect for the privileges of the rich? You must earn your keep at Cockfosters. Otherwise Gwenny's going to get very, very cross and cut you out of her will."

Gwenny shrieked, "Will you shut up, Harry!"

Deborah said soothingly, "He doesn't really mean what he says, dear. You ought to know that by now. He just loves pulling our legs." She laid a hand to my arm. "Do you think you could fetch me a small glass of sherry, Nig dear."

"Of course."

Already a great change seemed to have come over Deborah. She was no longer timid and apologetic. There was a sparkle in her eye and she looked ten years younger. She couldn't keep her eyes off George, and every time their glances met she blushed like a girl and a gentle little smile played about her lips. There was no doubt that she was head over heels in love with George, at the mercy of an autumnal passion that had flared up, suddenly, violently, and changed her whole personality. Whether George reciprocated her feelings I wasn't sure. I still couldn't make up my mind whether he was using Deborah to pique Gwenny, or whether, tired of Gwenny's tantrums and temperament, he was genuinely attracted to her sister. He was certainly making a fuss of her, setting a chair for her out of the sun, fetching her a cushion, whispering a word or two in her ear.

All this by-play didn't go unnoticed by Gwenny. She began joking with Harry in a loud unnatural voice, then whinnying with laughter. She made short work of her gin and Lillet, and asked me to fetch her another. Harry was obviously enjoying himself. During a sudden lull in the conversation, which had been growing noisier every minute, he bawled out:

"Gwenny! Gwenny! Gammon's at the decanter again. He ought to go easy. He looks as if he's suffering from high blood pressure."

Then he started on a gruesome tale about an American journalist he'd met in Pontecorvo, whose blood pressure was so high that he didn't dare bend to pick up a collar stud. I'm not sure if anybody was really listening, because by that time everybody seemed to be talking at once and at the top of their voices.

Then André Duconte came in and in a flash the whole atmosphere changed.

I don't know if Harry spotted him at first, but Duconte certainly noticed Harry. He'd sauntered into the loggia, his usual neat, glossy, smiling self. Then his smile flicked out as if turned off by a switch. I saw him grow pale and rigid and the sweat slowly break out on his forehead. His eyes seemed to recede into their sockets, darting this way and that, as if seeking a line of escape. His expression was one of sickly fear.

Then Gwenny was saying, "André, I don't believe you've met Harry Skeet," and Harry was glaring at the Frenchman with an expression of such loathing and contempt that everybody suddenly stopped talking and stared at him in astonishment. The next instant Harry lunged forward and, swearing under his breath, got his fingers round Duconte's throat.

The Frenchman made a curious rasping noise and struggled frantically to loosen Harry's grip. I could see the veins on Duconte's forehead standing out like cords as he laboured to get his breath. Then I saw his hand drop to his hip and, the next moment, a knife blade flashing in the sunlight.

Gwenny uttered a long shriek of alarm.

"Stop him, somebody! Stop him! He's got a knife. Harry, you fool...let him go!"

George and I got off the mark at the same instant, but we just weren't quick enough. I saw the knife blade go up and descend. As Harry's hands fell limply to his sides, I heard him draw in a sharp whistling breath. But before George and I could close in on Duconte, he'd ducked between us and slipped out through the garden door. We were after him in a flash, but he'd cut round the side of the house where several paths led through a thick shrubbery, beyond which was a wooded area of the park. We could only guess at which path he'd taken, but our guess was evidently wrong because we never caught a glimpse of him, not even in the distance. After ten minutes we gave up the search and returned to the loggia.

Harry, thank heaven, though he looked a bit shaken, was not seriously hurt. The knife had nicked his upper arm. Deborah was on her knees beside his chair bandaging the gash. Somewhere inside the house Gwenny was sobbing hysterically, and as there was no sign of Sheila I guessed she'd gone in to console her and calm her down.

It was from that moment the atmosphere at Cockfosters began to deteriorate. Not that it had been exactly amicable on my arrival. But now, beneath the surface pattern of all that was said and done during the next few days, I sensed an undercurrent of tension and hostility. And to make matters worse Sheila's attitude to me seemed to become less warm and friendly. We didn't have a row or anything like that. She merely became elusive and far less approachable. I had the idea that she didn't want to be too much alone in my company.

3

I NEVER DISCOVERED WHAT THE TROUBLE WAS BETWEEN Harry and André Duconte. Sheila was equally puzzled. It was obvious the two men had met before, but when, how, and in what circumstances we never found out. While Deborah was pinning the bandage round Harry's arm, George observed:

"Well, that was a ruddy mix-up and no mistake! What was it all about anyway?"

Harry merely grunted, "I could do with another drink," and shut up like a clam.

After that we went in to lunch. It was a good lunch, but nobody seemed to notice what they were eating. There was a '45 Beaujolais, but it might as well have been *vin ordinaire* for all the appreciation it received. There was an air of grim joviality about the meal that was unnerving. Nobody mentioned the incident in the loggia. Harry twitted us all in turn, told a couple of bawdy anecdotes that were genuinely funny, but he was a long way off form. We laughed loudly enough, then all stopped laughing at exactly the same moment, so that we

were left stranded on one of those uneasy silences that over-
whelm a gathering when the atmosphere is charged with tension. The conversation went forward in jerks, like a machine
that needs oiling. Half-way through the meal Gwenny said
she felt giddy and went up to her room.

Directly after lunch I saw Harry sneak upstairs. Then I
heard a door shut and I guessed he'd gone into Gwenny's
bedroom. George and Deborah went through to the loggia
for coffee. Sheila said something about "Aunt Deborah's
never going to get around to those wretched flowers" and
disappeared into the lounge. Not wanting to be a third to the
couple in the loggia, I decided to slip up to my room and put
a new spool in my camera.

As I went by the door of Gwenny's bedroom, I heard
Harry say, "I've my own reasons for what I did. They needn't
concern you. But you're going to do as I ask or I'll finish you
for good..."

I hadn't wanted to eavesdrop, but Harry was evidently in
a temper and his voice had risen to a shout. I didn't catch
Gwenny's reply, but it sounded to me as if she were crying.
Ten minutes later I heard the slam of her door and the thud
of Harry's footsteps pounding down the stairs. I stayed up in
my room for another twenty minutes, sitting in an armchair
by the window, smoking, and reading a magazine. I thought
I'd let things settle down a bit before going in search of Sheila.
I was going to suggest a row on the lake, which lay about a
quarter of a mile from the north side of the house. There was a
little island in the middle of the lake, where a ring of flowering
shrubs half-concealed an ornamental summer-house. Sheila
and I often slipped over there when we wanted to be alone.

I made a bee-line for the lounge. The flowers had evidently been arranged in the vases, but there was no sign of Sheila. I met Daisy, the parlourmaid, in the hall, and she seemed to think that Sheila had gone through to the loggia. But she wasn't there either. Just Deborah and George talking quickly and earnestly together, their heads almost touching. They looked like a couple of anarchists planning an assassination. When they heard my footsteps behind them, they jerked round with a startled look and hastily drew apart. Deborah looked sheepish and confused. There was a scowl on George's beefy, drink-coarsened face.

I apologised for breaking in on their conversation and said I was looking for Sheila. Deborah seemed surprised.

"But, Nig dear… I thought you knew. She walked back across the park with Harry about a quarter of an hour ago. Didn't she tell you she was going to the village?"

"She never said a word."

George had pulled out his big drooping pipe and was stuffing tobacco into its porcelain bowl with his stubby fingers. The sun was now well overhead, flooding directly in through the glass roof. George was sweating in every pore and his shirt front was darkened with moisture. He looked shockingly out of condition. He asked, "No sign of that Duconte fellah, I suppose?"

"No."

"Well, we can't wonder at that…pulling a knife on Skeet like a damned crook. You can bet your bottom dollar we shan't see him here again."

"What about his clothes?"

"If he's got any sense he'll cut his losses and keep out of

Gwenny's way. She'll side with Harry. She's always had a soft spot for old Skeet. Heaven knows why. He treats her abominably." George paused to light his pipe and added between puffs, "By the way...where...is she?"

"Up in her room."

Deborah said with a sigh, "All these horrible upsets... they're so degrading. Gwenny has only herself to thank. I can't understand why she invited that man to stay here in the first place. The moment I set eyes on him I thought he looked shifty. You thought so, too, didn't you, George?"

George nodded complacently.

"Too smooth and plausible—that was my opinion. But Gwenny was always a bad judge of character. When I first met Duconte down on the Riviera I remember thinking to myself, 'This chap's a gigolo or I'm a Dutchman!' Heaven knows how he wormed himself into Gwenny's favour."

It was funny to hear George, the "toady-boy," talking like this. It made me realise how blind people are to their own shortcomings. I think his air of righteous indignation was genuine. He couldn't see that for the last twelve months or so he'd been no better than a kept man—the latest and, to my mind, one of the most obnoxious lovers to appear on Gwenny's pay-roll. And now, what was even more loathsome, he was making a pass at poor Aunt Deborah. Gwenny, of course, was quite capable of looking after herself. She knew only too well how to crack the whip and bring men like George to heel. But Deborah's innocence was childlike and her infatuation as unreasoning and compelling as a schoolgirl's. Harry might make a joke of this secretive affair, but to me it seemed tragic. I felt I wanted to warn Aunt Deborah that George was not to be trusted, that she was being used as a cat's-paw to further some deep and furtive game of his own.

But when I saw the way she looked at him I knew it would be useless. And besides...what *was* George's little game? To make Gwenny jealous? But that was only a guess. It was even possible that George had really fallen in love with Deborah— possible but not probable. I couldn't see George chasing after a woman whose sole assets were a three-roomed cottage, a pre-war car, and a mediocre talent for writing light romantic novels. Of course, there was her figure. But George had never struck me as being particularly virile. I couldn't help wondering if that were the reason why Gwenny had lost interest in him. The reason, too, why George was drinking so heavily... to deaden his sense of inadequacy.

II

I could see I wasn't wanted in the loggia, so I mumbled something about having a couple of letters to write and drifted upstairs again to my bedroom. To my surprise, I heard, for the second time, a man's voice speaking sharply and urgently behind Gwenny's door. At first I wondered if Harry had returned to the house while I was out in the loggia. Then I realised it was André Duconte.

I guessed at once what he'd done. Instead of dashing off through the shrubbery and clearing off across the park, he'd merely slipped round to the north side of the house, entered the front-door and sneaked up to his room. For some reason or other none of us had thought of looking in his bedroom. We took it for granted that he'd want to put all the distance he could between himself and Harry Skeet. Instead, all during lunch, he'd been sitting only a few feet above our heads. No doubt he'd been awaiting an opportunity to see Gwenny alone—perhaps with his door ajar, so that he could see and hear all that was going on in the corridor. The moment I'd gone downstairs he'd evidently nipped into Gwenny's room.

Although both their voices were raised I had no clear idea of what they were talking about. They were speaking in French, and although my German's passable, my French has always been pretty weak. True, I caught an odd word or two—words like "pourquoi" and "jamais" and "alors"—but that wasn't much help. And twice I heard Gwenny mention the Villa Paradou, which was the name of her villa at Cap Martin, on the Riviera. I daren't linger too long, because at any moment the door might open, and I knew Gwenny was quite capable of kicking me out of the house if she thought I'd been eavesdropping.

Back in my room I tried to assess the mood of the conversation from the tones of their voices. I don't think they were exactly angry with each other. Duconte sounded frightened, desperate and insistent. At one point he seemed to be threatening Gwenny. She, on her part, seemed to be reassuring Duconte. Her voice was shrill and anxious, yet incisive. I had the impression that she was working out a plan of action—not for herself, but for Duconte.

All this, of course, was little more than pure speculation. But one thing was certain. The feeling of foreboding, of apprehension, that had overwhelmed me when I'd first caught sight of Cockfosters had been more than justified. There was a devil of a lot going on around me that I couldn't understand.

Why was George setting his cap at Deborah? Why had Harry tried to choke the life out of Duconte? And on whose side was Gwenny—Duconte's or Harry's? And how was it that Harry was allowed to stroll into Cockfosters whenever he pleased and throw his weight about? And why had Sheila, without a word to me, suddenly gone off with Harry across the park?

I'd reached this point in my reflections, when I was aware of stealthy activity in the corridor. I heard doors being opened and shut, a subdued murmur of conversation, then the sound of footsteps going discreetly down the stairs. After that there was silence for a time. Then, round in the stable-yard, I heard a car being started up and, coincident with this, a quick padding of footfalls on the landing.

The main window of my bedroom faced north, which meant that I looked out directly on to the drive. Jumping up, I crossed to the window and looked down. It was just as I'd anticipated. Gwenny's powerful and expensive Panther saloon was just nosing up to the steps which led down from the front-door, with Gwenny herself at the wheel. The next instant I saw Duconte come down the steps two at a time, carrying a suitcase and an overcoat. A quick scramble and he was inside the car. I heard the slam of the door, the crackle of tyres on the gravel, the sudden quickening drone of the engine. Ten seconds later the car had disappeared round the bend in the drive at the bottom of the steep incline that mounted to Cockfosters.

A split second after that, George Gammon came pounding round the side of the house. I saw him stare down the drive, scratch the back of his head with the stem of his pipe, shrug, and, at a more leisurely pace, make his way back to the loggia.

It was a beautiful day. Not a cloud in the sky. I screwed up my eyes against a dazzling gleam of blue where the lake lay in the hollow, half-concealed by a misty green belt of larches. I was on holiday, staying under the same roof as Sheila and the weather was superb. I ought to have been feeling on top of the world. But I wasn't. I felt strangely uneasy and depressed.

III

A little after four Sheila returned to Cockfosters. I met her in the hall.

I said rather surlily, "Where have you been?"

"Over to the windmill with Harry."

"You might have let me know you were going."

"I didn't know where you were."

"Up in my room. You could at least have given me a call."

"I'm sorry, Nig."

I persisted.

"After all, if you wanted to have a private talk with Harry, I could at least have strolled over later and met you."

Sheila uttered a sigh of exasperation.

"I've already told you…I'm sorry!"

She usually confided in me about everything and I waited for her to tell me why she'd suddenly gone off with Harry Skeet. But I realised at once that I wasn't going to get an explanation. It was then that I first had the illusion that Sheila was separated from me by a wall of glass. There was something distrait and distant about her manner. All the time she was talking to me, her mind seemed to be following an entirely different train of thought. I had the impression that she was bewildered and worried, preoccupied with some personal problem about which she was unprepared to talk.

I guessed at once that Harry was responsible for her abrupt change of mood. He'd asked her to walk back to Wendhurst with him because he had something to tell her. And since Sheila had made no attempt to rope me into the party… something private. But what? Something about Gwenny? Or was it tied up with the sudden eruption of violence that had occurred in the loggia? Perhaps Harry was anxious to justify his attack on Duconte, because even if he didn't give a damn for anybody's opinion of him, I think he made an exception of Sheila. He really valued her respect because he was genuinely fond of her.

Tea had just been served in the loggia and we drifted through and dropped into a couple of wicker chairs. There was no sign of Deborah and George. Nor had Gwenny returned as yet in the car. It struck me as a good opportunity to let Sheila know what had been happening in her absence.

She said, "So he was here all the time!"

I nodded and asked, "Do you think he and Gwenny have gone off somewhere together?"

Sheila said practically, "Did Aunty have time to pack?"

"No."

"Then she's probably driven André to Canterbury station. She wants him out of the way. He'll have plenty of time to catch the night ferry from Dover."

"On his way to the Villa Paradou?"

"It's possible."

I hesitated a moment, then took the bull by the horns.

"Look here, Sheila darling—did Harry tell you what he's

got against Duconte? They'd met somewhere before. No doubt about that. Perhaps he told you where and when they first bumped into each other."

Sheila said shortly, "He never referred to the incident. He didn't even mention André."

So they hadn't been discussing Duconte. And Sheila had been quick to see that in asking these questions I was trying to pump her about Harry and the reason why she'd sneaked off without letting me know. I tried to clamp down on my curiosity, but it wasn't easy. I felt if she'd only let me in on her troubles I could help her to straighten them out. But whenever I got on to the subject of Harry she edged me aside and retired behind that wall of glass.

After a cup of tea and a slice of cake she excused herself and moved towards the inner door. Then she turned and said:

"By the way, I shouldn't say anything to George or Deborah about André going off in the car with Aunt Gwenny. If they're going to hear about it, it had better come from her."

"All right."

"And I wouldn't say anything to Gwenny herself unless she mentions it. She might be furious if she thought you'd been prying on her."

I flared up at that.

"Damn it all! I wasn't prying on her."

Sheila smiled rather wanly.

"No, but she'll *think* you were. She's got a pretty low opinion of human nature."

And with that, she went into the house.

4

GWENNY RETURNED HOME THAT EVENING JUST AS Sheila had anticipated and joined us at dinner. She said absolutely nothing about André Duconte, so I held my tongue about all that I'd seen and heard that afternoon. She made only one reference to the scene in the loggia. Addressing nobody in particular she asked:

"Does anybody know what possessed Harry to act as he did this morning? I'd be grateful for an explanation."

We all looked at each other blankly and shook our heads.

Then Deborah murmured, "We're no wiser than you are, dear. It's all very upsetting."

It was an odd question and I couldn't see why Gwenny had asked it. I was convinced she knew the answer. I could only suppose she pretended to ignorance to pull the wool over our eyes. Admittedly I'd heard Harry shouting at her, "I've my own reasons for what I did. They needn't concern you," but I felt sure she'd managed to wheedle the truth out of Duconte.

I'd never seen Gwenny so subdued and negative as she was

that night. Usually when she was around it was difficult to get a word in edgeways. But for most of the meal she sat silent and preoccupied, while the rest of us worked like hell to keep the conversation alive.

All these events had happened on the Wednesday and Thursday preceding the Easter week-end, and for the next few days there was a kind of brooding hiatus before things got cracking again. On Easter Sunday, Sheila, Deborah and I attended morning service at the Wendhurst parish church. We'd seen nothing of Harry, and as he wasn't on the telephone we'd been unable to make an enquiry about his arm. After lunch on Easter Monday I suggested to Sheila that we walked over to the windmill to make sure that he was all right. I was a bit worried that the wound might have turned septic, and the poor devil had nobody to look after him if he suddenly went sick.

Sheila said, "I've got the most frightful headache, Nig. Would you mind very much if I didn't come?"

I swallowed down my disappointment and said of course if she was feeling like that I'd go on my own. I didn't believe in her excuse, but I had to accept it. The incident naturally fostered my growing suspicion that Shelia, for some enigmatic reason, didn't want to spend too much time alone in my company. I was surprised that she hadn't brought up the tricky subject of our marriage again. But she never once mentioned it. And in her present touchy and evasive mood I felt it was best to keep off the subject myself.

It took me about twenty minutes' brisk walking across the fields to reach Wendhurst. The fine weather was still holding up. More than once I heard the cuckoo—at one moment close up, at the next a long way off. The vague thought went through my mind that to cover the distance in the time it would have to exceed the speed of sound, until I realised, of course, that it was two cuckoos calling to each other. Being a Bank Holiday all the village shops were closed, but there were quite a few people idling in the streets or working in their gardens. The black sail-less windmill stood out like a paper-cut against the china-blue sky. As I walked up the rutted track between the whin bushes, I was suddenly struck by its air of desolation. Its windows and doors were shut. The iron bar on the garage doors had been swivelled into its socket and padlocked.

I went up the staircase, tried the studio door and found it was locked, but by leaning outward over the rickety rail I was able to see in through one of the windows. The room looked more than ever as if a hurricane had swept through it. There were clothes and books and sketches lying all over the floor. I could see the quivering hindquarters of a mouse projecting from a loaf of bread that had been left on the table. The bed was empty and unmade. There was no sign of Harry.

When I got back to the road I realised that all my movements had been watched by an old man, who was standing up close to his garden hedge, leaning on a hoe. He spat ferociously from the side of his mouth and croaked:

"There ain't nobody there."

"So I see."

"'E's gone. Went Good Friday."

I was surprised. That was the day after he'd been up to Cockfosters and Sheila had walked back with him to the studio.

"You're sure?"

"I should be. My boy runs the only taxi in Wendhurst. 'E drove Mr. Skeet Good Friday morning over to Folkestone."

"Do you know where he's gone?"

"Italy it was...or Germany...somewheres across the Channel. Dick put him down at the harbour, so he says. Be some time before we see him around here again, I reckon."

I thanked the old boy, who touched his hat and bobbed down behind the hedge to get on with his hoeing. As I was about to move off his head shot up and he called after me.

"They say down at the Bull he's an old devil with the wimmin. A proper old he-goat." He cackled lewdly. "Can't keep his hands off 'em."

Then he ducked down behind the hedge again and I heard the furious clicking of his hoe biting into the sods.

II

When I got back to Cockfosters I found that during my absence the lid had blown off. Gwenny and Deborah had evidently had the father and the mother of a row. Deborah was sitting in a corner of the loggia, red-eyed and still softly weeping. Sheila was hovering round her with a cup of tea, trying to console her. She signed to me to take a chair and held a warning finger to her lips. Deborah threw me a blank and miserable glance, scrabbled for her handkerchief, dabbed her eyes and, gulping out her thanks, accepted a cup of tea.

Sheila said, "I shouldn't take it too much to heart. You know what Aunt Gwenny is. I'm sure she didn't mean half the beastly things she said."

But Deborah was in no mood to be mollified. There was no doubt that she'd been cut to the quick by the sharp edge of her sister's tongue.

"But to accuse me of...*that*! It's unbelievable. That the thought should have ever entered her mind. And the slur on poor George's honour! I shudder to think what he'd do if he knew how he'd been insulted."

"You intend to tell him?"

Deborah looked profoundly shocked.

"Oh no, no—I couldn't. Not a thing like that!"

Sheila asked, "Where *is* George? I haven't seen him since lunch."

"He borrowed my car to drive over to Folkestone. He's some friends there. He'll be back to dinner." Adding with a little wail of misery, "Oh, I can't imagine what's got into Gwenny. She's often difficult, I admit, but you wouldn't believe the horrible things she said about George and me. I shall never feel the same about her again. How can I, dear? To accuse me of...*that*! I can't get over it. My own sister...to suspect such an infamous thing..."

I'd never seen Deborah in such a bitter and rebellious mood before, and it made me realise how keenly she resented Gwenny's insinuations. To be accused of "that" was, in Deborah's opinion, the deadliest insult one woman could hurl at another. And when that woman was one's own sister...! If it hadn't been for George's presence at Cockfosters, I think Deborah would have packed there and then and rushed home to Honeypot Cottage. But although her pride was wounded to the quick, she just hadn't the courage to cut short her romance when it was only just getting into its stride.

After another little weep she got her feelings more or less under control and announced that she was going to take a walk round the lake. It was a lovely, windless evening and she thought it might help her to calm her nerves. There was no doubt that Deborah was overwrought, tottering all the time on the brink of hysteria.

The moment I was alone with Sheila, I said, "Harry's gone abroad. He went last Friday."

Sheila's surprise seemed genuine.

"Gone abroad? Where?"

"Italy, Germany...the old boy in the cottage across the road wasn't sure. But, good heavens, didn't Harry tell you he was going away?"

"No. Why should he?"

"You were with him on Thursday afternoon and he evidently left early on Friday morning. It's odd that he didn't tell you."

Sheila said with a little shrug of indifference:

"I don't think it's odd at all. Harry's always slipping off like this without a word to anybody. I don't see any reason why he should have told me."

Then, piqued by her air of detachment, I gave way to my irritation and said the wrong thing. The moment the words were out of my mouth I could have kicked myself.

"Well, you and Harry have always seemed as thick as thieves. Look at the way you sneaked off with him the other afternoon. He seems to have some sort of influence over you and I wish the devil I knew what it was."

Sheila said coldly, "So that's what you think." She gave another exasperating little shrug. "Oh well, in that case..."

And she left me standing there, trying to stammer out some sort of apology, wondering why everything seemed to be falling apart between us, when only a few days before she'd been sitting up in the window of the music-room, watching and waiting for the first glimpse of my car.

III

Dinner that night was the most painful meal to date. Deborah and Gwenny were not speaking to each other. Nor were Sheila and I. George hadn't shown up. How we ploughed through the inevitable four courses without suddenly screaming our heads off heaven alone knows! I did my best to lure Gwenny out of her shell, but her response was discouraging. The only time she showed a flicker of interest was when I told her about Harry's sudden flit across the Channel. She asked one or two pertinent questions, and then went silent. She was obviously startled and disturbed by the news.

Then, to make matters worse, just before we rose from the table, George rolled in as tight as a tick. I'd never seen him in such a state of bliss before. He stood in the doorway, rocking slightly on his heels, beaming and chuckling at us, with one eye wide open and the other half closed. He said to Gwenny:

"Sorry if I'm late. Dello lot of traffic on the road to-night... dello lot..."

Then he tried to give Gwenny a bit of a bow and nearly pitched forward on his face.

Gwenny got up slowly and with great dignity, drawing herself up to her full height, so that her figure was shown off to almost indecent advantage. She never uttered a word, but I knew exactly what was going to happen and I braced myself for yet another violent and disagreeable scene. The slap echoed in the room like a pistol shot. I saw George put up a hand to his cheek, and in his eyes an expression of childlike bewilderment, that gave way in about ten seconds to one of murderous fury. Deborah uttered a shrill bleat of alarm and distress and, hastening towards him, took him by the arm and helped him to a chair.

Gwenny had left the room at once and I wasn't slow in doing the same. Sheila came out into the hall almost on my heels, but as she took no notice of me I turned aside and went upstairs to my bedroom.

I suppose this incident really marked the climax to all the tension and enmity that had been building itself up during the last few days. The explosion, as it were, at the end of a slow fuse. Things couldn't possibly go on as they were. Gwenny would see to that. And as we were all there as her guests it was pretty obvious what line of action she would take. In short, the time was now ripe, even overripe, for this ill-fated house-party to break up.

I don't know if the others anticipated that the end of their stay at Cockfosters was in sight. If not, then Gwenny wasn't long in making it clear to them. Half-way through breakfast the next morning she announced abruptly:

"I'm closing the house on Friday and giving the staff a fort-night's holiday. I shall expect you to make your own arrange-ments about leaving. I'm crossing to France with the car early on Friday morning. I'm telephoning Madame Fougère at once, telling her to open up the villa ready for my arrival."

She reminded me of a colonel laying out a tactical scheme

to his subordinates. No loophole for questions. She was going to do precisely this and that, and if we didn't like it we could damn well lump it. Her attitude was insufferable because it denied us our status as individuals. Like bad servants, we were no longer wanted in the house and so, at very short notice, we were being dismissed.

I admit, of course, that George had behaved like the boor he was and deserved to be treated in this peremptory manner. But what had poor Deborah done? It wasn't her fault that she'd fallen for George Gammon. I can't imagine any woman deliberately *wanting* to, and she couldn't be expected to reason herself out of love with him.

And what had I done to upset Aunt Gwenny? Asked for her consent to marry Sheila? I suppose that was it. But when she'd said "No" I hadn't argued with her or lost my temper or pulled a fast one on her by driving Sheila off in the car. I'd swallowed down my disappointment, and done my damnedest to comport myself around the place like a civilised and grateful guest.

And now we'd got our marching orders…

Sheila asked submissively, "And what about me, Aunty? Am I coming with you to the villa?"

"No. I'm ringing Hester Mellicot and asking her to have you for a week or two. I'm sure she will. She doesn't enjoy many visitors, stuck away there in that great house of hers in the wilds of Scotland."

Scotland! Gwenny must have noticed my change of expression, because she suddenly fixed me with a spiteful glance and flashed me a viperish little smile. She'd guessed what had gone through my mind. That with Sheila buried in the depths of Scotland I'd have no chance of getting in touch with her while Gwenny was down on the Côte d'Azur.

Before breakfast came to an end, I'd decided to hang on to the last minute at Cockfosters in the hope of winning Sheila over to a more forthcoming state of mind. I was determined to find what had come between us and why her attitude had changed so suddenly towards me. In particular, why Harry Skeet had wanted to see her alone. I still felt that it was something he'd said to her that was at the root of her present standoffishness.

It was now Tuesday, and I made up my mind to leave for London directly after lunch on Thursday.

5

I WONDERED WHAT GEORGE WAS GOING TO DO. HE'D
been living with Gwenny for the past twelve months or so and
now, without warning, he was out on his ear. I knew Deborah
wouldn't leave until he did, because one could see with half
an eye that she treasured every minute spent in his company.
She must have felt frantic about the future. After all she must
have realised that, when the moment came for them to part
at Cockfosters, there was a chance they'd never meet again.

I mooned around the garden for a time, smoking one cigarette after another, trying to sort it all out. Sheila was busy
with her household duties. George and Deborah had unac-
countably faded away, and I suspected that they'd gone for
a long walk in the woods. Through the open window of the
study I heard Gwenny on the telephone to the A.A. making
her reservations on the Friday morning Dover–Boulogne
car-ferry and arranging with them about the necessary
documents.

I was just taking a turn through the kitchen garden when,

unexpectedly, Sheila showed up. She said without preliminary, "I want to talk to you. Let's walk down to the lake."

There was a little more cloud about than there had been
during the last few days. It looked to me as if the fine weather
were about to break up. When the sun went in the wind was
chilly, and clear of the walled garden it was blowing quite
freshly. The surface of the lake was grey and ruffled, and the
reeds along its banks were hissing like a nest of serpents.

I said, "Shall we row out to the island? It's a bit nippy here.
It'll be more sheltered in the summer-house."

"All right."

There was a small boat-house at either end of the lake,
each housing a row-boat. We headed for the nearest and,
in a few minutes, I was sculling over the choppy water. The
concrete landing-stage with its iron mooring-rings was out
of sight round the far side of the island. As it came into view,
Sheila suddenly said:

"Stay a moment, Nig. There's somebody there."

I twisted round on my seat and saw the second boat
swinging idly at the end of its painter, and, at the same time,
I heard voices coming from behind the flowering shrubs that
screened the summer-house. I said *sotto voce*:

"George and Deborah."

Sheila nodded and, as the oars were squeaking a little in
their rowlocks, signalled me to stop sculling. No doubt she
felt it would embarrass the couple if they discovered we were
there. Although we couldn't actually see them, they were less
than half a dozen yards away and everything they said was
startlingly clear.

"So you've nowhere to go?"

"Nowhere. Given a little more time I might have been able to get in touch with an old army pal of mine in Barcelona. He owns a little hotel there on the Ramblas. I think he'd be prepared to give me a job looking after the accounts. But he's away at the moment...er...in Majorca."

"Do you want to live in Barcelona?"

"I'd hate to, but beggars can't be choosers. I've got to get a job of some sort...and at my age it isn't easy. Fact is, I get a small remittance every three months from an uncle of mine in Buenos Aires. And just at the moment"—George registered extreme embarrassment—"well, I'm a bit pressed for ready money."

One could hear his tale fairly creaking, but Aunt Deborah never suspected for a moment that he was romancing, that when it came to the hard-luck story George was a past-master. She sounded almost tearful in her distress. She said again:

"So you've nowhere to go?"

"Nowhere."

And then, causing Sheila and I to stare at each other in disbelief, we heard Deborah proposing that George should come and stay with her at Honeypot Cottage. Temporarily, of course. Until such times as he was able to find a job worthy of his talents. George kept saying over and over again in a kind of lecherous undertone:

"But I say, old dear... I say..."

But such was her infatuation she wasn't going to let a little matter like the conventions stand in the way of her happiness. The last thing we heard her saying as the boat drifted out of earshot was:

"You really needn't worry about what people will say.

The cottage is very isolated. And if there's anything you want in the village I can always fetch it. We've only got to be discreet..."

Such innocence, I thought, was both disarming and dangerous.

II

In the end Sheila and I fetched up in the music-room, and I asked her at once what she'd wanted to see me about. She hesitated a moment and then said:

"You won't understand, Nig, but I want you to have patience. I'm in a most awful fix and I don't know what to do."

"About us?"

"Partly."

"You no longer think it's a good idea that we should get married?"

She said slowly, "I think we should let matters rest as they are at the moment."

"Because of that seventy thousand?"

She flushed.

"I think that's vile of you. You know it's not true."

"Then why this sudden coolness towards me? Have I done or said anything to upset you?"

"No."

"Then what...?"

"I can't possibly explain. I wish I could. But I didn't want you to go away feeling all the wrong things about me."

I said, "Do you think it'll all come right in the end?"

But she wasn't very reassuring.

"It might. There's so many things…" Then she broke off and added, "By the way, when are you leaving?"

"Thursday—after lunch. And you?"

Sheila made a sour grimace.

"So far Aunt Gwenny hasn't issued her orders."

III

I wondered what had been the outcome of the little discussion in the island summer-house. I didn't doubt that, after a conventional protest, George would jump at Deborah's offer to put a roof over his head. All this talk about getting a job was merely eyewash. George was bone idle and, as far as I could make out, he hadn't done a stroke of work for years. Of course, he wouldn't find the same comforts and cuisine at Honeypot Cottage as he had at Cockfosters, but half a loaf was better than no loaf, particularly if one didn't have to earn it by the sweat of one's brow.

Even if they had agreed to go off together, they naturally weren't going to shout the news from the housetops. After all, if Gwenny got wind of this development, she was quite capable of altering her plans just to spite her sister and taking George off with her to the Villa Paradou. And at the prospect of a holiday loafing around Cap Martin George would go like a lamb, leaving poor Deborah high and dry.

At least that was my opinion at lunchtime on Tuesday. By lunchtime on Wednesday I wasn't so sure. A curious change seemed to have come over George since he'd rowed Deborah out to the island. He looked at her quite differently, with real warmth and intimacy, almost with respect. He couldn't keep his eyes or his hands off her, trailing around after her like a hungry dog, talking earnestly to her in corners, fussing around her as I'd never seen him fuss around Gwenny. Luckily Gwenny was far too occupied with the arrangements for her departure to notice what was going on.

On Wednesday afternoon George borrowed Deborah's car and drove over to Folkestone again to see his friends. I don't know how he fitted them into his story about having nowhere to go, but he probably told Deborah that they hadn't got a spare room or something of that sort. For my own part I suspected these friends to be a myth. Considering George's condition when he'd returned from his last jaunt I guessed he'd made a round of it with some of his pub acquaintances. He'd been long enough at Cockfosters to nose out a few scroungers and bounders like himself in the neighbouring towns. After all, any chap living under the Damoclean sword of Gwenny's temperament couldn't be blamed if he sneaked off for an occasional pub crawl. I prayed to heaven that he wouldn't come back drunk.

But he didn't. He arrived back just after dinner, cold sober and oddly preoccupied. Gwenny and Deborah still weren't speaking to each other and we'd had another silent and sulky meal. After a little starchy conversation over coffee in the lounge, we all went up early to bed.

Much to my surprise Gwenny joined us at breakfast on Thursday morning. She wasn't looking quite so grim and, although she refused to address herself to her sister, she was a little more affable to the rest of us. I think she felt relieved because all the hostility and hoo-ha of the last few days was due, in a few hours, to come to an end.

Somewhere about the toast-and-marmalade stage, George suddenly looked across at me and said:

"I don't want to be a damned nuisance, but could you drive me over to Canterbury station this morning?"

"Of course. What time's your train?"

George told me and I realised at once that he was aiming to catch the London express. I was puzzled. Was he really turning down Deborah's invitation to stay at Honeypot Cottage? That particular train certainly didn't stop at any intermediate station. Then, intercepting a quick little smile that flashed between George and Deborah, I tumbled to his little game. He'd made that request in front of Gwenny because he wanted to deceive her.

Directly after breakfast I drove the car round to the front-door. A moment or so later, George came down the steps, portering a couple of battered and bulging suitcases, followed by Sheila and Aunt Deborah. There was no sign of Gwenny. When he'd solemnly shaken hands with the two women, he put his cases in the boot and climbed in beside me. A few noisy farewells, a wave or two, and we were soon out of sight among the trees of the park. We weren't two hundred yards up the lane beyond the drive gates, however, when George said:

"Look here, old man, I haven't been quite straight with you. I'm not going to the station. That touch about catching the London express was all my eye and Betty Martin. I want you to drop me at the Varley cross-roads."

I turned and stared at him, hoping to disconcert him, but he returned my gaze with a wonderfully frank, though rather bleary look.

"Am I allowed to ask why you've had me on a string?"

"I'd rather you didn't, old man."

"You wanted Gwenny to think you were leaving for London?"

"That's about it."

I had to pretend, of course, that I knew nothing of what they'd been discussing behind the flowering shrubs on the island. But I guessed George wouldn't have long to wait at the cross-roads before Deborah came along in her little car and picked him up. He begged me not to return directly to the house, because if I got back too soon Gwenny might start asking awkward questions. I told him that was fine because I really did want to go to Canterbury. The fan-belt on my car was worn and I hadn't been able to pick up a replacement at the local garage.

I dropped George on the corner, where the lane joined the main Canterbury–Dover road, shook him by the hand, took one final look at his red and raddled face and thanked God that I should probably never see him again. Of course, there was always the chance that Aunt Deborah might make a new man of him. But I doubted it, because George wouldn't stay with her *that* long.

As I anticipated, when I reached the cross-roads on my return run there was no sign of George and his suitcases. And no sooner had I garaged my car and gone into the house than Sheila appeared from the sitting-room and said:

"Aunt Deborah's left. She seemed to make up her mind in a hurry. She's sorry she didn't see you to say 'Good-bye,' but she sends you her love."

I then told Sheila how George had asked to be dropped

at the Varley cross-roads, and we hung about for a time discussing the astonishing change that had come over Aunt Deborah. Then, flying off at a tangent, Sheila said:

"I had a postcard this morning from Harry. He's in Coblence. He talks of moving on by easy stages to the Black Forest."

After a little more chit-chat, during which Sheila stubbornly steered the conversation clear of our personal relationship, I went upstairs to pack. With Gwenny getting ready to leave early the next morning the whole house was in chaos. There were doors opening and shutting everywhere and the staff were almost run off their feet trying to catch up with Gwenny's constant stream of orders. Sheila, it seemed, was not due to leave until after lunch on Friday, several hours after Gwenny, when she was to catch the two-thirty at Canterbury. She was spending a long week-end in town with Hester Mellicot who was coming down from Scotland to meet her.

We had lunch rather hurriedly at one end of the long refectory table—just Gwenny, Sheila and myself. Gwenny made no reference to Deborah's hasty departure, and she certainly didn't suspect that George had sneaked off with her to Honeypot Cottage, because she suddenly turned to me and asked:

"What does George think he's going to *do* in London? He hasn't a penny to his name. And, if I know anything about it, most of his friends are as shiftless and incompetent as he is."

I stammered something about him hoping to get a job. Gwenny gave a cynical little laugh and said with a snort of scorn:

"George was always an optimist. Who's going to employ

a drink-sodden wreck of a man like that? I've never seen any-body go to pieces so quickly. He's only himself to thank if he finds himself up against it. I did my best for him."

The time then came for me to make my round of farewells. After I'd said "Good-bye" to the kitchen staff, I drove the car round to the front-door and stowed my cases in the boot. I'd seen Gwenny go up to her room, and I intended to take leave of her up there, so that I could edge Sheila into the lounge and have our last few minutes in private. But it didn't work out that way. Gwenny probably guessed my intentions because she said, "So you're going now, Nig darling. I'll come down and see you off."

"But you're busy...you really needn't trouble."

"But I want to, darling. You've behaved very well these last few trying days. It's been nice having you around. Such a pity I've had to cut your visit short." She stumped down the stairs, shrieking at the top of her voice, "Sheila! Sheila darling! Where are you? Nig's just off!"

And that was how it all finished up. With Sheila and I dumbly shaking hands, and Aunt Gwenny standing by with a fatuous smile on her face, saying, "Aren't you going to kiss each other?" so that I felt like strangling her, because I knew that Sheila was feeling as wretched and frustrated as I was. It was a proper fiasco. Just as Gwenny had intended.

After that I jumped into the car and drove off as quickly as I could, turning only once to wave at the bottom of the hill before the house was hidden by the trees. It was a day of low cloud, with a hint of rain in the air, and the colour seemed to have gone out of everything. More than ever Cockfosters looked like a barracks, grim and grey against the skyline, with the two doll-like figures standing on the steps, answering my wave.

And I wondered when and in what circumstances I would visit Cockfosters again. Perhaps I should never return. Perhaps Aunt Gwenny… But what was the use of speculation? Gwenny was a law unto herself and as unpredictable as the weather. And yet something told me that where Sheila and I were concerned she'd never change her mind. She was determined to keep us apart. Why, I couldn't say. Nor could Sheila. I remembered her saying, "There's something more to this than we imagine."

Later, of course, I realised how right she was! But that was after the police had stepped in and the truth, after a tireless and brilliant investigation, had been brought to light.

PART II

POST MORTEM AT THE VILLA

6

AFTER A SILENCE THAT HAD LASTED AT LEAST FIVE MIN-
utes, Fougère took the pipe from his mouth and observed:

"*Eh bien*...what can you expect? It's always the same...
chopping and changing...never knowing her own mind for
more than two minutes on end."

Madame Fougère looked up from her knitting, nodded
sagely, and said:

"That's true enough. Too much money's like a maggot in
the brain. It eats away common sense. You never know where
you are with a woman of her sort. She's enough to try the
temper of a saint."

They sat in their handkerchief of garden on the slopes
above Menton, gazing down placidly at the blue waters of
the Golfe de la Paix, watching the Sunday traffic threading its
way along the promenade. A little to their right the wooded
headland of Cap Martin thrust out into the sea. Somewhere
out of sight among the parasol-pines near the apex of the cape
was the Villa Paradou.

The Fougères were discussing Madame Marrable. Not continuously, but in fits and starts, drowsing in the hot sunshine among the espaliered apricots and pear trees, content to sit and say nothing for a time, ruminating on the fickleness and stupidity of their mistress. Fougère tended the garden and did odd jobs about the villa. His wife was cook and general housekeeper. Even when Gwenny was in residence the couple never lived in. At seven every morning they mounted their ancient bicycles and rode at a snail's pace out to the villa, returning home at seven in the evening, with their handlebar baskets groaning under the weight of choice vegetables, half-empty bottles of wine and other tit-bits that had come from Gwenny's table. For forty years Fougère had worked as a railway porter at Toulon. Now that he'd retired, their employment at the Villa Paradou afforded a welcome means of adding to his meagre pension.

The smoke from Fougère's pipe hung in swathes on the windless air. His wife was knitting a sock with her eyes half-closed against the brilliance of the day. Peace reigned in the little garden. Down on the *plage* the fronds of the palm trees hung limp and unstirring.

Presently Fougère enquired, "It was from Lyons she sent it?"

"Yes—Lyons."

Silence came down again, enveloping them like a mountain cloud, shutting them away with their reflections. Madame Fougère was seeing the telegram again, reading it over in her mind, experiencing again the exasperation that had moved her when it had been delivered the previous day out at the villa. DELAYED. DON'T EXPECT ME UNTIL

TUESDAY AFTERNOON—MARRABLE. When the boy had cycled up the drive, she'd been sitting on the terrace, in the shade of a vine, polishing the silver. Sunday afternoon, she'd said over the telephone from Cockfosters. That was to-day. Now madame, for some inexplicable reason, had suddenly changed her plans and the villa was to remain locked and shuttered for another two days.

Fougère's thoughts had moved on from the telegram and were now hovering round an incident that had deeply impressed and disturbed him. The evening before, his old friend Pialou, the window-cleaner, had cycled out to the point for a couple of hours' fishing. By the time he'd packed up his gear and scrambled back over the rocks to the road where he'd left his bicycle dusk had come down and it was almost dark under the parasol-pines. He was a few yards short of the entrance to the Villa Paradou when he'd seen the figure of a man dart across the road and slip up the drive. His curiosity aroused, Pialou had left his bicycle by the roadside and cautiously followed the figure. He was just rounding the bend in the drive when, only a little way ahead, he'd seen the man mount the terrace steps and, after a moment's hesitation, walk in through the front-door. Pialou had then crept towards the house, tried the door and found it locked. After that he'd made a circuit of the place, staring up at the shuttered windows, expecting somewhere to see a glimmer of light shining through the slats. But the place had remained in darkness, and after hanging about for some five minutes Pialou had shrugged his shoulders and returned to the road.

When he'd told Fougère his story, the old man had stared at him in disbelief.

"It is impossible, *mon ami.*"

"But with my own eyes…"

"It is impossible! Marie and I have one set of keys to the villa. All the other keys are held by madame herself. That he should have gone in through the front-door is inconceivable."

"All the same…do you expect me to doubt the evidence of my own eyes?"

"It was a man?"

"Yes—but don't ask me to describe him. It was too dark for that."

"Through the front-door, you said?"

"Yes—the front-door."

After Pialou had joined him in a glass of wine and continued on his way home to the Rue St. Michel down by the harbour, Fougère had crossed himself and mumbled a prayer to the Virgin, humbly soliciting that this ghost might be exorcised from the villa. For he didn't doubt that what Pialou had seen was no mortal man. Neither he nor Madame Fougère had ever suspected that the Villa Paradou might be haunted and they decided, there and then, that there was no pressing reason for them to visit the house until Madame Marrable arrived on Tuesday afternoon. During Saturday night a heavy shower of rain had fallen, so there was no need for Fougère to water the garden. The larder was stocked. The dust-sheets had been removed from the furniture. Madame's bed was made. Everything, in fact, had been ready for madame since yesterday afternoon.

And now they weren't to expect her until Tuesday, April 26th…

II

Tuesday, April 26th.

Fougère went to the little shed at the end of the garden and wheeled out the bicycles. It was just after two o'clock and a shimmer of heat lay over the pan-tiled roofs of the town. The sea was like a shining plaque of blue enamel, with streaks of indigo and pale green brushed across its surface. As Fougère stood waiting at the gate for his wife, he could see the café parasols planted along the *plage* like a border of full-blown flowers. He called out impatiently.

"Well, don't take all day about it."

"I'm coming, Jean."

"And about time, too!"

Madame Fougère was dressed in black silk. A white straw hat was perched on her dark pyramid of hair. She looked as if she were just setting off for early Mass. She took the second bicycle from her husband and the couple, mounting their saddles, trundled off down the hill at a pace that was barely sufficient to keep them from overbalancing. At the bottom of the hill they turned right along the Promenade Maréchal Joffre and were soon in the shade of the pines that fringed the east side of the cape. Fifteen minutes later they were propping their bicycles against the terrace balustrade of the villa.

As the old man stirred around in his pocket for the keys, his eye wandered over the pink façade of the house, making sure that all the shutters were still closed as he had left them. Then, followed by Madame Fougère, he went up the steps to the front-door, turned the handle and tugged it vigorously.

"*Tiens!* it is locked securely enough."

"Of course it's locked."

Old Fougère said slowly, "I was thinking of Pialou's story. He's not the sort of chap to imagine things."

"No. Pialou's sober enough. I've never known *him* the worse for drink. With five children and a sick wife to care for he can't afford it."

Fougère looked meaningly at his wife, crossed himself rather furtively, and said in a sepulchral voice, "Well, there you are then…"

His hand shook a little as he fitted the key into the lock, and when the door was open he stood aside so that his wife could precede him into the hall. That wasn't the usual way of things. If he and Marie arrived together at a door or a gate, Fougère was always the first through because he considered it right and natural that a married man should take precedence over his wife.

Madame Fougère said, "It's as dark in here as the inside of a cow. Hurry up and open the shutters, you fool!…standing there twiddling your cap. Anybody would think—"

There was a clatter, a little cry of pain and, to his surprise, Fougère saw his wife stumble forward over a big, black object that was lying a few feet inside the door.

"What is it? Are you all right?"

"Of course I'm all right. Help me up. And how should I know what it is? Something you left lying about after you'd locked up the other day…that's about the measure of it."

With her husband's help, Madame Fougère scrambled to her feet, stooped for a moment to rub her shins through her skirt, resettled her hat, and ordered Fougère to switch on the chandelier. A blaze of light suddenly washed the shadows out of the hall. They turned and looked down at the object over which Madame Fougère had stumbled. A look of incredulity crossed their features, giving way to an expression of alarm, almost of panic. Fougère muttered:

"So she's here already. Now we'll start off badly and no mistake. Though why she should have locked the door behind her and left all the shutters closed…"

Madame Fougère had already taken a quick look in the lounge and dining-room. Now she went to the foot of the stairs and listened carefully. Not a sound in the house. Everything was so quiet that they could hear the throbbing of the pleasure steamer as it rounded the headland on its way back to Monte Carlo.

"Madame! Madame Marrable! It is me…Marie. Are you there, madame?"

In the meantime Fougère had gone down on one knee and was gazing at the huge black cabin-trunk, wondering how madame had managed to get it single-handed up the terrace steps and into the house. He knew that cabin-trunk only too well, with its brass edges, massive clasps and the initials G.E.M. stencilled in white on the lid. After his first unsuccessful attempt to manhandle it upstairs he'd been forced to construct a rubber-tyred, two-wheeled trolley so that he could get the monstrous thing into madame's dressing-room. Fougère was proud of that trolley. Madame had complimented him on his ingenuity. But as a retired porter he felt secretly ashamed of his inability to swing the trunk on his shoulders and carry it upstairs. It was the biggest trunk he'd ever seen. A man could have curled up inside it with the lid down and still have found room to blow his nose.

Madame Fougère said, "She's not in the house. She must have left the trunk and driven off again in the car."

"How did she get the trunk into the house? Tell me that."

"Perhaps…"

"Well?"

"Perhaps she had somebody with her in the car. Perhaps a man…"

"Did she say over the telephone last Tuesday that she was bringing a guest to stay at the villa?"

"She said she was coming alone. But if she can change her mind over one thing she can change it over another."

But Fougère was no longer interested in the argument. He'd noticed that the safety catches of the two clasps were not in position, and it suddenly occurred to him that the trunk was probably unlocked. Idly he slid aside the spring locks. The hasps flicked up with a snap. Before Madame Fougère could stop him, he'd raised the lid and, still at the mercy of his childlike curiosity, peered inside.

"Mon Dieu!"

His exclamation split the silence of the house from top to bottom, though Fougère was not even aware that he'd opened his mouth. He could hear the blood pounding in his ears and, somewhere outside the terrible confusion that had taken possession of him, his wife's anxious enquiry: "What is it? What's the matter?"

Fougère slammed down the lid and one by one, fumbling in his haste, fastened the clasps. He could feel his heart thudding behind his ribs and the sweat breaking out on the palms of his hands. A sudden wave of nausea swept through him. He got shakily to his feet and stared at his wife with a dazed and terrified expression. His mouth was so dry that his voice was little more than a croak.

"We must ring the police."

Madame Fougère was saying over and over again:

"What is it? What's the matter?"

The old man didn't seem to hear her questions, for he went on muttering almost to himself.

"We must ring the Commissariat at Menton. It's nothing to do with us. We must make that clear at the start. They'll begin asking questions. Perhaps they'll try to catch us out. But we've only got to keep our heads…"

Madame Fougère's voice was almost frantic. She was glaring at her husband as if he'd taken leave of his senses. She shrilled out, "Will you tell me what's wrong, you fool! All this talk about ringing the police… What have we got to ring the police about?"

Fougère's eyes were still clouded with bewilderment, but at last he seemed to grasp what his wife was saying.

"Madame Marrable."

"What of madame?"

"She's doubled up inside the trunk…dead. Murdered, for all I know…and naked as the day she was born…"

7

FOUGÈRE HAD OFTEN SEEN INSPECTOR HAMONET SITting in the Café Floreal just round the corner from the Commissariat, playing *belote* with his friends, but he'd never spoken to him. He looked a good-natured fellow in his off-duty hours, but now, with his *kepi* on and his face unsmiling, there was, in Fougère's opinion, something menacing about him. He'd brought along a sergeant, who kept scribbling notes in a little black book. Two loops of string had been slipped round the hasps of the trunk so that it could be opened without touching it.

"All right. I've seen all I want to here. Let's go through to another room. The doctor will be along any minute. He won't want you around while he's making his post-mortem."

Madame Fougère led the way into the kitchen. At a signal from Hamonet, the sergeant flung back the shutters and the room was suddenly drenched in sunlight. Almost at once the temperature of the room began to rise, and soon Fougère was mopping his brow and rubbing his hands on his trouser-legs.

"What made you open the trunk?"

Fougère looked at the floor and stammered.

"I don't know. I wish now I hadn't seen what was inside it. Of course, it's nothing to do with us. We're as much in the dark as you are."

The inspector turned to Madame Fougère.

"This telegram you spoke of…have you still got it?"

"Yes…here."

She pulled it from the pocket of her dress. Hamonet smoothed it out, read it and handed it to the sergeant, who slipped it between the pages of his notebook.

"You were expecting Madame Marrable to arrive here by road?"

"Yes. She was crossing to Boulogne from Dover early last Friday. Let's see…that was the twenty-second. She spends most of the year at her house near Canterbury."

"*Did* she cross on the twenty-second?"

Madame Fougère said tartly:

"How am I to know? But she sent that telegram from Lyons sometime on Saturday, and it would take her at least two days to drive there from Boulogne."

Fougère put in querulously:

"We haven't been near the villa since Saturday afternoon. My wife will swear to that. So it's no good thinking we had anything to do with it."

But Hamonet took no notice of the old man. He went on questioning Madame Fougère in his flat, clipped voice, not hurrying her, but never allowing her for an instant to wander from the point.

"She was driving down alone?"

"So she gave me to understand."

"It's a powerful car?"

"Yes."

"How long did Madame Marrable usually allow herself for the journey from Boulogne to the villa here?"

"Three days."

"When was madame last down at the villa?"

"In January...for three weeks."

"And since then the house has been shut up?"

"Yes."

"Has she any enemies?"

"Not that I know of."

"A husband?"

"She's a widow."

The catechism went on and on. Noticing an electric fan on the refrigerator, Hamonet crossed over and switched it on. The sergeant was scribbling as fast as he could, his pencil hissing on the paper, the leaves of his notebook fluttering in the sudden flow of air. Old Fougère mightn't have been there for all the notice taken of him, and he kept shuffling round the room, muttering over and over again:

"We can't tell you anything about it. It's nothing to do with us. Perhaps you're hoping to catch us out...perhaps that's it!"

Suddenly Hamonet, irritated by his mumblings, swung round on him and rapped out, "Did you think of looking in the garage to see if madame's car was there?"

"Well...no. As a matter of fact—"

"Then you'd better find out at once."

No sooner had Fougère gone out of the back-door than there was a ring at the front. The sergeant went down the hall and opened up. It was the police surgeon. Hearing his voice, Hamonet said:

"All right, Madame Fougère, that'll do for the moment. You'd better stick in here in case there are other questions I want to ask you."

Hamonet carefully shut the kitchen door and walked down the hall to where the doctor was already kneeling in front of the open trunk. He was short and bald and the armpits of his grey tussore jacket were darkened with sweat. As he leaned over to make his examination drops of moisture trickled from his forehead on to the lens of his glasses, and more than once he took them off to polish them. The dead woman's knees were drawn up against her stomach so that she lay almost doubled up in the trunk.

The doctor observed, "In a position like this I think we can reasonably assume that she was pushed into the trunk soon after she was killed…before the onset of rigor mortis. Death was unquestionably due to suffocation."

Hamonet asked, "Suffocation due to being shut up in the trunk?"

"No. I should say from the compression of the nose and lips that she'd been smothered…by a pillow or a cushion, perhaps."

"No other marks of violence on her body?"

"None, as far as I can see from a preliminary glance."

"And death occurred…?"

The doctor lifted his shoulders.

"Three days ago…perhaps longer. It's not easy to be accurate. The trunk would be more or less airtight. The ordinary processes of decomposition and so forth have naturally been arrested."

The doctor's examination became more specific and his observations more technical. But Hamonet wasn't really listening. He was thinking that if the woman had been dead for three days then she must have been murdered at some point between Lyons and Cap Martin. The telegram had been sent off at 12.10 P.M. on Saturday. Exactly three days ago. Why the body had been brought to the villa, he couldn't say. It seemed a crazy act on the part of the murderer to risk being spotted at the villa lugging the trunk up the steps from the car. And how had he got in? Presumably by means of the keys he'd found in the woman's handbag or the dashboard pocket of her car.

The doctor broke in on his thoughts, "Well, that's about all I can tell you. You'll be arranging for an ambulance to take the body to the mortuary?"

Hamonet nodded.

"Until we can get in touch with her next-of-kin. The Fougère woman can probably help me there."

The doctor finished lighting his short black cigar and held out his hand.

"I'll make out my written report for the examining magistrate."

"Good. Only I won't be seeing this case through myself. It'll be handed over to Nice. We've already let them have a preliminary report and they're sending a man over. I don't know yet who'll be in charge of the investigation, but I'll put you in touch with him."

When the doctor had driven off, Hamonet turned to the sergeant.

"Better take a look at the upstairs rooms. I'm going to have another talk with the Fougères."

The old man had partly opened the kitchen door on his return from the garage, and he had his ear to the gap, trying to make out what was taking place in the hall. On hearing the inspector's footsteps approaching, he silently closed the door and shuffled away to the window. Madame Fougère had fetched a bottle of cognac and three glasses from a cupboard and set them out on a table. In case the inspector should refuse a drink, she and Fougère had already fortified themselves with a nip or two.

"Well, was the car in the garage?"

"No—it's empty."

Madame Fougère nodded towards the bottle.

"You'll take a little something, Inspector?"

"Not at the moment, madame. There are one or two points about which I'm still not clear. You say Madame Marrable telephoned you from England when she first told you she was coming down to Menton?"

"Yes—last Tuesday."

"You took the call here at the villa?"

"No, m'sieur. We don't live in."

"Then how…?"

"We have a telephone at home. Madame paid for us to have it put in, so that if there was any little thing she wanted us to get in the town—"

"Why didn't she telephone you from Lyons on Saturday morning instead of sending a telegram?"

"Perhaps she did and found us out. All Saturday we were over here making ready for madame. If she got no reply she may have thought we were shopping or something of the sort."

"What of her next-of-kin?"

"That would be her adopted daughter…or her sister, per-haps. But I don't know how you're going to get in touch with them. Madame told me on the telephone that the house was being shut and the staff sent on holiday. Mam'selle Sheila has gone to stay with a friend. I don't know where."

"And the sister?"

"I haven't got her address either."

The old man had just finished giving Hamonet the regis-tration number and description of the missing car when the sergeant entered the kitchen. He said importantly, "Can you come upstairs a minute."

Hamonet nodded.

"Very well." Up on the landing he said sharply, "Well, what is it?"

"In here…"

It was one of the guest-rooms at the back of the villa, overlooking a rose garden. The sergeant had pushed open the shutters and the room was filled with a blaze of honey-coloured light. The usual appointments—a divan bed, a big built-in wardrobe, an armchair by the window, a table or two, a door in one corner, half-open, giving into a bathroom. The bed had not been made up, but it was evident that somebody had recently been sleeping on it, for the coverlet and peach-coloured blankets were flung down and the pillow bore the imprint of a head. One or two empty wine bottles had been rammed neck-downward into the wastepaper-basket, and the ashtray on the bedside table was filled with cigarette stubs. On the foot of the bed was a copy of *France-Dimanche*. Hamonet picked it up and glanced at the date. April 24th—last Sunday's edition. He crossed to the bathroom. There was a soiled towel flung over the rail and a rime of dirty soap clinging to the washbasin.

"What the devil's been going on here?" he said.

"Ask me another. Perhaps the Fougères have got an explanation."

But the old couple were obviously nonplussed. True, Madame Fougère hadn't looked into the room since she'd dusted and polished it about a week ago. That, of course, was after she'd received Madame Marrable's instructions to get things ready at the villa. But everything in that room, as in every other room, had been left as clean and tidy as one could wish.

"So it's no good asking me what's been going on up there. I don't know any more about it than you do. What's more, we left the house locked and shuttered, so how anybody managed to get in…"

All through his wife's recital Fougère kept nodding and grunting and sucking his teeth. The bottle of cognac on the kitchen table was almost empty and the old man's breath was reeking of brandy. Every now and then he lifted his shoulders in a hopeless gesture and muttered "*Eh bien*, what is one to make of *that*?" He seemed dazed by the sudden pressure of events. It was difficult now to remember how ordinary everything had seemed cycling along the road under the pine trees, with the fishermen perched on the rocks, and the little pleasure yachts drifting over the glassy water.

Suddenly Fougère was aware that Hamonet's steely eyes were fixed on his.

"You haven't seen anybody hanging about the place during the last few days?"

"No...nobody. Not that we've been over here since Saturday. You see, it's just as I said. It's no good looking to us to help you out. Perhaps if you asked in the houses round about..."

Suddenly the old man broke off and stood staring at Hamonet with his mouth hanging open. How had he come to forget it? Pialou's story. The room upstairs where somebody had evidently slept the night. Perhaps, after all...

Hamonet said, "What is it? You've remembered something?"

"Perhaps... I'm not sure."

His weak eyes were watering in the strong sunlight that poured through the window. He felt fuddled by all these questions. His mind couldn't keep up with them. And the brandy wasn't helping to keep his thoughts in order. He glanced across appealingly at his wife, as if to enlist her help in dealing with Hamonet. Madame Fougère guessed at once what was troubling him.

"It's Pialou's story—that's what he's thinking of. I suppose you ought to know. It happened last Saturday evening..."

Before the old woman had finished telling her tale Hamonet's mind was full of conjecture. Suppose for the moment he ignored that telegram from Lyons and assumed Madame Marrable had turned up at the villa on Sunday night. Suppose the unknown man had been in the house when she arrived, and as soon as she'd entered the house, for some reason or other, he'd attacked her. In his hand, perhaps, a pillow from the bed on which he'd been lying. Perhaps he had no thought of murder in his mind. Perhaps he'd held the pillow over her face to stifle her screams, fearing they might draw somebody to the house. But by the time he'd removed the pillow the woman was dead. What to do with the body? Where to conceal it? He'd seen the cabin-trunk in the car outside. Either it was unlocked or he'd found the keys in his victim's handbag or the like. He'd emptied its contents into the back of the car, dragged the trunk into the hall and, stripping off the dead woman's clothes, forced the body inside it. Then, perhaps, an interruption, a scare of some sort, a moment of panic. Voices in the road, footsteps approaching, the slam of a door upstairs—something, at any rate, that had broken his nerve, so that he'd hurriedly locked the door of the villa, jumped into the car and driven off as fast as he could. No doubt he'd actually intended to drive the body away in the trunk. But as it was…

Hamonet's reflections were brought to a sudden halt. Somewhere in the house the telephone was ringing. Madame Fougère looked at him enquiringly. Behind her back the old man was just emptying the dregs of the cognac bottle into his glass.

Hamonet said, "It's all right. I'll take it."

He went through quickly into the hall and picked up the receiver. Through the open door he could see the sergeant moving about among the cactus plants in the garden, where he'd been sent to search the grounds.

"Hullo."

"Villa Paradou?"

"Yes. What is it?"

There was a moment's silence, as if the caller were put off his stride by the inspector's abrupt and authoritative manner. Then the voice, a man's voice, said in English:

"I'd like to speak to Madame Marrable. *Comprenez-vous?* Madame Marrable... I'd like to speak to her. Is she there?"

Hamonet knew enough English to understand the question, but he had to think quickly before he decided how to answer it.

"Who is it that speaks, please?"

His English wasn't bad but his accent was atrocious.

"It's Mr. Derry—Nigel Derry. I'm ringing from my hotel in Menton."

"But, of course. Madame Marrable has expected you to telephone. She is not here at the moment, but she leave the word that she desire you to come over at once."

8

BACK IN THE KITCHEN THE OLD MAN WAS DODDERING, half-asleep, at the table, his head clasped in his hands. Madame Fougère, at last giving way to her distress, was sitting opposite him, the tears running down her purple cheeks. Hamonet said:

"It was a M'sieur Derry enquiring for Madame Marrable. He's English. Do you know anything about him?"

"Nothing. He's never stayed at the villa."

Hamonet took up the empty cognac bottle, glanced at it and put it down again. Madame Fougère, struggling to control her emotions, nodded to the cupboard.

"Perhaps you'll join us now? There's another bottle."

"Thanks. I will."

Fougère was fast asleep and snoring. His head had fallen sideways to the table, and every now and then he blew out his lips as if throwing a kiss. When Madame Fougère had poured out the drinks Hamonet began to question her about the guests who had stayed at the villa during Madame Marrable's last few visits. But before the housekeeper could reply, the sergeant's head suddenly appeared round the door.

"Well, what is it?"

"The inspector's arrived from Nice. He's out in the hall now, taking a look at the body. You'll never guess who they've put on to the job!" The sergeant was evidently finding it difficult to control his excitement. "Blampignon! We're in luck's way. It isn't often we get a chance to work in with a big shot like that."

Hamonet was impressed but he wasn't going to let the sergeant see it. Blampignon was the most experienced and successful detective along the Côte d'Azur. He was a personality in the police world and the stories told about him in the bars and cafés along the coast would have filled a full-length book. Hardly a month went by without his name cropping up in the papers. Once or twice Hamonet had attended his lectures on criminal investigation, but he'd never exchanged more than a dozen words with him. He said to the sergeant, "You found nothing in the grounds?"

"Nothing."

"All right. I'll come through."

Blampignon had evidently concluded his examination, for the trunk was shut, and he was just heaving himself up off his knees. His fat, good-humoured face was gleaming with perspiration and he was wheezing and puffing with the effort of raising his sixteen stone into a vertical position. With every movement his huge body quivered like a jelly. Without saying a word he shook hands with Hamonet, loosened the top button of his white ducks and pulled out a packet of *Bastos*. The sergeant hurriedly lit a match and held the flame to the tip of Blampignon's cigarette. Beneath the inspector's silk shirt, which was clinging to him like a second skin, Hamonet could see a shadowy pelt of hair. Blampignon said abruptly, "Well, what have you found out?"

"Little enough. But there are one or two facts that may prove of interest."

Blampignon nodded towards the open door of the lounge. "Very well. Let's go in there."

The windows were still shuttered, but a certain amount of light filtered into the room through the slats. The sergeant was about to open the shutters, but Blampignon stopped him. They made themselves comfortable in the big armchairs, with their legs stuck out, their faces scarcely visible in the airless twilight. All the time Hamonet was handing on the details of what he'd learnt Blampignon never uttered a word. But for his gusty breathing one might have thought he'd slipped from his chair and tip-toed out of the room. When Hamonet had finished talking, Blampignon demanded forcefully:

"But the woman…what do you know about *her*? What have you found out? What sort of woman *was* she?"

"So far…it's difficult to say…"

"*Eh bien!* then we must find out." Blampignon had heaved himself to his feet and was now tramping heavily about the room, rattling the ornaments. "In nine cases out of ten, the solution to the problem posed by a murder case is to be found in the character of the victim. What sort of company did she keep? Was she generous, spiteful, mean, bad-tempered or easy to get along with? Did she drink, gamble, go to church, interest herself in good works? A widow, you say. Very well… she might have been hot stuff. A widow of forty…you know how it is. Or perhaps she was loyal to the memory of her husband. That's equally possible. Then her financial affairs… there may have been members of her family with expectations. You see what I'm driving at?"

Hamonet said, "Perhaps this Englishman may have something to tell you. That may be him now." A car had just come to a stop on the drive and they could hear a quick murmur of voices. Evidently the young man had hired a taxi to bring him out to the villa. "Do you want us to stay?"

"No. I'll see him alone."

"Very well then, we'll be getting along. I'll arrange for an ambulance to take the body to the mortuary. I'll see that the men don't leave their dabs all over the trunk. What about the Fougères? They're still in the kitchen."

"They'd better hang on for the moment. I'll want their fingerprints. I'll come on to the Commissariat when I've finished here."

Blampignon went to the windows and, one by one, threw open the shutters. For a moment he was blinded by the sudden onslaught of light. The taxi was just backing to turn and go off down the drive. The young man was standing at the foot of the steps looking up curiously at the house. Blampignon called out in excellent English, "In here if you will."

He walked over to the door and met the young man stepping round the trunk in the hall. He pushed out his hand.

"M'sieur Derry…my name's Blampignon. I'm a detective-inspector attached to the *Sûreté Nationale*. I'd like to have a talk with you."

Derry was obviously puzzled and a little suspicious. There was no doubt that Blampignon, in his pink striped shirt and white duck trousers, was not his idea of a detective. But he followed the inspector into the room and was ushered into a chair facing the window. Blampignon, on the other hand, had his back to the light so that he could watch every change of expression on the young man's face. He said:

"You called here expecting to see Madame Marrable?"

"Yes. I rang the villa—"

Blampignon flipped up a hand.

"A moment, M'sieur Derry. You've got to know the truth sooner or later. I prefer you should know it now. About two hours ago Madame Marrable's dead body was found curled up inside that trunk in the hall. There seems to be no shadow of doubt that she's been murdered. So far we don't know why she was killed or who's responsible for the crime. I'm here to find out."

At first the young man seemed too surprised and shocked to utter a sound. He stared at Blampignon with a stupefied expression, sitting bolt upright, his hands gripped tightly over his knees. Then he blurted out:

"But...but it's impossible!"

Blampignon shrugged. That's what they always said. "Impossible!" As if murder were something one merely read about in novels and newspapers, something that could never touch one personally.

"You knew Madame Marrable well?"

"Yes...very. She was my godmother, a friend of my mother's. I've known her for years. I've recently been staying at her place in England."

"And now, perhaps, she has invited you down here?"

"Yes...unexpectedly. She sent me a telegram from Le Touquet asking me to join her here at once."

"When did she send the telegram?"

"Last Friday."

"You've still got it?"

"No. I'm afraid I—"

"Well, we needn't worry about that. Can you remember how it was worded?"

"Yes, of course, MUST SEE YOU URGENTLY—JOIN ME VILLA PARADOU MONDAY—GWENNY."

"This urgent business—have you any idea what it was?"

"I haven't a clue. I've been trying to puzzle it out. But she was like that. Always acting on impulse, expecting everybody to be at her beck and call… to toe the line."

Blampignon smiled.

"Nevertheless, you toed the line yourself."

The young man reddened slightly. For a moment he seemed at a loss. Then he stammered out:

"As a matter of fact, I thought it might have something to do with Sheila… Sheila Marrable, her adopted daughter."

"You're in love with her, perhaps?"

"Yes. I'd even asked Mrs. Marrable to consent to our marriage, but, for some reason or other, she flatly refused. Naturally when I received that telegram I wondered if she'd had second thoughts about the matter and wanted to talk it over with me."

"So that's how it is! *Eh bien*, M'sieur Derry, you can be of great help to me in trying to get to the bottom of this tragic affair. I want you to tell me all you can about Madame Marrable. Her family, for instance… her friends, her household. The kind of life she led. Something of her character, her background, perhaps. Every detail is important to me."

"I can speak in confidence?"

"Of course."

There was no doubt that Derry was nervous, uneasy, still trying to adapt himself to the grim atmosphere that hung like a cloud over the villa. In the stifling heat of the Midi afternoon he seemed out of place in his thick tweed jacket, brown corduroys, and stout brogue shoes. Blampignon was appropriately dressed yet even he was sweating like a pig.

"She had plenty of money, of course. I expect you realised that. Her husband left her a pretty sizeable fortune…"

It was all rather halting at first, as if the young man found it embarrassing to talk intimately of an old friend in front of a stranger. But gradually, prompted by the shrewd questions that Blampignon slipped in from time to time, he began to speak more freely.

"She wasn't an easy person to get along with. I admit that. You never quite knew where you were with her. She wasn't exactly touchy, but temperamental. I suppose, with so much money, she'd got used to having her own way…"

Blampignon had lighted a second cigarette from the butt of the first. His heavy-lidded eyes were half-closed, his hands crossed on his stomach like a man enjoying a siesta. Every now and then the ash from his cigarette showered over his shirt-front, but he didn't even trouble to lift a hand and brush it away. Anyone who didn't know him would have said he was doddering on the brink of sleep.

"She just couldn't get along without having a man around the place. There was this chap George Gammon, for instance, and a Frenchman called Duconte…"

At one point the ambulance turned up and Blampignon

could hear the men under Hamonet's instructions grunting and shuffling with effort as they carried the trunk out of the door and down the steps.

Presently Derry said, "Well, that's about all I can tell you. The last we heard of Mr. Skeet he was in Coblence heading for the Black Forest. As for this chap Duconte, I imagine he's returned to his place here at Menton. But I can't tell you exactly where he lives."

"You know Mam'selle Marrable's present address?"

"Yes."

Blampignon wrote it down.

"And the sister...Mam'selle Gaye?"

He wrote that down, too, pushed himself up from his chair and crossed to the window. With his back to the young man, he asked, "When exactly did you arrive down here?"

"About eight o'clock yesterday evening."

"By train?"

"Yes."

"What did you do then?"

"I took a taxi from Menton station direct to the villa."

"And then?"

"I didn't quite know what to do. You see, the place was locked and shuttered and nobody about. I couldn't imagine what had happened to Mrs. Marrable because I knew she expected to arrive here on Sunday at the latest. Luckily I hadn't paid off my taxi, so I returned to Menton and checked in at a cheap hotel. I rang twice this morning to see if anybody had turned up, but I didn't get any reply. It wasn't until I rang this afternoon—"

"What are your plans now?"

"I don't know. I haven't had time to think. I suppose either Miss Gaye or Miss Marrable will have to come down to arrange about the funeral and all that. I'll probably hang on at my hotel for the moment in case I can be of any help."

Blampignon said:

"I've just got to see the Fougères and take a look round the house and grounds. If you care to wait another twenty minutes or so I'll run you back to your hotel."

"Thanks. I'd be grateful."

II

It was just after seven o'clock. The day was beginning to cool. In the shopping streets of the town the sun was laying the long shadows of the plane trees along the pavements. The holiday-makers were drifting from the café tables along the prome-nade and making their way leisurely back to their hotels for dinner. The little flotilla of pleasure yachts had long since returned to their moorings in the harbour. Somewhere across the Italian frontier a scrub fire was burning on the mountain-side and a pillar of tawny smoke rose in the air.

Blampignon and Hamonet were sitting over a couple of Pernods in the Café Floreal just off the Rue Partenou. The place was almost deserted. Just a couple of workmen leaning on the zinc-topped bar, a little old man with an ashen face and a perpetual sniff hunched over his *anis* in a corner. Hamonet had told Magali, the *patron*:

"If any of the usual crowd come in tell them I don't want to be interrupted."

As a concession to the falling temperature, Blampignon

had put on a snuff-coloured jacket and fastened the collar button of his shirt. But he still looked like a tramp. He'd dropped Derry at the Hotel Mimosa and looked in at the Commissariat to pick up the Menton inspector and put in a report to Nice. Already Nice had taken action on his report. A call to Scotland Yard, asking them to get in touch with the dead woman's next-of-kin. A general alert to their own police throughout the country to keep a watch out for the missing car.

Hamonet said, "Well, what's your idea? Do you think she was murdered somewhere between Lyons and the coast?"

Blampignon narrowed his eyes against the smoke rising from his cigarette.

"Unless that telegram to the Fougères was sent by the person who killed her."

"Yes—exactly. It struck me that as the Fougères were on the telephone…"

Blampignon was canted back in his chair, his legs pushed out, eyeing the upturned toes of his *espadrilles*. Now he cut in.

"On the other hand, that telegram could have been genuine. Perhaps Madame Marrable met somebody in Lyons, and it was this meeting that caused her to alter her plans. She may have arrived at the villa with this person and been attacked the moment she stepped into the house."

Hamonet asked, "What did you make of the young Englishman?"

"He was ready to talk. I think what he told me was too circumstantial to be false. I know something now about that woman's character, the sort of life she led, the background against which she moved. She's no longer just a naked body doubled up in a trunk…"

He had a reason for telling Hamonet all that he'd found out about Madame Marrable. He intended that the inspector should work in with him. Hamonet didn't strike him as a particularly clever fellow. Just a hard-working, efficient policeman with good local knowledge, which was the kind of subordinate Blampignon favoured when he was preoccupied with a case.

"Of course, if she was playing around with men it puts a different light on things."

"That's my opinion." Blampignon slopped a little water into his Pernod and watched it go cloudy. "Did you bring along that map as I asked?"

"Yes…here."

Hamonet spread it out on the glass-topped table and dragged his chair round a little so that he and Blampignon could study the map together. He was still wondering why Blampignon had chosen to discuss the case in such a public place as a café. He hadn't yet realised how Blampignon hated police-stations with their shiny varnished walls, bleak furnishings, and endlessly tapping typewriters. Somehow he'd never been able to think clearly with the dusty smell of officialdom tickling his nostrils. He was a man of the streets, brought up in the back-parlour of a little *bistro* near the docks at Marseilles. A man who knew little about the finer points of the law, but a great deal about the seamy side of life.

Already his stubby forefinger was jabbing here and there about the map.

"Three probable routes which she might have taken from

Boulogne to Lyons. Here…see?…direct through Paris…to the east of Paris through Amiens and Troyes…to the west through Rouen, Chartres, Moulins. The Fougères said she allowed three days for the trip from Boulogne to the villa?"

"Yes—three days."

"That's a distance of about eight hundred miles—an average, shall we say, of two hundred and seventy miles a day. *Eh bien!* on my way to the Commissariat I made an enquiry at the *Syndicat d'Initiative*. The early morning car-ferry docks at Boulogne at 11.25. So the first day's run would not be as long, perhaps, as the other two. Say, two hundred miles." Blampignon had thumbed a stub of blue pencil from the breast-pocket of his jacket. Now, for an instant, he held it poised over the map. "So that on the first night Madame Marrable must have stayed somewhere about"—with a flourish he drew three quick circles on the map, with Paris enclosed in one of them—"here or here or here. That means she probably registered at an hotel. No doubt one of the more expensive hotels. Very well. We'll get the police in these three areas to make a special check-up on the matter. That was Friday night. If she really sent that telegram then we know that by late Saturday morning she'd arrived at Lyons. Perhaps she stayed there the second night. That's another thing we can find out. Or she may have driven on, say, to Valence, even Avignon. It would have been possible in a fast car…"

The café was slowly filling up. One or two of Hamonet's friends came in and moved over to his table, but Magali hurriedly intercepted them. Presently Hamonet saw them sitting away near the window, every now and then glancing in his direction, talking volubly among themselves as they got out the cards for the inevitable game of *belote*. There was no doubt that Blampignon's presence in the bar had set the whole place by the ears. As Magali whisked around with the drinks, everybody was plying him with questions.

"Don't ask me. Hamonet knows when to hold his tongue. But a big shot like that...it's bound to be a murder case."

"It's Blampignon, isn't it?"

"Of course."

"What a character! He looks like a beachcomber!"

Blampignon seemed unaware of the stir he was causing. No doubt he was used to being pointed out in public places. He seemed to move around in a private sanctum of his own, like a snail in its shell, indifferent to the stares and nudges and speculation. He was talking now, quietly, fluently, the cigarette jutting from the corner of his wide mouth jumping up and down, his gross body quivering with animation, his hands every now and then fluttering in the air like big brown butterflies.

"This man seen by the Fougères' friend, the window-cleaner...no question that he was the chap who'd been dossing down in that upstairs room. We know he was there on Sunday. That copy of the *France-Dimanche* told us that. Perhaps Madame Marrable actually arrived at the villa on Sunday and it was he who murdered her. Though how we're going to fit that in with the medical evidence..."

Hamonet said, "Yes. I thought of that," and went on to enlarge on his theory. Blampignon listened, occasionally nodding his agreement or taking a sip of his Pernod. Eventually he said:

"This chap Duconte...it might be interesting to get our

hands on him. He was staying with Madame Marrable in England and came down here about ten days ago. He evidently lives somewhere in the town. Ever heard of him?"

"Never. But if he's still living here, we'll trace him all right."

Blampignon was leaning over the map again, running his pencil this way and that along its tracery of roads. They had both finished their Pernods and Hamonet was trying to catch Magali's eye so that he could order up another round.

"Le Touquet. But why Le Touquet? That telegram she sent to Derry...why did she send it from Le Touquet?"

It was certainly strange. Hamonet saw at once what was puzzling the inspector. Le Touquet was on the coast road from Boulogne to Abbeville. True, on her journey south, Madame Marrable would have certainly driven through Abbeville, but the main road from Boulogne ran further inland through Montreuil. Why then had she made this détour along the coast?

Hamonet said, "The young chap showed you the telegram?"

"No. I gathered he'd destroyed it."

"Then perhaps he was mistaken about the place from which it was sent."

"It's possible, of course." Blampignon was looking for the ashtray which was hidden under the map. Unable to find it, he dropped the butt of his cigarette on the red-tiled floor and stamped on it with his heel. "Or perhaps that telegram was never sent. Have you thought of that?"

"I don't follow."

"Remember, our young friend didn't expect to find us at the villa. When you answered the telephone he probably thought it was a servant. *Alors!* when he walks into the villa, he finds the police in possession and has to think quickly."

"You mean he may have had something to do with the murder?"

Blampignon shrugged.

"I mean he may have had to think up a quick excuse for his presence down here on the Midi."

"But what positive motive…?"

"He wanted to marry Madame Marrable's adopted daughter and she'd refused her consent."

"He told you this himself?"

"Yes."

"But surely, if he'd done the job—"

"He'd have held his tongue, eh? Perhaps, perhaps not. Sometimes it is better to hide behind the truth than a pack of lies. Suppose I get to hear of the facts from somebody else… at once my suspicions are aroused. As it is he's quite open with me, and I'm naturally inclined to believe he's innocent."

Hamonet said, with a dubious expression, "All the same…"

Blampignon chuckled wheezily, "You don't really think he killed her, eh?"

"No."

"*Eh bien!* neither do I." He heaved himself round in his chair and shot up a hand. "Waiter!… two Pernods."

"No. This one's on me."

"Very well. If you insist…"

9

ARRIVING VILLA PARADOU THIS AFTERNOON—PLEASE
PREPARE ACCOMMODATION FOR THREE—GAYE.

WHEN MADAME FOUGÈRE HAD READ OUT THE CABLEGRAM,
the old man said, "That's the sister, isn't it? The mousey one?"

"Mam'selle Deborah, of course. She stayed down here
about a year ago. Well, this means we ought to get out to the
villa at once. It's past twelve o'clock. You'd better fetch the
bicycles."

Grumbling and muttering to himself Fougère wheeled
the bicycles down the front path and the couple set off at
their customary snail's pace down the hill. Most of the way
they rode abreast, but as usual they didn't have much to say
to each other.

Once the old man observed, "The fat man from Nice...
the detective... I said to him 'It's no good taking *our* fingerprints. We don't know anything about it. It's the chap Pialou
saw...he's the one you want to look for.'"

Madame Fougère said tartly, "*Tiens!* I suppose he knows what he's up to. Do you think he's going to take advice from an old fool like you?"

The heat struck up off the road as if they were riding along a strip of red-hot metal. There wasn't a breath of air. Not a ripple on the water. Under the parasol-pines the shadows lay blue and shimmering. At every downthrust of his pedals Fougère's bicycle creaked and complained as if it were about to fall apart. Presently, sweating and short of breath, they turned into the entrance to the villa.

The events of the day before had left the old man unnerved. Already he'd been at the cognac bottle, but it hadn't done much to ease the apprehension out of him. He'd heard it said that, more often than not, a murderer will return to the scene of his crime. Perhaps it might be that way up at the villa. Perhaps when he and Marie were sitting at the kitchen table shucking peas or peeling the potatoes, they would hear the sound of stealthy footsteps padding down the hall, and then, slowly, the door would swing open…

His wife's voice broke in on his reflections.

"*Mon Dieu!* was it you who left the ladder leaning against the balcony? You must be out of your senses!"

The old man's eyes were nearly popping out of his head. He couldn't believe the ladder was actually there. The last he'd seen of it was hanging high up on the garage wall. That was the evening before, when he'd gone round the place making sure that everything was securely locked and shuttered. He gasped out:

"It's none of my doing. What did I say? There's things going on around this place that none of us can put a name to."

"Yesterday evening, before we left…did you lock the door of the garage?"

"No."

"Why not?"

"Because you don't put a cork in an empty bottle. Of course, if there'd been a car in the place…"

"All the same, the ladder was there. And now see what's happened. There'll be trouble over this."

As he unlocked the front-door and went into the house, the old man was shaking like a leaf. He shuffled around opening up the shutters as quickly as he could, glancing warily this way and that, standing for a moment at the bottom of the stairs, his head cocked sideways, listening. Then suddenly, filling him with terror, he heard footsteps coming up the terrace steps behind him.

"Well, what's all this? What's going on? That ladder outside, for instance…have you got the window-cleaners here?"

It was Blampignon. The couple hadn't heard him arrive in his car, because he'd parked it in the shade a little way up the drive. The Fougères, each trying to get in an explanation, began gabbling at the top of their voices.

"All right. One at a time. You, madame?"

"We noticed the ladder there when we came up the drive just now. The old fool forgot to lock the garage. That's where they got hold of it. If you ask me, somebody's forced the shutters to get into an upstairs room."

"*Eh bien*, we can soon make sure about that. You stay here."

Madame Fougère was right. The shutters in one of the front bedrooms had been prised apart and the lock wrenched from its screws. A single push and they swung back revealing the top rungs of the ladder projecting above the edge of the little iron balcony. Blampignon thought: Now what the devil's been happening up here?

He glanced at the bed. The coverlet was undisturbed. It was obvious that nobody had stayed a night in the room. Everything, in fact, looked pretty much in order. That was at a first glance. Then Blampignon noticed something that suddenly whipped up his interest. Scoring the polished surface of the walnut bed-head was a long jagged gash. On a table in the centre of the room were the shattered remnants of a big cut-glass vase. Moving to the bed Blampignon took a closer look at the splintered woodwork. Then he uttered a little grunt of surprise. Embedded in the gash was a small distorted lump of lead that he recognised at once as a bullet from a small-calibre automatic. There was little doubt what had happened. Somebody standing on the balcony or in the window—perhaps even on the top rungs of the ladder—had fired into the room. At a second person, no doubt, standing back somewhere in the shadows. But in the darkness they'd missed, and the bullet had evidently smashed through the glass vase and finished up in the bed-head.

Probing the bullet free with his penknife, Blampignon slipped it in his pocket and, after a long and patient examination of the room, during which he found nothing further of interest, he went down to join the Fougères in the kitchen.

"It's just as you suspected, madame. Somebody broke in again last night. They knocked a vase over on the table by the look of it. You'd better get upstairs with a dust-pan and brush and sweep up the pieces." He swung round on the old man. "As for you...what about taking that ladder back into the garage. And this time make sure the place is locked."

The old man began querulously, "Well, you can't blame me. In the circumstances there didn't seem much point..."

But Blampignon had turned his back on Fougère and was addressing himself again to the housekeeper.

"I've had a telephone call from the British police. There's a party of three flying into Nice airport this afternoon. I'm driving them straight over here to the villa. Did you know anything about this?"

"Yes, m'sieur. Mam'selle Gaye—that's the sister, of course—sent me a cablegram this morning. Everything will be ready for them when they arrive."

"You can expect us about half-past four."

"Very good."

As he went down the drive Blampignon was already trying to fit this latest incident into the framework of the murder case. But he couldn't make head or tail of it. Just as he couldn't make up his mind about the man Pialou had seen walking into the villa on Saturday night. The trouble was he didn't know when the trunk had been dumped in the hall. Saturday, Sunday, Monday? The medical evidence suggested that Madame Marrable had been dead for about three days, but it didn't follow, of course, that the trunk had been in the villa for the same length of time.

He'd driven out to Cap Martin that morning because he wanted to make a few enquiries at the houses in the near vicinity. About half a dozen villas in all. Just three questions to which he wanted an answer. Had anybody seen a large grey saloon entering or leaving the grounds of the Villa Paradou during the last few nights? Had anybody noticed a man prowling around the place after dark? Had anybody seen or heard anything near the villa which appeared, in retrospect, unusual or suspicious?

He didn't get anywhere at first. The news of the Fougères' discovery had already leaked out. Through the Fougères themselves, no doubt, who wouldn't be able to resist talking about the sensation with the other domestics in the neighbourhood. Everybody, in fact, was ready to discuss the affair with Blampignon, to put forward their own wildcat theories, even to offer him advice, but nobody had anything to tell him. At least, not until he cross-questioned the kitchenmaid at the Villa des Roches.

"No, I haven't seen a car drive into the place for months. And that's not surprising, because the house has been shut up since last January. Of course the Fougères turn up now and then to keep the place aired and water the garden. But it wasn't them I saw last night. No question about that. It's only in the daytime you see the Fougères around."

"And last night?"

"I was walking up the road to post a letter to my young man in Limoges. The box is on the corner at the top of the hill. I suppose it was about half-past eleven."

"Well?"

"I was on my way back when a car went by. I wouldn't have seen the couple if they hadn't come out of the gates just as the car was passing."

"A couple, you say?"

"Yes. A man and a woman. I saw them clearly enough in the headlights. I didn't notice all that much about the girl, but I couldn't help feeling I'd seen her before somewhere. In the town, perhaps...a waitress or something of that sort. About twenty-five. Perhaps younger. But it was the man who really caught my eye. I remember thinking to myself 'He's a foreigner. You'd never see a Frenchman dressed like that!' He couldn't have been a day under sixty and there he was dressed like a kid of ten. Like a Boy Scout—that's what I remember thinking."

"He was wearing shorts, perhaps?"

"Yes—that's it. Shorts and little socks and white tennis shoes. You never saw anything so funny! No hat on his head, and his bald head as brown as a nut. A real comic!"

"You weren't close enough to hear what they were talking about?"

"No. They were off down the hill before I reached the entrance to the drive."

"One other point. A little before that, you didn't by any chance hear anything in the nature of an explosion? A pistol shot, for instance?"

"Yes—I did. Just after I'd posted my letter. I thought it was a car backfiring."

"Just a single explosion?"

"Yes."

So much for that. A few minutes later Blampignon was back at the Villa Paradou. The old man, with a basket on his arm, was bobbing about among the pea-rows in the kitchen garden. Blampignon strolled over to him and asked without preliminary:

"This man seen entering the villa on Saturday night by your friend Pialou...was he wearing shorts?"

The old man screwed up his eyes, slipped a forefinger under the brim of his hat and began to scratch his scalp.

"Well now...Pialou never mentioned it. He said it was too dark to see the fellow properly. But why not ask Pialou yourself? He lives over Penelli's, the bakers, down on the Quai Laurenti. He eats in the café next door because his wife has just gone into hospital. You'll catch him there now if I know anything about it."

II

It was a sleazy little café with two rows of tables set out on the pavement under a faded blue awning. A scrawny cat picked its way delicately among the iron legs of the chairs and tables. A smell of garlic and fish soup wafted through the bead curtain that hung in the doorway of the restaurant. Every now and then a girl of about fifteen pushed her way through the clattering beads, banged down a loaded tray, and went back into the café calling out a fresh order. Somewhere inside a mechanical piano was tinkling out a waltz. Blampignon's eye travelled this way and that among the customers, trying to make up his mind which of them looked like the window-cleaner. There was no doubt that he was in the place, because the two-wheeled cart, to which his ladders were strapped, was drawn up at the kerbside.

"A table, m'sieur?"

"No. I'm looking for M'sieur Pialou."

The girl grabbed a handful of the beaded strings and pulled them aside.

"He's inside. That table over there. Will you be ordering anything to eat?"

"Perhaps later. I haven't made up my mind."

Blampignon crossed to the table indicated by the girl and held out his hand.

"M'sieur Pialou?"

"That's me."

"I'm from the *Sûreté Nationale* at Nice." Blampignon flashed his official card under the other's nose. "There's a question or two… Do you mind if I join you while you finish your lunch?"

Pialou hurriedly wiped his mouth on the back of his sleeve and gestured to the chair opposite. He was an undersized man with a head too big for his body, and little bloodshot eyes that blinked and twinkled under a pair of grizzly eyebrows. He mumbled through a mouthful of spaghetti:

"It's about that affair up at the villa, I suppose. It's all over the town about the murder of the Englishwoman."

Blampignon nodded.

"In particular about this man you saw entering the house on Saturday night."

"What do you want to know?"

He was respectful enough but certainly not intimidated by the presence of the detective. He obviously didn't allow himself much time for lunch, because all during the interrogation he went on shovelling the food into his mouth and glancing up anxiously at the wall-clock.

"For one thing…the clothes he was wearing. Did you notice anything unusual about the way he was dressed?"

"I can't say I did."

"It was too dark to see, perhaps?"

"That's about it."

"But he was wearing an ordinary lounge suit?"

"Yes. I'm sure of that…and a dark hat. Slimly built and not very tall. A youngish chap, I should say. But if you asked me to pick him out in a crowd…" Pialou gave an expressive shrug, filled his wine glass from the carafe at his elbow, pushed back his empty plate and added cryptically: "All the same, you won't have to look far to find him."

Blampignon stared at the fellow in surprise.

"Oh, and what makes you think that?"

"It's this way. Apart from Madame Marrable only the Fougères had the keys of the villa. The old man will tell you that. And that young chap had a key right enough. I heard the scroop of it in the lock. No fumbling either. And that's a point too. Mind you, it's not for me to air my opinions. But I should say he'd got Madame Marrable's permission to sleep at the villa. I mean, unlocking the door like that and just strolling in…it's obvious he knew his way about the place…"

III

After Pialou had gone off down the quayside, pushing his hand-cart, Blampignon ordered the *plat du jour* and a half-bottle of *San Georges,* and some forty minutes later drove up through the old town to the Commissariat. Hamonet was in his office, scribbling away diligently at his desk, with his sleeves rolled up and his jacket slung over the back of his chair. Blampignon gave him a limp handshake, took off his green sunglasses, and lowered his bulk into a chair by the open window.

"Well, how goes it? Anything to report?"

Hamonet nodded.

"I've been trying to get you on the telephone at Nice. I've picked up some information about that chap, Duconte."

"You've found out where he's living?"

"Where he *was* living, to be exact…lodging with an old girl called Gonville just off the Cours de Castellar."

"And now he's cleared out?"

"Yes. He turned up there about ten days ago—Friday the fifteenth, to be precise—and left the same day."

"Well, that fits in with Derry's story. According to him Duconte crossed from England on the fourteenth. *Eh bien…* let's hear the rest of it."

The facts weren't exactly sensational, but they set Blampignon off on another fascinating train of speculation. Duconte had turned up about five o'clock on Friday afternoon and told Madame Gonville that he no longer required his room. He'd only a handful of personal belongings, and these he'd hurriedly stuffed into a suitcase. He'd seemed nervy and apprehensive. Madame Gonville had asked him for a forwarding address, but Duconte had told her that he wouldn't have a permanent address for the next few weeks. He was travelling by easy stages down through Rome and Naples to Sicily. A business trip, he said, which Madame Gonville had taken with a pinch of salt, because during the twelve months or so that Duconte had been with her he'd never appeared to be in any form of employment. Hamonet went on:

"The fellow evidently hadn't two sous to rub together. He paid Madame Gonville eight hundred francs a week for his attic. You never saw such a hole! Just a table, a chair, and a rusty iron bedstead. Not even room in the place to swing a cat…"

The only decent things he seemed to possess were the clothes he stood up in. When and where he took his meals the old woman never found out. Most of the day he'd lie in bed, reading the newspaper and smoking cigarettes. Then in the evening he'd dress, spruce himself up and saunter off into the town. He never got back to his attic until the small hours of the morning.

"There was a girl in his life. I found out that much. An assistant behind the perfume counter at the Monoprix in the Rue Partenou. Madame Gonville and her neighbours had often seen them about the town together in the evenings. They reckoned it was the girl who kept him in food and cigarettes…even paid for the rent of his room…"

But it was months now since anybody had seen Duconte with his arm round the young woman's waist, strolling with her along the lamplit promenade or sitting, with their chairs touching, at a café table. At the turn of the year, in fact, Duconte's fortunes seemed to have changed. It was rumoured that he'd been taken up by a wealthy English widow with a villa out at Cap Martin. Once Madame Gonville had seen him driving with the Englishwoman in a large and expensive car. A neighbour had spotted them coming out of the Hotel de Paris in Monte Carlo. He still rented his attic room, but often for days on end he wouldn't set foot in the place. Suddenly he seemed to have money in his pockets and new suits to his back. Hamonet continued:

"A run of luck at the tables…that's what he told the old woman. Not that she believed him. She was too shrewd for that. She knew well enough where his money was coming from, but she held her tongue because she couldn't afford to lose the eight hundred francs he paid for his room. And then, one evening about a fortnight ago, when Duconte was in England staying with Madame Marrable, the girl from the Monoprix turned up. Still head over heels in love with Duconte. No doubt about that. And Madame Gonville, who felt sorry for the girl, let on about the widow. After that the fat was properly in the fire. The girl nearly had hysterics. The old woman did her best to calm her down, but she went off swearing that she'd get even with Duconte if ever he dared show his nose in the town again...

"Well, since then the girl's been seen hanging about outside the old woman's cottage. Always after dark, of course, because she doesn't leave her job until six. It was during the afternoon when Duconte finally turned up and collected his belongings, so that, in the long run, the girl missed him. The next night Madame Gonville waited for the kid to show up and told her what had happened. I think she only half-believed that Duconte had cleared out. Anyway, she was up there again last Friday and Saturday night. Since then she seems to have stayed away. No doubt she's made up her mind that the old woman was telling the truth...that Duconte really had started on that trip of his down the Italian coast. If," amended Hamonet cautiously, "he ever intended to start. Frankly, I think the old woman's right. This business trip's all eyewash. I've a feeling Duconte's still somewhere in the locality."

Blampignon flicked the stub of his *Bastos* out of the open window. His right eyelid drooped in a knowing wink.

"So have I," he said.

10

A LITTLE AFTER THREE, BLAMPIGNON WAS BACK IN HIS office at the Nice headquarters of the *Sûreté Nationale*. There was a message on his desk-pad—the summary of a telephone call that had been put through from Scotland Yard.

Ascertained from Customs and A.A. officials at port of Dover, Marrable crossed to Boulogne, car-carrier S.S. Lord Warden, 9.45 a.m. Friday, April 22nd. No passenger. Luggage included large brass-bound black cabin-trunk. Marrable subsequently cleared Customs at Boulogne Maritime at (circa) 11.45 a.m. Full details of car, as set out in A.A. Carnet de Passage, appended herewith...

The description and registration number, in fact, matching up with the information already obtained from old Fougère. But this was the only message that had come in. No news of the missing car. No word from Paris or any of the police stations in the districts to the east and west of the capital, where Blampignon believed Madame Marrable might have checked in at an hotel at the end of her first day's run. Nothing either from Lyons, Valence, or Avignon.

It was a fantastic situation, to say the least of it. At 11.45 A.M. on Friday, April 22nd, a woman drives out of the Customs sheds at Boulogne Maritime. Four days later—on the afternoon of Tuesday, April 26th, to be precise—the dead body of this woman is discovered in a trunk some eight hundred miles away. Nothing as yet to suggest where she had slept the nights *en route*. Nothing to indicate where or when and why exactly she'd been murdered. Clear of the Boulogne docks she, presumably, heads the car south, and thereafter... not a word of her, not a sign. It was as if the car had sprouted wings and journeyed down the length of France at twenty thousand feet!

But wait!—that wasn't exactly true. Somebody had seen her after she left Boulogne. What about the assistant in the post-office at Le Touquet who had handled her telegram to Derry? It might be as well...

Blampignon's hand reached out to the bell-push on his desk. It was now ten-past three. He still had twenty minutes in hand to get out to the airport and meet the London plane. Even before the door had fully opened, he was saying:

"See here, Emile. I want you to get in touch with the police at Le Touquet. At once, you understand. On Friday, April 22nd, probably about midday, a telegram was sent from one of the post-offices in the town by a middle-aged Englishwoman. The telegram read..."

He couldn't describe her clothes, of course, because the only time he'd set eyes on Madame Marrable she hadn't a rag to her back. But a handsome, auburn-haired woman and a foreigner into the bargain...surely she'd be remembered in a small-town post-office, particularly as her telegram had been sent in English.

And all the time he was issuing his instructions, the thought was floating around at the back of his mind:

"But why Le Touquet? Why did she take the coast road to Abbeville, when the fastest and most direct route would have been through Montreuil?"

II

Out at the airport there was no respite from the sun. It beat down pitilessly on the flat-topped buildings, glaring down from a brassy sky, blocking out square black shadows on the concrete forecourt, mocking the few shade-trees that straggled up through the hard baked earth. The wind-sock hung limply from its staff. Beyond the runways the sea was a burnished strip of blue, shimmering in the molten air.

"The London plane?"

The car-park attendant raised a forefinger to his cap-peak.

"Just in, m'sieur. The passengers are now clearing Customs."

Blampignon pushed through the swing-doors into the cool and echoing reception hall and made his way down a corridor to the Customs shed. The first passengers were already drifting through the barrier. The inspector's eye travelled swiftly this way and that among the little groups clustered about the steel-topped counters. It didn't take him ten seconds to spot the trio he'd come to meet. A few minutes later he was saying:

"Mam'selle Gaye? Inspector Blampignon of the *Sûreté Nationale.* I've a car waiting to take you to the villa."

The unhappy woman looked at the end of her tether. She scarcely seemed able to stand. There were mauve shadows under her eyes and her skin was the colour of parchment. At one moment, seeing her sway, Blampignon thought she was about to faint.

"Can I get you something, madame...a little brandy, perhaps?"

"No, please don't trouble. I'm quite all right. Just a little passing giddiness. It's the plane that's upset me. Let me introduce my niece...Miss Sheila Marrable...and Mr. Gammon, an old friend of my sister's..."

They were both very much as Blampignon had imagined. The girl fresh and charming, with a troubled nervous look in her clear blue eyes, obviously distressed by the tragedy that had suddenly clouded her young life. The man, unprepossessing, ruddy-faced, with the hoarse voice of the habitual alcoholic and glazed uneasy eyes. He was portering two small suitcases, one of which he put down, to shake hands with Blampignon.

"A shocking business, Inspector. It's good of you to meet us. I suppose, so far, you haven't any news...any idea that is...?"

"No. We've nothing to report."

They walked across to the car, the girl with her arm through that of the older woman, who'd now opened her handbag and taken out a bottle of smelling salts, which she was wafting to and fro under her nose. Blampignon didn't fail to notice their little sidelong glances. They were obviously taken aback by his appearance, no doubt expecting him to be dolled up like a *gendarme* in cloak and *képi*, with a twirling baton in his white-gloved hand!

They didn't speak much in the car. A desultory remark or two about the weather, about their journey down, but no mention of the matter that must have been uppermost in their minds. It was all very constrained, discreet and English. Not that Blampignon minded, because he'd never been much of a hand at small-talk. And besides, he liked to drive fast and that, on the crowded littoral road, meant watching one's step. In less than five minutes they were in the thick of it, nosing through the crawling traffic along the Promenade des Anglais. Once clear of Nice, however, Blampignon swung the car on to the Moyenne Corniche and the going was quicker.

Presently, breaking one of the many long silences, he said, "Perhaps you didn't know…but M'sieur Derry arrived down at Menton on Monday evening. He's staying there now at the Hotel Mimosa."

"Nigel in Menton! But it's impossible. What on earth is he doing down here? Are you sure about this?"

It was the girl, of course, sitting beside her aunt in the back of the car.

"Quite sure. Madame Marrable sent him a telegram from Le Touquet last Friday, asking him down to the villa."

Gammon said, "That's odd. Why the devil didn't she ask him the day before? He didn't leave Cockfosters until after lunch on Thursday."

Blampignon shrugged.

"She was a woman of impulse, perhaps."

"That's true enough. But even then...to invite him down like that, on the spur of the moment."

Blampignon pointed out, "She evidently wished to see him on an urgent matter."

The girl asked quickly, "Did Mr. Derry say what this matter was?"

"No, mam'selle. He didn't appear to know himself. Now, I imagine, he never will. Unless, of course, *you* happen to—?"

"No. I'm completely at a loss."

For a time they discussed the matter among themselves, suggesting this and that, but in the long run they gave it up and once again fell silent. Although the windows were open the heat in the car was stifling. In the mirror Blampignon could see Mam'selle Gaye lying back with her eyes closed, fanning herself languidly with a magazine, her plump body giving to every sway and jolt of the springs. The girl was gazing down at the endlessly shifting panorama of the coastline, drumming her fingers on and on against the metal clasp of her handbag. Every now and then, obviously embarrassed by the silence, yet not knowing what to say, Gammon cleared his throat and shifted uneasily in his seat.

Blampignon was thankful when, some twenty minutes later, he turned the car off the road between the entrance pillars of the Villa Paradou.

III

The Fougères were waiting at the foot of the terrace steps to welcome them. The old man had doffed his battered hat and was holding it clasped like a poultice over his stomach. Madame Fougère, evidently overcome by emotion at the last minute, was dabbing her eyes with the hem of her apron.

When the housekeeper had ushered the two women into the house, followed by Fougère with the baggage, Gammon turned to the inspector.

"You'll come inside and have a drink?"

"Later, perhaps, when you have eaten, and the ladies have had time to compose themselves after the journey. At a moment like this I don't like to worry them, but, naturally, there are a number of questions…"

"Of course. Then we'll be seeing you anon?"

"In about an hour's time, if that's convenient."

"Yes, that's fair enough."

Blampignon was just turning out of the drive, when a taxi swung in through the gates. The young Englishman was perched on the edge of the back-seat, thumbing frantically through a wad of notes, evidently making ready to pay the fare. He certainly hadn't wasted much time in getting out to the villa. No doubt he'd rung up and learnt from Madame Fougère the time that the visitors were expected to arrive. He could imagine Derry and the young woman, after their unexpected reunion, speculating on the meaning of that telegram, wondering, perhaps, if Madame Marrable had suddenly withdrawn her opposition to their marriage, puzzling over the reason for her abrupt change of heart. A tantalising enigma to which now they would probably never know the answer.

The whole case was like that. One mystery added to another. Bits and pieces of information that did nothing to clarify the events that had led up to the murder. Strange and seemingly unrelated incidents adding further confusion to an already tangled skein of circumstances. And so far he hadn't been able to solve one of the problems confronting him!

Ten minutes later at the Commissariat, Hamonet was saying, "No. There's little enough to report. I looked in at the Monoprix this afternoon to check up Madame Gonville's story with the girl behind the perfume counter. Simone Berthode. I got her name and address from the manager. The girl's evidently walked out on her job. She hasn't been seen there since last Saturday."

"*Eh bien*...so what?"

"I went round to her house in the Rue Longue, and it was the same story there. She walked out of the place on Saturday evening, and so far hasn't come back. Her mother, as you can imagine, was almost off her head with worry. She was just making up her mind to come and have a word with us here." Hamonet took up a photo from his desk and handed it to Blampignon. "That's the girl."

A slim, dark girl, not exactly pretty, not exactly plain. Yet striking in a way, with a mass of soft hair swept back off a wide forehead and large expressive eyes. Blampignon said:

"I'll keep this photo, if it's all the same to you."

"Of course."

A minute or so later Blampignon was on the telephone to Nice.

"It's Emile I want to speak to."

A few seconds' delay, then, "Emile speaking."

"About that enquiry you were making for me at Le Touquet..."

"Yes. There's nothing doing. They checked up at every

post-office in the town. Nobody remembers seeing the Englishwoman or handling the telegram in question."

"*Merdre!* And apart from that?"

"No…nothing. Nothing to report."

After a short discussion with Hamonet, Blampignon went out to his car and set off back to Cap Martin. Not as yet to the Villa Paradou, but the Villa des Roches. A light breeze was drifting off the sea, ruffling the glassy membrane of the water, blunting the edge of the heat. A convoy of lilac clouds was sailing slowly across the horizon. Inland, against the dark sweep of the mountains, the little villas, like coloured cardboard boxes, stood out square and neat in the sharp evening light. A group of fishermen, barefooted, with their trousers rolled above their knees, were hauling a net on to the promenade. A couple of buxom girls, with brown muscular legs, their bicycles propped against the kerb, were taking a snapshot of the scene. As he drove by Blampignon leaned through the window and waved to them, and they called out something in a language he imagined to be Dutch.

The kitchenmaid at the Villa des Roches was squatting on an upturned cask by the back-door, scraping potatoes into a big earthenware bowl. A dog was curled up asleep on the cooling stones of the courtyard, which was roofed in with a gigantic vine. On seeing Blampignon, the girl hastily smoothed down her skirt, put aside her bowl and got to her feet. The inspector took out the photo of Simone Berthode.

"This photo, mam'selle… I want you to take a careful look at it. Have you ever seen this girl before?"

Evidently she was long-sighted, for she held the photo almost at arm's length and gazed at it through half-closed eyes.

"Perhaps... I'm not sure."

"She serves behind the perfume counter at the Monoprix in the Rue Partenou."

Then she got it. She said excitedly:

"Of course!...that's where I've seen her...that's why I thought her face looked familiar. It's the girl I saw coming out of the Villa Paradou last night with that odd-looking foreign chap."

"You're sure?"

"I'd be surprised if I was mistaken."

Back in the car, which he'd parked a little way down the road from the villa, Blampignon glanced at the dashboard clock. It was six-fifteen. Very well, he'd give the visitors up at the Villa Paradou another fifteen minutes before breaking in and badgering them with his questions. It was cool and pleasant there in the aromatic shade of the pines. Dragging out the inevitable packet of *Bastos*, he lit a cigarette and gave himself up to his reflections.

So Simone Berthode had been up at the Villa Paradou last night. Because of Duconte, of course. Perhaps somebody had tipped her the wink that Duconte had moved into the villa on clearing out of his room at Madame Gonville's. Or was she, perhaps, just following a hunch, knowing nothing of the murder, believing that Madame Marrable had returned to the villa and Duconte had scuttled off to join her?

And the man Pialou had seen letting himself into the villa on Saturday night, the man who had slept in the spare room and left a copy of *France-Dimanche* on the bed...everything now suggested that it was Duconte. And Simone Berthode had broken into the place with intent to murder him, seeing him in the shadowy darkness of the room, firing that single ineffectual shot.

With a petulant, almost feminine gesture Blampignon flicked the ash from his cigarette. *Tiens!* it was all very well as far as it went, but it didn't go far enough. He'd re-enacted this little drama in his mind and left one of the characters in the wings. What of the elderly foreigner in shorts? How did he come into the picture? An accomplice, perhaps. Somebody enlisted by the girl to help her in the grim business of liquidating her one-time lover. That might be the explanation, of course. On the other hand, a curious and unlikely combination. The little assistant from the Monoprix, this elderly eccentric, who, in the kitchenmaid's opinion, was certainly no Frenchman.

But this shooting incident mustn't be allowed to distract his attention from the Marrable murder. It was another affair entirely, demanding a separate dossier—the Simone Berthode Case. But Duconte, of course, still not cleared of suspicion where the widow was concerned. If he'd been sleeping at the villa then he could well have committed the crime. Death had occurred three days before the Fougères had discovered the body in the trunk. That, with reservations, was the doctor's opinion. So the Englishwoman might have driven up to the villa late on Saturday night, perhaps even knowing that Duconte was there, having given him the keys of the place, and it was then that he'd killed her. But *would* he have killed her? The goose that laid the golden eggs...?

No. It was Derry who'd now captured Blampignon's interest. Derry, at least, had motive. Madame Marrable had slammed down a shutter between him and her adopted daughter, refusing to countenance their marriage, Then, for some mysterious reason, she'd sent that telegram, inviting him to the villa. A telegram that Derry had unfortunately destroyed. If, indeed, it had ever been despatched. A telegram existing only in the young man's imagination, perhaps, serving as an explanation for his presence down on the Côte d'Azur.

What had Derry said? That on Monday night, the day before the discovery of the body, he'd taken a taxi from the station direct to the Villa Paradou. Then, finding the house locked and shuttered, he'd returned at once to Menton and booked in at the Hotel Mimosa. They only had to question the taxi-driver, who'd be easy enough to trace, to check up on this part of Derry's story. And the young man was intelligent enough to be aware of this. So this abortive journey of his out to the villa might be no more than a blind.

Just Derry's word for it that he'd arrived at Menton on Monday evening. It might have been Saturday night. Which meant that the man Pialou had seen unlocking the front-door of the villa might not have been Duconte, as Blampignon had been inclined to suspect, but Derry. And it was Derry who'd been making use of that spare room. Derry, perhaps, who was lurking in the house when Madame Marrable turned up... sneaking down the stairs with a pillow in his hand, creeping up behind her...

But, like all the clever ones, he'd tripped up. Le Touquet... that was where he'd gone wrong. Madame Marrable, in the ordinary run of events, wouldn't have passed through Le Touquet on her journey south. And it was this fact that had urged Blampignon in the first place to make enquiries about that telegram.

True, the young man didn't look or act like a murderer. But nine times out of ten, of course, they never did. Particularly the clever ones!

11

Blampignon was saying,

"Your sister made up her mind in a hurry to shut up her house in England and come down here?"

Deborah nodded.

"She only decided three days before she left."

"Who knew of her plans?"

"All of us at Cockfosters, of course... my niece, Mr. Gammon, Mr. Derry, and the servants. And a friend of my sister's in Scotland, who was having Sheila to stay with her. And, naturally the Fougères."

"And M'sieur Duconte?"

"Perhaps...but I don't really know."

They were seated in a little room to the left of the hall. Evidently a kind of study, for there was an escritoire set against the wall between two glass-fronted bookshelves. Otherwise, quite sparsely furnished. Just a few dumpy armchairs upholstered in leather, a small couch under the window. In a corner, a set of golf-clubs, a couple of fishing-rods in waterproof

cases. Almost a masculine room. One looked for a pipe rack
on the wall, a tobacco jar on the mantelpiece.

Certainly no setting for the timid feminine creature opposite, with her tired eyes and sagging, unhappy face. The horror
and shock of her sister's sudden death seemed to have left
her on the verge of a nervous collapse. There was something
pathetic and defenceless about her that made this interview,
from Blampignon's point of view, all the more distasteful. It
was always the same in a murder case, this questioning of the
victim's relatives and friends. One had to remain impersonal,
unmoved, and yet it was difficult at times to conceal one's
sympathy. In this case, for instance. Every question he put to
her…it was like hurling a stone at a wounded bird. But the
law had to be served. It wasn't his job to comfort the bereaved.
That was for the priest. It was his job to pry and probe, to
analyse and deduct, to arrive, in the long run, at the truth.

Yet there was little she could tell him that he hadn't already
learnt from Derry.

At first Blampignon's omniscience obviously puzzled her.

"But how do you know all this? It's quite true, I admit. But
how did you find out?"

Then, suddenly, it occurred to her.

"It's Nigel… Nigel Derry. You've been talking to him,
of course. It was he who told you that my sister and I had
quarrelled."

Blampignon inclined his head.

"Over certain insinuations she'd made about you and
M'sieur Gammon. That's what I was given to understand."

He saw a slow flush creeping up her neck, suffusing her
pallid cheeks, the sudden unexpected flash of anger in her

eyes. For a moment she couldn't speak. Then she said in a low voice:

"There are some things one can never forget or forgive. One does not speak ill of the dead...but even now.... How could she have *said* such things—to me, her sister? It's dreadful to think that we parted like that...in anger. And now we shall never...never..."

But she couldn't go on. She just sat there, mute and stricken, trying to choke back her sobs, a handkerchief pressed to her mouth.

For a time Blampignon kept silent, pretending to study the notes he'd jotted down in a little blue book. Then he said quietly, "And when you left your sister's house to return to your cottage, M'sieur Gammon came with you?"

At first she didn't seem to hear the question. Then she looked up, quickly lowering her glance again, and said almost in a whisper, "He felt it was wrong to accept my invitation, because of what people might say. He knew that I lived alone at the cottage. But my sister's decision to shut up the house was so sudden. He had nowhere else to go. And he's been so good to me...so kind and considerate."

"And he stayed on with you until you left for London this morning to catch the plane?"

"Yes."

"*Eh bien*, mam'selle... I have only one more question to put to you. Do you know of anybody among your sister's acquaintances who—how shall I put it?—bore her a grudge, who had anything to gain by her death?"

"No. Nobody."

II

Then it was Gammon's turn. An easier interview this. No feminine susceptibilities to study here. He came into the room with a breezy, almost familiar air, nodded affably to Blampignon and made a bee-line for the nearest armchair. His vinous complexion was ruddier than ever. He looked as if his collar were choking him. When he tried to light his pipe he couldn't bring the match to the bowl, almost as if his eyes had lost the power to focus. It was obvious he'd been drinking. He wasn't exactly drunk. Just mellow. His every movement deliberate, as if each gesture were the result of a conscious effort of will.

Yet there was a wary light in his eyes, something uneasy about them, the look of an old dog who keeps a watchful eye on his master's boot. He jerked his thumb at a tray of drinks on a table beside the desk.

"I see they've looked after you all right. What do you say to a little something before we—?"

"Not at the moment, if it's all the same to you."

Gammon shrugged.

"It's a nasty business this. What's your idea about it?" Blampignon smiled blandly but said nothing. Now that Mam'selle Gaye was no longer in the room he'd already stuck a cigarette between his lips. Gammon went on thickly, "If you ask me, there's a lot of things that look fishy about this case. There's young Derry, for example. What's he really doing down here? In my opinion, that telegram from Le Touquet... it's all eyewash. If I were in your shoes—which, thank God, I'm not—I'd keep a close eye on that young chap. Sooner or later, they say, a murderer will always give himself away." Adding hastily, "Not that I really think he did it, of course. Don't run away with that idea…

"And then there's that gigolo, Duconte. What about him? He's a murderous little runt if ever I saw one! Has anyone told you yet about him and Harry Skeet?…about the way he pulled a knife on him? I wouldn't trust Duconte further than I could kick him. The moment I set eyes on him, I said to myself…"

There was no need for prompting here. It was a monologue. Blampignon simply lay back on the couch, his hands cupped under his head, his eyes closed…listening.

"And Harry Skeet himself…he's supposed to be in Germany, taking a trip down the Rhine. But you never know. There was a damned odd relationship between him and Gwenny Marrable. He'd got a hold over her of some sort. I'd take a bet on that. The way that bounder threw his weight around…it stuck in my gullet. I've often asked myself…"

Somewhere in the house a telephone was ringing. There was the distant slam of a door, footsteps clacking down the parquet of the hall, the sudden cessation of the jangling bell.

"You're not going to tell me that a woman like Gwenny Marrable went through life without leaving a lot of bad feeling in her wake. *De mortuis*, of course…but that woman was a proper bitch at times. She never thought of anyone except herself. Take the way she'd treated her sister—"

There was a knock on the door. Blampignon heaved himself round on the couch and lowered his feet to the floor.

"*Entrez!*" It was Madame Fougère. "For me?"

"No. For M'sieur Gammon."

Snatching the pipe from between his teeth, Gammon asked sharply:

"Who is it?"

"A gentleman, but he wouldn't give his name."

With a vaguely anxious air, Gammon followed Madame Fougère into the hall, closing the door behind him. Blampignon heard the housekeeper stumping away up the passage towards the kitchen. He thought: That's strange. Who the devil knows that Gammon's down here on the Midi?

It couldn't be Derry. As he'd ushered Mam'selle Gaye into the writing-room, he'd caught a glimpse of the young man through the half-open door of the lounge, talking earnestly with the girl. And if not Derry?

Soft-footed as a cat for all his sixteen stone, Blampignon moved to the door and cautiously twisted the handle. At first, even with the door ajar, he couldn't hear a sound. For a moment he thought Gammon must have hung up and slipped into the lounge to pass on some message to the others. But he was wrong about that. Gammon was there all right, obviously with his ear glued to the receiver, listening for all he was worth!

"Yes, yes… I know that all right. But how the hell do you expect me to…by to-morrow?"

Evidently his caller was speaking almost non-stop, for it was only now and then that Gammon managed to slip in a word.

"But look here, I'm bloody well not going to…

"But I've told you already—it may not be possible.

"That's all very well, but you needn't think…

"To-morrow night…ten o'clock…the Pénitents-Blancs…

"Hullo? Hullo? Are you still there?"

But the caller had obviously rung off. Silently, without haste, Blampignon shut the door and tip-toed back to the couch. As he came in, Gammon said, "I'm sorry about that," and crossed at once to the drinks tray. He flipped a hand at the generous array of bottles. "Sure I can't persuade you?"

"Later, perhaps."

"Well, if it's all the same to you…"

He poured himself a stiff peg of whisky and dropped again into his chair. The aura of good-fellowship that had previously enveloped him had now evaporated. The hand holding his glass was shaking. He kept sucking his upper lip and baring his teeth. A curious performance. No doubt some form of nervous tic.

He said in a flat voice, "Now what was I telling you when the Fougère woman came in?"

Blampignon prompted him and he began to talk again, no longer rambling on, but in fits and starts, evidently unable to keep his mind on what he was saying. In any case, most of what he said was little more than ill-tempered gossip, which from Blampignon's point of view didn't add up to much. For all his shaggy tweeds and big drooping pipe he was no better than some mean and tattling old woman. Now that he'd been at the bottle the expression on his perspiring face was more stupid than ever.

Presently Blampignon asked, "After you left Cockfosters, I understand you went to stay with Mam'selle Gaye?"

"Yes. It was good of Deborah to put me up, knowing darn well what sort of construction all the nice-minded people in the village would place on my visit. Between you and me she's worth two of Gwenny. It's taken me a long time to arrive at that conclusion, but now that I have…well, I've given the matter a lot of serious thought. I mean, a woman like that, living alone, trying to make ends meet…she needs somebody to look after her."

Cocking an eyebrow, Blampignon threw him a shrewd, almost mocking glance.

"*Eh bien*, she won't be so badly off in the future. I imagine she'll come into a tidy bit of money."

Gammon stared at him owlishly.

"She might, of course. It's more than possible. Frankly, what with this, that and the other, the idea hadn't occurred to me."

The lie stuck out like a sore thumb, but he never batted an eyelid. He certainly knew how to lay on an act. But that wasn't surprising. Most of his life, no doubt, he'd been laying on an act, living on his wits, on other people's gullibility, buttering them up, sponging on them, thumbing a nose at them behind their backs.

A crafty customer, to say the least of it…slippery as an eel, with his eye always on the main chance. An unlikeable chap.

Suddenly, struck by an idea, Blampignon got up, crossed over to Gammon and held out his hand.

"If you've got it on you, I'd like to see your passport."

"Of course. But what's the idea?"

Was there a note of apprehension in his voice? It was difficult to say. Anyway, fumbling at an inside pocket, he pulled out his passport and handed it to Blampignon.

A flick through the pages and Blampignon was thinking: So that cat won't jump!

The passport carried the official stamp of the *Sûreté Nationale*, dated that day, indicating Gammon's entry into the country through the airport at Nice. The previous franking carried the date January 6th of that year, evidently a sea-crossing to Boulogne Maritime, when he'd accompanied Madame Marrable, no doubt, on her last visit to the villa. And between those two dates Gammon had certainly not set foot in France.

True, he'd already got his alibi. Since Thursday last he'd been staying with Mam'selle Gaye at her cottage in Sussex. She, herself, had corroborated this statement. But the evidence of his passport swept the last glimmer of doubt from Blampignon's mind.

Derry, Duconte, perhaps. That he still had to find out. Gammon, at any rate, was in the clear.

III

The girl next. Her blue eyes still clouded with unhappiness. Yet, unlike her aunt, she had her feelings firmly under control. He went through it all again with her—the set-up at Cockfosters before the little house-party had broken up in an atmosphere of enmity and suspicion. But her assessment of Madame Marrable's character was less acid and uncompromising than Gammon's.

"My parents died in a car accident in South Africa when I was only two. Ever since then Aunt Gwenny's treated me as if I were her own daughter. I shall always be grateful for what she has done for me."

Blampignon noticed that the girl never referred to her as "mother." It was always "Aunt Gwenny." He said:

"Since you left Cockfosters you've been staying with a friend in Scotland?"

"Yes."

"When did you leave your aunt's house?"

"Late on Friday morning."

"After she'd left to catch the ferry?"

"Yes."

"What time did *she* leave the house?"

"As far as I know…about half-past six."

"You're not sure?"

"No. As she was starting off so early, I said good-bye to her the night before."

"And the servants?"

"No. When my aunt caught the early ferry she never expected them to see her off. She always had a flask of coffee by her bedside and had her breakfast on the boat. The car was packed ready overnight, so that she could slip away without disturbing anybody. But she was like that. Terribly selfish and unreasonable at one moment. Terribly considerate at the next. She hated anybody imposing on the servants. We all had our little duties about the house…even Mr. Gammon."

The telephone was ringing in the hall again. The girl glanced towards the door.

"I wonder if I ought to…?"

"What about Madame Fougère?"

"She's gone home. I heard her arguing with the old man as they went off down the drive on their bicycles."

But by then the ringing had stopped and, a moment later, Gammon stuck his head in at the door. His bleary eyes swivelled to Blampignon.

"It's for you."

"Very well."

It was Hamonet ringing from the Commissariat. A note of repressed excitement in his voice.

"Nice have just come through. They guessed I might know where to get in touch with you."

"Well, out with it!"

"The car's been found."

"Where?"

"A few miles north of Le Touquet."

"Tiens!"

"It had been run off the road into some sand dunes, half-hidden among the bushes. Nothing's being touched until you turn up. They've posted a couple of men—"

"All right. I'll drive back to Nice at once. I'll have to charter a special plane to fly me to Le Touquet to-night. They'll jib at H.Q....the expense, of course. But if you're good you can always get your own way."

"You're in a hurry?"

"Yes. I've got to be down in Menton by ten o'clock to-morrow evening...without fail."

"You're on to something?"

"Perhaps."

"Any further instructions?"

"Not at the moment."

"Well, in that case..."

As he walked away from the phone there was a puzzled expression on Blampignon's massive countenance. He was thinking: Le Touquet again! Now what in heaven's name...?

12

THERE WAS A METALLIC TASTE IN HIS MOUTH. THE DRONE of the little piston-plane that had rushed him north to Le Touquet and back was still throbbing like a pulse in the crown of his head. Every now and then, as he lounged at the wheel of the car driving back from Nice airport to his office, his eyelids began to slide down and he gave a prodigious yawn. More than once he took a corner with two wheels on the wrong side of the white line. It was only the cigarette drooping slackly from a corner of his mouth that kept him on the safe side of sleep.

A rattling, exhausting night. A phantasmagoria of impressions. The plane sweeping through the sky over the black and featureless countryside. The tarmac at Le Touquet, wet with a sea mist, glistening in the lamplight. The police car roaring out of the silent and empty town, the local inspector bawling in his ear above the noise of the engine.

"It was a chap named Lafont who found it…a commercial traveller. If you ask me, it's Mother Nature we've got to thank for this slice of luck. You see, he'd pulled his car into the side of the road and gone round behind the bushes to relieve himself..."

A little group of them standing about the big grey saloon, going over it inch by inch in the light of their torches. Testing for fingerprints, of course—steering-wheel, dashboard, gear lever, door handles—getting nowhere, because the last thing the murderer had obviously done before abandoning the car was to rub over every surface from which a print might have been developed. The oncreeping of dawn, a little chill wind running over the dunes, the first sleepy piping of blackbirds in the stunted pines. Then back at the airport, a scrambled meal, a drink or two, a round of handshakes, and he was off again. Beauvais, Paris, Lyons, the great bastion of the Alpes Maritimes, the airport at Nice.

By eleven o'clock he was sitting in his office, studying the enlarged photographs of the fingerprints lifted from the trunk. One set Fougère's. The other that of a murderer, perhaps. It was Variot who'd come through from the laboratory with the prints. Blampignon had asked:

"Only two sets? Surely that's impossible? Many people besides the actual murderer would have handled the trunk *en route*. The English servants who, no doubt, placed it in the car, the Customs officials who examined it, Madame Marrable herself..."

Variot had shrugged.

"Well, there it is. You can't get around the facts."

Now, driving over to Menton, Blampignon was thinking:

"Perhaps it was Madame Marrable... On her journey down, she may have given the trunk a rub over with a duster, something of that sort. Otherwise..."

But it wasn't a very satisfactory explanation.

II

At Monte Carlo Blampignon stopped for lunch at a little restaurant near the Casino gardens. It was hotter than ever. The asphalt was soft to the tread, blackened here and there by the imprint of footsteps. The sprinklers were working overtime in the shade of the trees, where every blade of grass glittered with diamond-points of light. A *fiacre* went by with a jingle of harness. Under its striped and tasselled hood an elderly hag with a face like a mummy was sitting beside a little boy in a sailor's suit.

Blampignon bought a paper and studied it over lunch. There was a write-up about the murder, a photo of the Villa Paradou, his own face staring back at him from the centre of the column. A little information, a lot of speculation—that was about all it amounted to.

A little after two o'clock he was parking his car outside the Hotel Mimosa at Menton. An unpretentious establishment, but clean and comfortable enough, with a tall sallow-faced girl flashing a toothy smile at him from behind the reception-desk.

"M'sieur Derry?"

The girl opened a large black book and ran a finger down the page.

"It's the young Englishman, isn't it?"

"That's right."

"Well, he was in for lunch. I saw him leave the restaurant. Room No. 26. I'll see if he's in." She juggled about with a little red plug on the internal switchboard. "Who shall I say?"

"Blampignon."

Yes—he was in all right. The girl said, "The lift's at the end of the hall. It's the second floor."

Derry was waiting in the corridor outside his room. Blampignon nodded a greeting, but they didn't shake hands.

"Can you spare me a minute? There are one or two little matters..."

"Of course."

Even if he'd said it were inconvenient, it would have made no difference. Blampignon hadn't trailed half-way along the sun-baked littoral to pay a social call on the fellow. It wasn't only the vile taste in his mouth, his lack of sleep, the throbbing in his head that had scrubbed the good-natured expression off his face. As this moment had approached—a critical moment, perhaps—his mood had grown grimmer, more preoccupied. He went into the airless little room with an authoritative tread. There was something almost menacing about him as he lowered his ungainly bulk into the big basketwork armchair.

Even the young man seemed to be aware of the change in him. There was an anxious flicker in his eyes. Blampignon's silence seemed to embarrass him. Seeing that the inspector was smoking, he took out a packet of Player's, twiddled a cigarette between his lips and sat down on the edge of the sagging bed. Blampignon already had a lighter in his hand. Flicking it on, he leaned forward in his chair and brought the flame to the tip of Derry's cigarette.

But he didn't put the lighter back in his pocket. Instead, he held it out, not eighteen inches from Derry's face, snapping it on and off, his eyes fixed on the intermittent flame. A handsome chromium lighter, with initials engraved on either side. A singular performance, to say the least of it. The sort of trick one might perform to amuse a restless child. The young man obviously couldn't make head or tail of it. He stared at Blampignon, wondering, no doubt, if he'd taken leave of his senses. Then, suddenly, his eyes widened in surprise.

"Good God! where did you find that? It happens to be mine."

"You're quite sure it's yours?"

"Of course I am. Those are my initials—N.W.D.—Nigel William Derry. But where on earth—?"

"We'll come to that in a moment. But before we do…" Blampignon took out his notebook, opened it at a blank page, and handed it to Derry. "I'm going to dictate a few phrases to you. I want you to write them down."

The young man's bewilderment was almost comical. He stammered. "I… I don't get it? W-what's the idea?"

"No need to worry about that. Pencil?"

Derry shrugged.

"Oh well, you must have your reasons."

Blampignon had slipped a folded piece of paper from his wallet. Smoothing it out, he said:

"*Eh bien,* if you're ready…"

"All right—fire ahead."

"'At Bockingford Arms turn sharp left for Milldown, then right fork beyond village… right again after level-crossing…'"

Silence in the room save for the scribbling of the pencil, the clatter of a bucket in the courtyard below the window, the clang of the lift-gates, the whine of its descent.

"'…three miles beyond Marlow take left turn at cross-roads.' Well, have you got it down?"

"There you are!"

A quick comparison was enough. Blampignon's expression was grimmer than ever. It was just as he'd anticipated. The notebook, the slip of paper...the handwriting on each was identical. He said sharply, "Your lighter, this sheet of paper bearing your handwriting...you know where I found them?"

"I've no idea."

"On the floor of Madame Marrable's car."

Derry exclaimed, "So it's been found! I didn't realise..."

"That's beside the point. I want to know just how those things came to be in that particular car."

"I'm completely at a loss."

"You remember jotting down these notes?"

"I think so...some months ago. I was going to visit a friend near Ely and he gave me some details of the quickest route."

"And the lighter?"

"I first missed it about a fortnight ago. Just before I left London, in fact, to stay with Mrs. Marrable."

"During your recent visit to her house did you at any time make use of madame's car?"

"Never."

The catechism went on, but it wasn't very satisfactory. Blampignon couldn't make up his mind about the young man. At one moment he seemed nervous, flurried by the relentless pressure of the interrogation—at the next, almost truculent. No doubt that he resented the inspector's questions, yet he answered them readily enough. Was it, perhaps, the indignation of an innocent man who, unjustifiably, finds himself under suspicion? Or the false resentment of a criminal who, one by one, sees his defences crumbling and makes a last desperate attempt to bluff his way out of the corner into which he has been driven?

Yet he didn't look like a cornered man. A puzzled, exasperated man, perhaps, but not a guilty one.

"I'd like to see your passport."

He handed it over without a word. A tense moment for Blampignon, but one that quickly fizzled out. No getting around it. Derry, like Gammon, had got his alibi all right. He'd landed in France, just as he'd said, on Monday, April 25th. No matter if Madame Marrable had been waiting in the car at Boulogne to meet him off the boat. No matter if five miles out of the town, seizing the first chance that had come along, he'd murdered her and concealed her body in the trunk. How could he have got the trunk to the Villa Paradou that night, some eight hundred miles away? And, on top of that, driven the car another eight hundred miles north to the spot where it had been found abandoned?

Yet it was Derry's lighter Blampignon had picked up on the floor of the saloon. The same with the slip of paper. And the telegram sent off from Le Touquet that he claimed to have received from Madame Marrable had, by the look of it, never been sent.

The "pros" and the "cons." One didn't know what to think. The whole case was like that. This little group of people who, until recently, had evidently enjoyed the confidence and hospitality of the dead woman...they all seemed to have something to conceal. None of them was entirely open. And behind the stark reality of the murder, other furtive and shadowy events seemed to be working themselves out, with this person and that linked in obscure relationships, confusing an already complicated investigation.

"Do you mind if I take your fingerprints?"

"I suppose I could refuse?"

"Of course. But in your own interests..."

"O.K. It's all the same to me."

Before leaving the car, Blampignon had dropped the little tin box containing the ink-pad into his pocket. There were fingerprint forms always in his wallet. The job didn't take him thirty seconds. When it was done, he said:

"Your lighter will be returned to you in due course. But for the moment, I'm afraid—"

"I'm in no hurry for it...whenever it suits your convenience."

His indifference was galling. There seemed to be a hint of mockery in his voice as if he were saying:

"Of course, if you want to waste your time it's none of my business. Because, no matter what you suspect, no matter what you think you've got against me, it so happens that I didn't commit the crime!"

And the devil of it was that, balancing one fact against another, it now seemed probable that he hadn't!

III

Blampignon said:

"Cinzano-Seltz. I'll take that table in the corner."

He was almost asleep on his feet. He didn't want to see Hamonet. They'd nothing new to talk about. He didn't want to see anybody. He wanted to drowse at a café table with a long ice-cooled drink in front of him and let the murder case go hang. After the first flush of interest, of excitement, it was so often the way. One struck a bad patch, when nothing seemed to add up, when everybody and everything was out of tune, when progress in one's investigation slowed to a snail's pace and it was difficult to get off the mark again.

It wasn't one of the popular *apéritif* hours and the café was almost empty. Only two rows of tables as yet set out on the pavement. At one of them a couple of elderly cronies were crouched, unspeaking, over a game of dominoes. At another, a hard-faced woman, plastered with cheap jewellery and reeking of scent, kept staring angrily up and down the street and glancing at her watch. She was obviously waiting for somebody. To judge by her sour expression, the way she kept drumming her fingers on the table, it was probably her husband.

"Cinzano-Seltz."

The waiter flicked over the table with his napkin, slapped down a couple of papier mâché mats and set out the glass and siphon.

"I'll pay now."

"As you wish, m'sieur."

Every shady seat in the public gardens across the road was occupied. Mostly mothers with their children, gossiping among themselves, knitting with their noses in a book, rocking a pram. A few old men sitting placidly behind their pipes, staring into space. Somewhere out of sight behind the flowering orange trees the tinkle of a fountain. A tranquil scene. The little town basking in the afternoon sun, its streets and pavements almost deserted, brought almost to a standstill by the fierce and sapping heat.

A rug vendor drifted up, threw a calculating glance at Blampignon and passed on up the street. A dog pattered by. Every now and then the waiter appeared in the doorway of the café, took a listless glance around and went back with a melancholy air into the bar. The grim-faced woman was still waiting for her husband. Presently she called the waiter, paid her bill, and stamped off in the direction of the Casino. Barely had she turned the corner at the end of the avenue, when a rotund little man, with two wisps of white hair curling up like horns from under the brim of his hat, bustled into the place. He enquired breathlessly, "Madame Gallimard?"

The Gallimards were evidently *habitués* of the café, for the waiter replied at once, "Too late, m'sieur. She's just left."

"In which direction…?"

"Towards the Casino. You'll catch her if you hurry."

"*Mon Dieu!*—yes. I'll have to put my best foot forward. I was late yesterday and the day before. I'm for it this time all right!"

With a commiserate shake of his head, the waiter watched the little fellow trotting away under the plane trees, then once more went up the steps into the café.

The two old men were still bent over their dominoes. During the last fifteen minutes they hadn't exchanged half a dozen words.

Blampignon dozed. Twenty minutes slipped by. In the bar the waiter was saying to the proprietor's wife:

"A man ought to throw his weight about sometimes. Otherwise it's a dog's life. You wouldn't catch me running after my old woman like that…"

Blampignon was now sound asleep with his mouth

half-open. Every now and then he made a curious snuffling sound, which resolved itself at length into a slow and steady snore. A fly rose from the rim of his glass and settled on his forehead. A van drew up at the fruiterers next door. The driver jumped down and began carting boxes of peaches into the shop. The town seemed to be coming out of its siesta like a patient from an anaesthetic. There were now quite a few pass- ers-by strolling on the pavements and the traffic was begin- ning to circulate more freely. A *camion* thundered past the café, momentarily blocking out the light, rattling the glasses, leaving a stench of diesel oil in its wake.

Blampignon woke up with a jerk. For a moment he couldn't make up his mind where he was. He stared around him with a stupefied expression, gazing across at the children playing in the gardens, then up and down the street.

Then, in a flash, he was on his feet, weaving his way among the café tables. A man had just come out of the fruiterer's next door. About sixty, perhaps. No hat on his bald head, which was burnt to the colour of mahogany. A stocky, rather aggressive figure in a faded bush-shirt, khaki shorts and grubby white plimsolls. A woman with him—a loaded basket hooked over a naked brown arm—a fine figure of a woman, big-bosomed, wide-hipped, with the free swinging stride of a gipsy. Provençal? Italian? Spanish? It was difficult to say.

"Au revoir, m'sieur."

Blampignon raised a limp hand. Obviously the waiter had been watching him through the window, and seeing he was about to leave had hastened to bow him off the premises.

The couple were, perhaps, a dozen yards up the street. They didn't seem in any hurry. Several times they stopped to browse in a shop window, mostly food shops, and more often than not they went inside to make a purchase. Blampignon kept pace with them, hanging about when they did, moving on behind them in fits and starts, but always keeping his distance. Soon the woman's basket was loaded to the handle. Even the man was carrying a few parcels, stuffed into a string bag that he'd dragged from a left-hand pocket. Not without difficulty, for his left arm seemed to be stiff and awkward in its movements like the limb of a man who has suffered a slight paralytic stroke.

Something relaxed, casual, almost domestic in their attitude to each other. Yet Blampignon found it hard to believe that they were husband and wife. He couldn't say why. Really no more than a hunch and it might well be that he was wrong. Over their relationship, perhaps. But not in respect of the man's identity. Little question about that. He was the man seen by the kitchenmaid at the Villa des Roches leaving the Villa Paradou with Simone Berthode.

Presently the oddly-assorted pair crossed the Avenue Boyer and went down the Rue Partenou. Here the idlers and shoppers were more numerous and once or twice Blampignon lost sight of the couple. But never for long. Anyway, he could rest easy about one thing. They hadn't the slightest suspicion that they were being followed.

"*Pardon, madame. Pardon, m'sieur.*"

This was where he had to push a polite way through a crowd of rubbernecks watching a televised motor race through the window of a radio store.

Then in the Rue de la Republique there occurred an incident that put a yet keener edge on his speculation. Nothing very dramatic. He was probably the only person in the street to notice the occurrence. He was only a few yards behind the couple, when, suddenly, the man stopped dead, grabbed the woman by the arm, spoke a few rapid words to her, and hurried her across to the other side of the road. At first Blampignon couldn't make head or tail of the fellow's actions. Then he realised. A man was standing outside a newsagent's with his nose in the open pages of the *Continental Mail*. It was the young Englishman, Derry. No doubt that the older man had spotted him and, for some reason or other, taken pains to avoid him. But why? Because he was known to Derry, perhaps as a respectable *paterfamilias*, and had no wish to be seen in the company of this handsome, full-bodied woman, who, in all probability, was his mistress? It might be the explanation.

The couple had now quickened their pace and Blampignon was hard put to it to catch up with them without attracting attention. After all, there was something conspicuous about a man of sixteen stone trotting along the pavement in the full heat of the Midi afternoon. But gradually the distance between them shortened again. Beyond the *Mairie* they turned left and began the long climb up through the maze of streets that mounted to the cemetery. Presently they were on the fringe of the alleyways that marked the limits of the Old Town. The district wasn't exactly squalid, but decidedly down-at-heel. There wasn't a shutter, a door, a sign above a shop that couldn't have done with a lick of paint. The few people abroad seemed to slink like shadows through the sub-aqueous twilight that filtered down between the houses. Even the dogs had a furtive look.

At one of these houses the couple came to a halt. The man

took out a key, mounted the worn stone steps and opened what was probably the only door into the place. Then they disappeared inside, slamming the door behind them. Blampignon had also come to a stop, ostensibly to light a cigarette. Now he crossed to the far pavement and began to plod on up the hill. Little enough to be seen. All the windows in the house, except one, were tightly shuttered. But in that one window there was a face behind the grimy glass, the face of a girl peering down into the street. Something familiar about the large expressive eyes, the sulky mouth, the dark hair swept back from the broad forehead. True, he'd never actually set eyes on her before, only her photograph. But the likeness was unmistakable.

It was Simone Berthode, the girl who, until recently, had served behind the perfume counter at the Monoprix!

13

THERE WAS A RUSTY WIRE BELL-PULL TO THE SIDE OF
the door. Blampignon gave it a tug or two. A thin jangling
echoed in the house. He waited. No sound of footsteps coming
down the passage or running down the stairs. Dead silence. A
silence so complete that one had the impression of the occupants holding their breath, gazing at each other, rigid, tense...
listening. Blampignon rang again. The result was the same.

A seedy, middle-aged man was approaching up the street,
eyes on the ground, his flat feet scuffing wearily over the
paving-stones. Blampignon stepped down to intercept him.

"A moment, m'sieur." The man came to a stop and glanced
up at the inspector with lustreless eyes, his hands pressed to
his lungs, trying to get his breath. "Can you tell me who lives
here at No. 24?"

"Yes—the widow Cambremont. She came into the property when her husband died. It must be eight years ago now...
perhaps longer."

"She lives here alone?"

The fellow shrugged. There was a lascivious smirk on his sallow, unhealthy face.

"Except when the foreign chap, the Englishman, comes to stay with her."

"So that's how it goes, eh?"

"Yes, for the last five years or more. And not so long after he was first seen going around with the widow, she had to call in the midwife." The fellow leered and winked. "Well, you can make what you like of that, but the boy didn't get his blue eyes and fair hair from his mother! He was only three when they lost him. The little chap was playing in the street when he was knocked down by a motor-cycle and killed. They say the driver was drunk...scarcely able to sit in the saddle...and never even pulled up to see what he'd done."

"*Tiens!* And the police never got on to him?"

"Never. Just here where we're standing—that's where it happened. Some say madame and the Englishman were looking out of the window at the time...that they saw the motorcyclist swerve slap across the street."

Exhausted by his recital the man pressed his hands to his narrow chest again and began to cough violently. Waiting until the attack had passed off, Blampignon asked:

"By the way, is there a back entrance to the place?"

"No. The houses here join on to those facing on to the Rue St.-Roch."

It was just as Blampignon had thought. One door only into the house, and that door stubbornly closed against him. Apart from fetching an axe and smashing his way in, what else was he to do? Demand admission in the name of the law, perhaps, but at this stage of his enquiries he didn't want to rouse the whole neighbourhood. A tantalising, infuriating situation.

He glanced up at the second-floor window where he'd seen the girl gazing down into the street. The shutters had been stealthily closed. No doubt it was she who'd seen him cross over to ring the bell, and crept downstairs to tip the wink to the others.

But he couldn't hang about there cooling his heels until one of them left the house. It was a job for Hamonet. He'd have to set a couple of plain-clothes men to keep watch on the place.

Blampignon's car was still parked opposite the café in the Avenue de Verdun. Retracing his steps through the town, he slipped with a sigh of relief into the little pearl-coloured Vedette and drove to the Commissariat.

Hamonet said, "Did you have a good trip north?"

"Bumpy and boring. I took a good long look at the car, but I'm not sure that it's got me any further. The fact is…"

He gave Hamonet an outline of the day's events and came, as quickly as he could, to the matter of Simone Berthode.

"24 Rue Mirimar. You'd better get a couple of fellows up there without delay. The girl's got to be brought here for questioning. The man, too. It's only a matter of time before one or the other of them sticks a nose outside the door. But no hoo-ha, mind you. It's got to be done discreetly."

"I'll deal with it at once."

When Hamonet returned he found Blampignon seated at the desk, poring over the enlarged photos of the fingerprints taken from the trunk. Alongside these he'd set out the specimen prints taken from Derry in the hotel bedroom. From the open despatch-case that he'd brought in from the car, he took out a magnifying-glass and began to search for points of comparison. Five minutes went by. Hamonet knew better than to interrupt. Blampignon kept mumbling and grunting to himself, every now and then dabbing at his neck and face with a handkerchief. Suddenly he snapped out:

"Well, that settles that! Derry never handled the trunk. That's one more point in his favour. But if *he* didn't then who the devil…?"

He still wasn't happy about the fingerprint angle of the case. Only two sets of prints had been isolated on the shiny black varnish. Two sets, and one of those Fougère's. It was illogical. There should have been a jumble of different prints, some, of course, more recent than others. And yet when Variot had come to develop the…

"*Tiens!*"

"What is it?"

"It could be the answer to a problem. On the other hand…"

Blampignon lifted his shoulders as if to say, "Until you can prove a theory it's better not to talk about it."

He looked up at the wall clock. It had just gone five. Five hours to kill before he went up to the terraced square in the Old Town and settled down to keep watch on the Chapel des Pénitents-Blancs.

He said to Hamonet, "What about slipping round the corner to the Café Floreal?"

"It suits me all right."

Magali greeted Blampignon like an old friend, shook him warmly by the hand and piloted him with flattering deference to a table in the corner. The *patron* had evidently been making quite a song and dance about the famous detective's previous patronage of his establishment. When he'd taken the inspector's order, he moved stealthily among the crowded tables, whispering to first one and then another of the *habitués*.

"That's him…over in the corner, talking to Hamonet. You wouldn't think to look at him…"

Heads were turned. Everybody suddenly broke off their conversations, nudging each other, hawking the news around.

"It's Blampignon. He's working on that murder case out at Cap Martin."

"Magali's quite right. You can't imagine a chap like that having anything to do with crime."

"He dresses like a beach attendant. There's a wine stain on his shirt-front. I'd give my right arm to know what they're talking about."

As a matter of fact, Blampignon was saying:

"You must come along some time and see my wife's budgerigars. She's taught one of 'em to recite. It's taken her the best part of six months, off and on. You never saw such patience!" He half-closed his eyes, threw back his head and addressed the ceiling in a sing-song voice:

> "'*Un jour sur ses long pieds allait je ne sais où*
> *Le Héron au long bec emmanché d'un long cou.*'

"La Fontaine, of course. It can do a bit of Racine as well…" He took up his drink. "*Bon santé!*"

Their glasses of iced lager were already filmed over with a mist of condensation. As the café filled to capacity the little room grew hot as a furnace. Blampignon's silk shirt was sticking to his chest. He could feel the sweat breaking through every pore, trickling down his skin, collecting in his eyebrows.

Hamonet was saying, "For myself…I breed rabbits."

But it really wasn't much use trying to keep off "shop." A few minutes later Blampignon was off again, airing his views on the murder case.

"When was she murdered? Where was she murdered? Tell me that, and I'd be a good deal nearer to telling *you* who murdered her. You remember what the doctor said? She died three to four days before she was found in the trunk. Say, Friday or Saturday—the day she actually landed in France or the day after. *Eh bien*…then tell me this. How did the murderer make contact with her on this side of the Channel?"

Hamonet suggested, "A prearranged meeting, perhaps."

"*Tiens!* Could they have met any other way? And if the meeting was prearranged then the man we're after was known to Madame Marrable."

"The man? But how can you be sure…?"

"This isn't a woman's crime. No woman could have lifted that trunk and carried it into the house. And the placing of the body in the trunk, the stripping off of the victim's clothes, the planning, the general strategy of the crime…none of these factors suggest the murderer was a woman. No. It's a man we're looking for. And this fellow…somebody Madame Marrable trusted, no doubt, somebody in her confidence, somebody who knew she was making for the Villa Paradou."

"Unless she was assaulted out of the blue, as it were."

"The casual killer? Think again! How would *he* know where his victim was off to? And even if he did find out, he wouldn't have troubled to dump the woman's corpse on the villa doorstep. If you ask me, that was a deliberate move to suggest that somebody in the locality had done the job. Derry, Duconte, perhaps. The murderer knew they were down in this part of the world. And apart from that he had his own alibi to think of!"

"It's certainly a point."

Blampignon drained his glass and looked around, trying to catch Magali's eye. Silence for a space. Then Blampignon said abruptly:

"He's already hopped back across the Channel. What will you bet on that?"

"The murderer?"

"Of course. Once he'd rid himself of the body at the villa he drove flat out for Le Touquet. Because from Le Touquet—having run the car off into those sand dunes just outside the town—he could catch the next available plane back to England."

Hamonet said, "So we're just wasting our time. After all—"

"A moment!" Blampignon had at last got Magali's attention, lifting a finger to him across the intervening tables, jabbing it indicatively at their empty glasses. The *patron* beamed, nodded, and bustled off behind the bar-counter. "A waste of time? Don't you believe it. The murder was committed in France. We've no need to argue about that. But how and when and where? Our English *confrères* won't have much to go on unless we can tell them that. As it is…"

A man was edging his way towards them among the chairs and tables. Noticing him, Hamonet cut in.

"One of the clerks from the Commissariat. I wonder what…?"

It was a phone call from the *Sûreté Nationale* at Nice. If Hamonet could make contact with Blampignon he was to pass on the following information. The slip of paper handed over by the clerk read:

Original contents of trunk in Marrable murder found this morning hidden in rocks on Grande Corniche between Roquebrune and La Turbie. Contents collected and passed on to Variot for laboratory examination.

When he'd dismissed the clerk, Hamonet looked across at Blampignon.

"What do you make of this?" Blampignon shrugged but made no reply. "You think she was actually murdered up there on the Corniche?"

Again the non-committal shrug.

"It's a reasonable line of argument."

Hamonet persisted.

"But the trunk would have to be emptied to make room for the body. No question about that."

"None."

"Then surely…?"

"The murderer may have carried the contents around in the car until he hit on a suitable spot to dispose of them."

"There is that, of course," Hamonet admitted.

II

After another couple of drinks Blampignon took his leave of Hamonet and walked back to his car, which was parked outside the Commissariat. He was feeling depressed, on edge, at a loose end. Still another two or three hours before Gammon was due to keep his appointment at the Chapel des Pénitents-Blancs. Little scraps of information still drifting in, but nothing tying up. He'd arrived at one of those frustrating moments in a case when one seems to have exhausted every possible line of investigation. He looked in at the police-station and put through a call to Variot at his private address.

"The contents of the trunk? Yes, I've run the tape over them. If you're hoping for anything sensational, then you're going to be disappointed. Mostly frocks, underwear, shoes, toilet articles…just what you'd expect. I got a few clear fingerprints off a scent spray and the back of a silver mirror. But every one of them matched up with the specimen prints we took from the dead woman over at the Menton mortuary."

For once, as the sun began to wester, the air failed to cool. The heat, if anything, grew more unbearable. There was scarcely a man in the streets who wasn't carrying his jacket over his arm. Every time a car went by a flurry of gritty dust was whipped up from the gutters. The sun was like a gigantic spotlight slung low over the horizon, glaring pitilessly into every nook and cranny, blinding and distracting.

Blampignon drove slowly out of the town and, turning off the littoral road, swung on to the Grande Corniche. Not heading for any particular spot. Still killing time. Perhaps with the thought at the back of his mind that up on the mountainside it might be less oppressive. Somewhere beyond Roquebrune he pulled into the yard of a disused quarry and shut off his engine. Then, pushing up the windscreen, he lit a cigarette and gave himself up to thought.

One riddle, at any rate, to which he seemed to have found an answer. The lack of fingerprints on the trunk. It wasn't Madame Marrable, of course, who'd rubbed over its surface with a duster. It was the murderer. A politic gesture to polish away his own fingerprints—the last thing he'd done, no doubt, before sneaking out of the villa and driving away through the night in his victim's car.

And the prints, other than Fougère's, that Variot had pointed out? Those of the unknown man who'd been sleeping in the villa. The man Pialou, the window-cleaner, had seen entering the place on Saturday night. The man who Blampignon now believed to be André Duconte.

Easy to imagine what had happened. The intruder seeing the trunk in the hall, wondering why it was there, when it had arrived, who had delivered it. Nervous, apprehensive, because somebody had obviously entered the place during his absence. And since there was no sign that the house had been broken into, somebody, like himself, who was in possession of a key. Madame Marrable herself, perhaps? Her initials, at any rate, stencilled on the lid of the trunk. And so he'd fiddled with the hasps, found them unlocked and opened up the trunk. Then sickened, terrified, in a panic, he'd slammed down the lid, pushed home the clasps and...

Exactly. What then? Would he have had the temerity to sleep another night in the villa when, at any minute perhaps, there might be a swish of tyres on the drive, a scrambling of feet on the gravel, as the police threw a cordon about the place preparatory to breaking in? "Acting on information received"—that was the official phrase. How was he to know that the police at that time knew nothing of the murder? His own position dangerous, unequivocal, to say the least of it. Surely his one thought would have been to get away from the villa as fast as his feet would carry him?

And thanks to the copy of the Sunday newspaper he'd left up in that spare room, they knew that the fellow had entered the villa on Sunday night. Little doubt that it was then he'd first set eyes on the trunk. Which meant that it was Sunday when the murderer had driven up in the car and carried the trunk into the hall.

And Madame Marrable had been dead for about three days. Friday when she'd landed at Boulogne. So that it was somewhere in the north of France, during the first two or three hundred miles of her journey south, that she'd probably been attacked.

And the murderer had left the contents of the trunk in the car, hidden under a rug no doubt, until he'd disposed of them among the rocks on the Grande Corniche. To confuse the issue, perhaps—to suggest that Madame Marrable had actually met her death only a few miles from the Villa Paradou.

Early on Saturday afternoon the Fougères had received a telegram from Lyons sent ostensibly by their mistress.

DELAYED—DON'T EXPECT ME UNTIL TUESDAY AFTERNOON—MARRABLE.

But it wasn't genuine, of course. It had been sent by the murderer to suggest that, at that time, Madame Marrable was still alive, to make sure that the Fougères wouldn't go to the police when she failed to turn up on Sunday night as arranged.

Blampignon was slowly coming out of his mood of

depression. The fog was lifting a little, the picture was growing clearer. A fact here, a fact there—at first unrelated, now beginning to fit in. No clue as yet pointing to the identity of the murderer. Somebody whose name hadn't cropped up, perhaps, during his talk with Derry, with the others staying at the villa. No reason, of course, why the murderer should have been a member of that fractious house-party at Cockfosters. Admittedly they alone seemed to know of Madame Marrable's plan to shut up the house and travel down to Cap Martin. But she could have telephoned or written a dozen friends without their knowledge.

Duconte, for one. This fellow, Harry Skeet...

Skeet?

Suddenly Blampignon came upright in his seat. With a muttered exclamation he spun the stub of his cigarette through the open windscreen of the car. He was hearing again the glutinous voice of Gammon saying of Duconte, "Has anyone told you yet about him and Harry Skeet...about the way he pulled a knife on him?"

And Derry, speaking of the same incident, "As luck would have it, the knife only nicked him in the upper arm. Painful enough, of course, but when you think how it might have ended up..."

And, in a flash, Blampignon was back in time, watching a stocky, bald-headed figure walking away down the Avenue de Verdun. The handsome, opulent woman at his side, with a loaded basket bumping against her hip. The man easing a string-bag from his left-hand pocket, his actions cramped, cautious, as if he were in pain, his left arm curiously stiff.

The left arm of Harry Skeet, perhaps?

Yet he remembered Derry saying:

"The last we heard of Mr. Skeet he was in Coblence, heading for the Black Forest…"

But they were wrong. For some reason or other Skeet had led them up the garden path. He wasn't in Germany.

At that moment he was sitting with Madame Cambremont and Simone Berthode behind the shuttered windows of the widow's house in the Rue Mirimar. Perhaps aware by now that the house was being watched, keeping their voices down, discussing their dilemma, wondering what to do, their minds filled with uneasy speculation. Uneasy, because at least two of them had something to hide from the police. At least two of them were guilty of a crime. *That on the night of Tuesday, April 26th, at the Villa Paradou…* That's how the charge would run… *having fired a gun at one, André Duconte, with intent to murder him.*

It was their hatred of Duconte, no doubt, which had first urged them to form this murderous alliance—the girl from the Monoprix, this elderly English painter. Impossible to say just how or when they'd met. Perhaps chance had brought them together. Or Madame Cambremont. There were a dozen likely explanations.

But no explanation, as yet, for Skeet's presence down on the Côte d'Azur. Why had he misled his English friends over that trip up the Rhine? To give him his alibi, perhaps, if Duconte were picked up with a bullet through his brain.

Or was it to put him in the clear, because he knew that the body of Madame Marrable would, in due course, be found in a cabin-trunk at her villa on Cap Martin? Had Skeet been waiting for the woman on the quayside, when she drove off the car-ferry at Boulogne?

What was it Gammon had said?

"There was a damned odd relationship between him and Gwenny Marrable. He'd got a hold over her of some sort. I'll take a bet on that..."

And now, perhaps, that relationship had been brought, abruptly, irrevocably, to an end. And in its place a new and terrible relationship established. The deathless affinity between a murderer and the victim of his crime.

14

BLAMPIGNON STOOD BACK IN THE SHADOW OF THE doorway, rigid as a post, looking across at the spectral façade of the Chapel des Pénitents-Blancs. Not wanting to be conspicuous he'd put on a navy raincoat over his light drill suit. In any case there was no moon and the square was poorly lit. With the coming of darkness the air had cooled a little. In most of the mean little houses the shutters had been flung back and the windows stood wide open to the Mediterranean night.

In one of them, a blowsy woman in a nightdress was sitting up in bed, knitting. A man, still in his shirt and trousers, was stretched out on the bed beside her, a pipe in his mouth, his nose in a magazine. An old woman came out of a hovel across the way and emptied a bucket in the gutter. Two doors along a lad of about sixteen was squatting cross-legged on a cushion, strumming softly on a guitar. A little way off another youth had upended his bicycle under a lamp-post, and was busy mending a puncture.

Blampignon glanced at the luminous dial of his watch.

Two minutes to go. He wondered from which direction Gammon would eventually appear. Up the terraced steps from the quayside? Or from one of the obscure alleyways that mounted through the Old Town? And the man he'd arranged to meet…where was he? Blampignon's gaze shifted to the chapel steps. No sign of him there. Just a couple locked in an embrace, a dog sniffing at their legs.

The first of the town clocks chimed ten. Then another and another. The young man with the guitar had picked up his cushion and gone indoors. The woman in the nightdress was leaning out of the window calling shrilly to the boy with the bicycle.

"Are you going to be all night about it? It's time you got to bed. Mucking about with that blessed bike of yours…"

Then, suddenly, Gammon came into view at the top of the steps. Blampignon cupped a hand over the glowing tip of his cigarette and shrank back farther into the shadows. For a moment the Englishman paused to get his bearings, then, knocking out his pipe on his heel, he strode quickly towards the chapel. Almost at once a slight agile figure darted out of its high arched doorway and came down the steps to meet him.

"Well, have you got it?"

"Yes…here."

Although their voices were lowered, the words sounded startlingly clear in the sudden silence that had fallen on the square. The man spoke in English, but his accent was unmistakably French.

"All right then, hand it over, and look sharp about it! I'm not hanging about here any longer than I've got to."

Something passed between them. Blampignon was sure

of that, but he couldn't see what it was. He merely saw their hands come together as if in a limp handshake and quickly fall apart. His rope-soled *espadrilles* made no sound on the mosaic paving as he stepped forward out of the shadows. But the fellow must have had the eyes of a hawk, for in a flash he spun round and, with a hand clapped to his hat, raced for the dark maw of the nearest alley. No use attempting to give chase. That part of the town was like a rabbit warren. Besides, he'd got off the mark too swiftly.

Gammon was still standing his ground. He'd swung round to face the inspector, watching him approach, a wary light in his eyes.

"What the devil are you doing up here?"

He sounded nervous, yet faintly aggressive.

"I might ask you the same question."

"You could, of course. But it doesn't follow I'd satisfy your curiosity."

"Meeting a friend, eh?"

"Perhaps."

"The friend that rang you up at the villa last night?"

"That's an idea, isn't it?"

"Somebody you weren't too anxious to meet?"

Gammon's expression never changed. He wasn't giving anything away. He didn't even answer the question, just shrugged it aside and changed the subject.

"By the way, in case you didn't know, they brought the coffin out to the villa this afternoon. The funeral's fixed for to-morrow. We're laying on the whole thing regardless, of course—full choral service, floral tributes, the whole bag of tricks. Twelve o'clock at the Protestant church. You'll be coming?"

"I doubt it."

"Other fish to fry, eh?"

"That's about it."

"Ah well... I've a taxi waiting down on the quay. It's time I was getting along."

As he watched the fellow strolling off towards the steps, Blampignon cursed under his breath. A promising situation that had fizzled out in a frustrating anti-climax. Evidently Gammon wasn't such a fool as he looked. He knew when to talk and when to hold his tongue.

And the fellow who'd been lurking in the chapel? Slight, about thirty, perhaps, a Frenchman. But on no occasion had Blampignon been able to get a clear view of his features. Dark, well-waisted suit, dark hat, something of the dandy about him. The gigolo type.

It *could* have been Duconte...

II

It was only a short step from the Place St. Michel to the Rue Mirimar. The two men posted by Hamonet outside No. 24 were still hanging around. One of them was actually squatting on the steps of the house, playing with a kitten—the other pacing up and down on the far side of the street.

"How goes it? Anything to report?"

The man, recognising the inspector, sprang up and gently pushed aside the kitten with the toe of his boot. Keeping his voice down, he said:

"Yes. Madame Cambremont left the house to go to the wine-shop on the corner."

"When was this?"

"About an hour ago. We stopped her, as we'd been instructed, and questioned her about the other two...Simone Berthode and the Englishman."

"Well?"

"She made out she'd never even heard of them. If I hadn't known better I'd have sworn she was telling the truth. What an actress! For all that, we insisted on searching the house."

The second man had now crossed over to join them. He obviously wasn't going to let his friend, Raunay, do all the talking.

"Funny...but she didn't make any fuss about letting us in. Opened up every door of the place to us."

Raunay cut in.

"But we didn't see anything of the girl or the Englishman. We opened every cupboard, looked under the beds, poked around in every corner of the place. Not a sign of them!"

The other man, Loisel, had then returned to the Commissariat to report to Hamonet. He'd found him still round at the Café Floreal, playing cards with his friends. Loisel went on:

"The inspector thinks they must have sneaked out of the place before Raunay and I turned up."

It certainly seemed the only likely explanation. Now the two men were hanging around, hoping they'd catch the couple trying to slip into the house during the night.

One thing they *had* noticed. The largest of the two attic rooms had been set up as a rough-and-ready studio. There was an easel near the window. On it a full-length nude of Madame Cambremont, lying back with one knee drawn up on a big brass-railed bed, her black hair fanning out over the rumpled pillow.

"When we asked her who made use of the room she said it was rented out to an Italian chap called Mengoli. Sometimes, to earn a few more francs, she acted as his model. According to her Mengoli had just returned to Genoa because his mother had died. But if you ask me she was having us up a stick, making monkeys of us, because Loisel noticed that the other pictures in the room carried a signature, and the name wasn't Mengoli."

Blampignon was smiling to himself.

"It was Skeet, perhaps?"

The two men looked at him in astonishment, then at each other, as if to say, "Now how the devil did he get on to that?"

Finally Loisel nodded.

III

All the next morning Blampignon was at his desk, dealing with other matters than the Marrable affair. A week-old robbery at one of the luxury villas up on the heights at Super-Cannes. The owner of the villa had a pull in political circles and was ringing up the *Sûreté Nationale* at least twice a day, making himself unpleasant, demanding that the heads should roll...including Blampignon's. Which didn't help to improve his temper. There were other minor cases on which he was keeping a fatherly eye. Reports to read. Directives to issue. Letters to dictate.

Sometime about noon he put through a call to Hamonet.

"How's the situation up at No. 24?"

"Nothing doing. If Simone Berthode and the Englishman managed to get clear before Raunay and Loisel turned up, then they're still out and about. Madame Cambremont left the house with her basket shortly after nine…"

For a time they discussed this and that, threshing around, trying to find a new point of departure, a clue overlooked that would set their investigations on the move again. Hamonet still hadn't abandoned hope of picking up Duconte. Every *gendarmerie* along the coast had been given his description and warned to keep his eyes skinned for the fellow. The frontier police at Vintimille were making sure he didn't slip into Italy.

Blampignon went on:

"I'm driving over to Cap Martin this afternoon. Nothing really in mind. Just to see if anyone at the villa has anything further to tell us. They're all at the funeral this morning. So if you want to get in touch with me any time after three o'clock…"

There'd been a sudden unexpected break in the weather. Blampignon had turned up at the office in a grey flannel suit. During the night the temperature had plummeted twenty degrees. Low cloud was rolling in over the mountains. The sea was grey, wrinkled, like elephant hide. The terrace tables of the cafés along the promenade were deserted, their parasols folded down, the white-coated waiters lounging around behind the steamy windows staring out at the traffic, bored, irritable, thinking of their missed tips. The fronds of the palm trees rasped together like steel files in the chill and rising wind.

For once Blampignon had lunch at home with his wife. It

wasn't often they met at midday. To mark the occasion she'd stepped out early to the fishmonger's and prepared his favourite fish—fried octopus with seasoned tomato sauce, *Poulpe à la Niçoise.*

At three o'clock he was standing in the porch of the Villa Paradou, enquiring of Madame Fougère, "Are they in? Who's here? Did M'sieur Derry return with them after the funeral?"

The housekeeper's eyes were red and swollen. There were traces of tears on her round leathery cheeks. The air in the house was still heavy with the scent of flowers, and petals from the wreaths were scattered over the Persian mats in the hall.

"Yes, they're all here. The *avocat* from England turned up early this morning. He'd been travelling all night, poor man, so as to be in time for the burial. They're in the lounge now… reading the will. Will you wait in the study?"

"No. I'll come through to the kitchen."

Fougère was sitting at the table, a glass of cognac under his nose. He was still in the clothes he'd worn at the funeral. His shiny black suit reeked of camphor balls and he kept easing his scrawny neck inside his high starched collar. He'd already taken off his boots, which had evidently been pinching him. On seeing Blampignon he rasped out:

"*Eh bien!* Have you found the chap who did it yet? I'll wager you haven't. It's the man Pialou saw last Saturday night. He's the one you want to—"

Madame Fougère broke in derisively.

"Listen to the old fool! He's always this way when he's in his cups. To hear him talk you'd think he was President of the Republic. How he ever kept his job long enough on the railways to get a pension…"

The old man said querulously, "And that's another thing. Who'll get the villa now? That chit of a girl or the mousy one? We've our jobs here to think of. You couldn't feed a nest of sparrows on my miserable pension. Perhaps *we'll* be remembered in madame's will. Even a little windfall would come as a blessing…"

His wife nodded meaningly towards the door.

"We'll know soon enough. They can't be much longer. You'll take a glass, m'sieur?"

"Not now, madame."

There was a different atmosphere in the house. He could sense it at once. It was like a numbed body slowly coming to life again. The shock of the tragedy was wearing thin and, little by little, things were returning to normal. The old man was worrying about his job, his future. As, no doubt, the others, closeted with the lawyer in the drawing-room, were looking ahead, aware for the first time, perhaps, how profoundly their lives were going to be affected by Madame Marrable's death.

Presently a bell rang in the kitchen, and Madame Fougère, who'd been busy preparing tea, now wheeled the loaded trolley towards the hall.

"Shall I tell them you're here, m'sieur?"

"Please."

A few moments later she was back again.

"If you'd go through…it's the far door on the left."

15

YES, IT WAS A DIFFERENT ATMOSPHERE ALL RIGHT. MUCH of the strain and tension of the last two days seemed to have slackened off. As befitted the occasion, the little gathering wasn't exactly animated, but everybody appeared more relaxed, more sociable. Even Deborah, as she came forward to greet Blampignon, managed to summon up the shadow of a smile.

"You wanted to see me?"

"In due course, mam'selle. There are one or two little matters...nothing really of importance."

She insisted on pouring him a cup of tea, then led him away to be introduced to Featherby, the solicitor. The two men shook hands, exchanging a few pleasantries, sizing each other up.

When Deborah was out of earshot, Blampignon said, "In a minute, when you've finished your tea, I'd like a word with you in private."

Featherby glanced at him shrewdly.

"I rather guessed you might."

For a time the conversation was general, mostly about the funeral, the service in the church, the view from the cemetery, the sudden change in the weather. A stranger entering the room would never have suspected that the bulky figure in the grey, double-breasted suit was a detective investigating a murder. To Blampignon there was an air of unreality about it all—the clatter of tea-cups, the small-talk, the unemotional English voices, the discreet avoidance of any reference to the manner of Madame Marrable's death. It was as if their native common sense was slowly reasserting itself, as if they were saying to themselves:

"It's a terrible thing to have happened...that she should have been the victim of so brutal and senseless a crime. But, after all, life must go on..."

Presently, catching Featherby's eye, Blampignon nodded towards the door and the two of them slipped across the hall into the little writing-room. The moment they were seated the solicitor enquired with a hint of embarrassment:

"I suppose you've no idea as yet...?"

Blampignon shook his head.

"If only we could arrive at a motive... This theory, that theory. You know how it is. But nothing concrete on which to base a firm line of investigation." They talked for a time of the main facts surrounding the case, then Blampignon went on, "You acted for Madame Marrable's husband when he was alive?"

"No. I didn't take over her affairs until after Humphrey Marrable died. In fact, when she first bought Cockfosters about twelve years ago. My practice is in Canterbury, only a few miles from the estate."

"She was a wealthy woman?"

"By to-day's standards—very. I estimate that, with death duties and all other outgoings deducted, the net value of her estate should be in the region of two hundred thousand pounds."

"*Tiens!* And the chief beneficiaries under her will?"

For an instant Featherby hesitated, fiddling with the clasps of the brief-case that he'd laid across his knees.

Finally he muttered, "I admit I'd anticipated the question, but I'm not sure..."

Blampignon reminded him, "I could get the details from Mam'selle Gaye, no doubt. But since you've got the facts at your finger-tips, it would come better from you."

"Very well."

It was much as Blampignon had expected. Apart from a few minor bequests to servants, including one hundred pounds each to the Fougères, it was Sheila Marrable and Deborah Gaye who'd come into most of the property. In Featherby's opinion they would inherit about seventy thousand each. Cockfosters had been left to the sister. The villa to the girl. Featherby went on:

"At one time the girl's inheritance was contingent upon her not marrying until she was thirty. If she did, then the whole of Mrs. Marrable's estate was to go to her sister absolutely. But the day before Mrs. Marrable crossed to France she came into my office and said she wished to add a codicil to her will. In this she rescinded the conditions previously laid down, making the girl's inheritance unconditional in every respect."

Blampignon asked sharply, "Do you know why she did this?"

"No."

"She gave no reason for adding the codicil?"

"None."

Blampignon couldn't make head or tail of it. Why, when she was against the girl marrying Nigel Derry, had she troubled to alter her will? Surely if the girl knew of the conditions governing her inheritance she would think twice before plunging into an early marriage? True, she couldn't marry Derry without her guardian's consent until she was twenty-one. After that she was free to do as she pleased. But with that seventy thousand in mind wouldn't she hesitate even then, when in less than ten years' time...?

And why had Madame Marrable made the girl's inheritance conditional in the first place? Because, no doubt, she wanted this hold over the girl, to keep her as long as she could within the orbit of her influence. An ageing, possessive, self-centred woman, terrified, perhaps, of loneliness, of boredom, seeing in the girl an insurance against the empty years ahead.

"This M'sieur Skeet...he was an old friend of madame's?"

"A very old friend. They first met in Toronto some years before the war."

"Before madame was married?"

"So I believe."

"A very old friend...and yet she fails to remember him in her will!"

"There's really nothing very strange about that. After all, Mr. Skeet had already been handsomely provided for."

"Provided for? In what way?"

"I can rely on you to treat this confidentially?"

"Of course."

"Well, about four months after her husband's death Mrs. Marrable settled an annuity on Mr. Skeet. An annual income of about seven hundred pounds. At that time, of course, I wasn't acting for her. But when she moved down to Cockfosters the relevant trust deed was handed over to my firm with the other documents connected with Mrs. Marrable's affairs. A generous settlement, you'll admit. The benefits of which Mr. Skeet has now been enjoying for the past fifteen years."

Blampignon had drifted to the window. With his back to the lawyer he was gazing out into the garden, where the first big drops of rain were pattering on the dusty leaves. Once again he was hearing Gammon's voice, in this very room, talking to him of Skeet.

"There was a damned odd relationship between him and Gwenny Marrable..."

Odd? A relationship that had ensured for Skeet a life pension of seven hundred a year? Surely intimate would have been the better word? What did it mean? Perhaps the lawyer...?

But Featherby could tell him nothing. He, himself, had never been able to discover the reason for his client's surprising generosity. He'd met Skeet on a couple of occasions at Cockfosters. Like Derry and Gammon he'd been puzzled by the fellow's presumptuous, almost patronising, attitude towards his benefactress.

Turning in from the window, Blampignon went on:

"Where did Madame Marrable meet her husband? In Canada?"

"No—London."

"How long did the marriage last?"

"A little over two years. Humphrey Marrable was over seventy when he proposed to her. For all his wealth he appears to have been a lonely man—in fact, somewhat of a recluse—and I imagine he really married for companionship. He needed a woman to look after him. He'd never enjoyed good health. He suffered, I believe, from some sort of cardiac weakness."

"And shortly after madame returned from Canada, M'sieur Skeet followed her over to England?"

"As far as I know…yes."

"Between ourselves…do you think she was faithful to her husband?"

The bluntness of the question seemed to disconcert the lawyer. He said stiffly:

"I know nothing about Mrs. Marrable's private life. I met her solely in my professional capacity. She always struck me as a very capable and single-minded woman."

Blampignon put a few more questions, then, aware that Featherby had little more to tell him, abruptly held out his hand.

"*Eh bien*… I'm most grateful. Perhaps you'd ask Mam'selle Sheila to join me in here."

II

A distressing and distracting day for the girl, no doubt. First the funeral, then the reading of the will, the sudden realisation that she was now a young woman of means, of independence, free to make what she would of the future, no longer forced to conform to the pattern of existence laid down for her by her guardian. Yet she was still wonderfully self-possessed. Blampignon set a chair for her and moved away again to the window. The rain was now a steady downpour, hissing in the trees, drumming on the flagstones of the terrace.

Silence for a moment in the little room. Then, twisting round a chair, Blampignon straddled it, his arms folded on its back, leaning towards the girl.

"I've just had a talk with M'sieur Featherby about the terms of Madame Marrable's will. May I congratulate you on your good fortune?"

"Thank you."

"Until this afternoon, you'd no idea that a codicil had been added to the will?"

"No idea at all."

"Madame had spoken to you about the original conditions governing your inheritance?"

"Yes—about a fortnight ago."

"When she knew that you and M'sieur Derry wanted to get married, perhaps?" The girl nodded. "Apart from yourself and the solicitor, who knew of these conditions?"

"Nigel, of course. Aunt Gwenny told him before she told me."

"M'sieur Derry. Nobody else?"

"No, I don't think…" A thought seemed to occur to her, for suddenly she broke off and added after a moment's reflection: "No—wait. I remember now. I mentioned the matter to Mr. Skeet the day before he left for Germany."

"He knew that you and the young man were hoping…?"

"Yes, I told him that same afternoon. He's always liked Nigel and I guessed he wouldn't be against the idea of our

marriage. You see, I couldn't understand why Aunt Gwenny
was being so unreasonable, and I just had to talk it over with
somebody. Naturally, I thought of Mr. Skeet."

"He's a good friend of yours?"

For some reason the girl suddenly lowered her glance and
flushed scarlet. Still without looking up, she nodded, saying
nothing, as if not trusting herself to speak. Puzzled by this
strange evasiveness, Blampignon went on:

"Do you think it was M'sieur Skeet who persuaded
Madame Marrable to alter the terms of her will?"

"It's possible, of course. If so he must have seen her that
night, because he crossed from Folkestone early the next
morning."

"He had a great deal of influence over your aunt?"

Again the queer evasive lowering of her glance, the blood
mounting to her cheeks. In one so direct and open it was
inexplicable. A simple enough question and yet she seemed
unable to find a ready answer to it. What was she trying to
conceal? Certainly something. Evidently something to do
with Skeet.

At length she spoke with an uneasy little smile.

"I think she found him amusing, but I'm not sure that she
took him very seriously. They were old friends, of course.
Aunt Gwenny met him long before she was married."

"What makes you think M'sieur Skeet is in Germany?"

"I've had a couple of postcards from him—one posted in
Coblence, the other in Mannheim."

"You've received postcards from him on other occasions
when he's been abroad?"

"Never. He's always been a shockingly bad correspondent."

"Then how do you account...?"

"I don't know. Nigel and I have been puzzling over it. He must have suddenly decided to turn over a new leaf."

After that he put a few general questions about the painter, but it was evident that there was one side of Skeet's life about which the girl knew nothing. About Madame Cambremont, for instance, the *ménage à deux* in the Rue Mirimar, the tragic death of the child that Skeet had obviously fathered.

"And Duconte...what was the trouble between him and M'sieur Skeet?" She didn't know. "Where and when had they first met?"

She didn't know that either. Everybody at Cockfosters had been puzzled by the violent flare-up in the loggia, but Skeet had obstinately refused to be drawn on the subject.

Blampignon rose and set his chair back tidily against the wall.

"*Eh bien,* mam'selle... I needn't keep you longer." He moved across and opened the door for her. "You haven't decided yet when you'll be returning to England?"

"Not yet. We shall be staying on for another few days, at least."

"Before you leave, I'd like you to get in touch with me."

"Of course."

III

A miserable evening. A premature dusk had brought the lights on early in the town. The heavy rain had given way to a slow fine drizzle that hung like a sea-mist between the houses. Only a few people abroad in the streets. The cafés and *bistros,* on the other hand, were crowded, mostly with workers who'd looked in for a quick drink before returning to their families. A few bored holidaymakers, huddled in their raincoats, stood about under the dripping awnings gazing into the windows of the trinket shops.

The Café de la Mairie. It wasn't much to look at. Half a dozen marble-topped tables, a few fly-blown mirrors on its varnished walls, the usual garish advertisements, an atmosphere you could cut with a knife. The sort of place in which Blampignon felt at home, rousing in him boyhood memories of his father's little *bistro* on the waterfront at Marseilles.

Elbowing his way through the throng round the bar, he ordered a cognac and sat down at one of the tables. Only two chairs were set to it, the other being occupied by a sleek-haired young man with his head in an evening paper. Blampignon made no attempt to strike up a conversation. He didn't want to talk. He wanted to relax, to roll the brandy round his tongue, smoke an unhurried cigarette, to savour the racy comments, the rough speech, the exuberant vitality of the good fellows about him. It was more like a club than a bar, for every time the door was pushed open to admit a newcomer every head swung round, and a dozen voices bawled out a greeting. The *patron* and his buxom wife were almost run off their feet trying to catch up with the quickening stream of orders.

Presently, in spite of the ever-mounting babel, the jostling elbows, the constant slamming of the street door, Blampignon's eyelids began to droop. He'd stubbed out his cigarette. His glass was empty. But he just hadn't the strength of will to get up and walk away. His great bulk seemed fettered to his chair by this sudden overpowering desire to sleep. He no longer attempted to fight it. His chin sank down, his eyes closed, the sounds around him receded and tapered out into silence. A few seconds later he was dead to the world.

He was awakened by a crash, a sudden uproar, a surge of thick-set bodies milling about his table. The young man opposite was on his feet. His chair had fallen to the floor. There was a knife in his shaking hand. Everybody seemed to be shouting at once.

"For God's sake, you crazy fool..."

"Get round behind him, can't you?"

"Hold the other one, else he'll be at his throat again!"

Blampignon was now fully awake, his eyes snapping this way and that, sizing up the situation, seeing the stocky, bald-headed figure in the blue gaberdine cloak struggling to break free from the sturdy hands that gripped him, the straining stringy muscles of his neck, the savage glitter in his eyes.

"Drop that bloody knife, will you!"

Somebody had edged round, jerked back the young man's head and caught him a cracking blow across the wrist. One could almost hear the sigh of relief as the knife clattered to the floor. In a flash the fellow spun round, raced for the door, jerked it open and slipped into the street.

"Get after him, somebody! He went off to the left... Jacques! Louis!"

A couple of men were already pushing through the door. Behind the bar-counter, the *patron's* wife was wringing her hands, shrilling at the top of her voice, "What's it all about? Will somebody tell me that! What's happened?"

One of the customers had picked up the knife and was gingerly examining it.

"Well, I wouldn't like to have that in my guts…"

Blampignon moved ponderously round the table and, with an authoritative air, held out his hand.

"All right—you can hand that over. My name's Blampignon. I'm from the *Sûreté Nationale* at Nice."

A sudden silence descended. For a moment everybody seemed nailed to the floor. Every eye was fixed on the detective. Then a gruff voice called out:

"In that case you'd better arrest this chap for starting a brawl. It's this sort of thing that gets a place a bad name. I've never had any trouble with the police before and I'm not—"

"Are you the owner of the café?"

"Yes."

"I'll want to collect a few statements. There's a room at the back, perhaps, where I can…?"

"If you'll come this way… Mind that chair and the broken glass. I'll lift the bar-flap for you."

"A couple of witnesses will be enough. You can sort that out among yourselves." For the first time Blampignon's gaze rested on the lined and cynically humorous face, half-hidden in the upturned collar of the cloak. "After that it'll be your turn, M'sieur Skeet. I'll leave it to you two fellows to see that he doesn't try to make a break for it."

16

"WHAT THE DEVIL DO YOU KNOW ABOUT DUCONTE?"

Blampignon shrugged.

"Just a fact here, a fact there."

"And you're hoping I'll fill in the gaps?"

"Exactly!"

They were sitting in the untidy little parlour behind the café—Skeet and the inspector. On the other side of the door things were evidently returning to normal. The street door was slamming again. Everybody was calling for drinks and talking at the top of their voices, no doubt arguing about the recent scuffle, taking this side and that, wondering what was happening in the little room behind the bar.

Decidedly nothing dramatic. If Skeet were in a tight corner then he certainly knew how to control his feelings. He was sitting in a rattan armchair, his cloak flung back, his hands clasped firmly over his bare and bony knees, a mocking expression on his weatherbeaten face.

"What is it you want to know?"

"For one thing…just now in the café, when you first noticed Duconte sitting at the table…why didn't you put a bullet through the fellow? Damn it all! at that range, you couldn't have missed."

"Possibly. But I just don't happen to possess a gun. Otherwise, perhaps…"

"So the gun belonged to Simone Berthode?"

Skeet said innocently, "The gun?"

"The one that was fired in that front bedroom out at the Villa Paradou."

Skeet ran a hand round his unshaven jowl.

"May I ask how you got to know about that unfortunate episode?"

Blampignon nodded. He was enjoying this moment of omniscience, the fellow's obvious bewilderment, the flicker of reluctant admiration in his glance.

"You and Simone Berthode were seen coming out of the villa drive together, a moment or so after a shot had been fired. *Eh bien*…since the gun isn't yours, it was obviously Mam'selle Berthode who took that pot-shot in the dark. But it was you, I imagine, who placed the ladder against the balcony?" A nod. "Believing Duconte was in the house?" Skeet nodded again. "And the girl had the same idea, no doubt, when she climbed up the ladder after you?"

"The devil she did!" Skeet's mouth was twisted in a caustic smile. "But luckily for me her aim wasn't as good as her intentions."

"And until that night you'd never met the girl?"

"Never. But she had all my sympathies from the start. Duconte had played fast and loose with that kid…he'd dealt her a really shabby hand. For months on end she'd skimped and saved to keep that little rat on the right side of starvation…head over heels in love with him, of course. Then somewhere or other Duconte met Gwenny Marrable, and that put Simone out in the cold. Can you blame her for wanting to get even with the fellow? With a girl like Simone he was just sticking his neck out. Her brother had fought with the Maquis. She happened to know where he kept his automatic…"

Nothing mocking about him now. He was putting up a case for the girl, defending her actions, seeing her as the victim of a gross injustice, driven to desperation by Duconte's callous and cynical behaviour.

"That night, when we met out at the villa, she was just about at the end of her tether. For three days and nights she'd been roaming the town with that gun in her pocket, looking for Duconte. Every bar and café, all his old haunts… I doubt if she'd had a square meal since she'd left home and started tramping the streets…"

She was terrified of returning to her parents' house, so Skeet had taken her back to the Rue Mirimar. While she was asleep he'd sneaked the gun from her pocket and thrown it into the sea.

"I wasn't going to have that kid involved in a murder case. Duconte was my responsibility, my pidgin… I'd been waiting a hell of a long time to settle my score with him, and I wasn't going to be cheated by—"

There was a scraping of heavy boots on the stone steps that led up from the bar level, a rap on the door. The *patron* stuck his head into the room.

"Jacques, Louis…they've just come in."

"Well?"

"They got on to the fellow all right—chased him through half a dozen back streets—but somewhere up near the station he gave them the slip. They stuck around, keeping their eyes peeled, but they didn't have any luck."

"Put up a couple of drinks for them. I'll pay on my way out."

When the *patron* had closed the door, Blampignon turned to Skeet. There was a sympathetic light in his eyes. He said quietly, "It was the child, wasn't it?"

"The child?"

"The little boy?"

Skeet stared at him, dumbfounded.

"Georges! But how in heaven's name…?"

"The drunken motor-cyclist…it was Duconte, of course?"

Skeet nodded. His hands were trembling. He suddenly looked tired, shrunken, pathetic. An old man, in fact. His eyes were no longer focused on Blampignon. His gaze seemed to be reaching back in time, clouded with grief and bitterness, moving with his memory into the past.

"It was an afternoon like any other…not much traffic about, the street almost deserted. Nearly eighteen months ago now. Georges was pulling his wheeled horse up and down the pavement. It was just after lunch. I was standing in the doorway, enjoying a pipe…" He seemed to be speaking to himself, almost inaudible, jerking out the phrases, trying to control the quaver in his voice. Yet the scene he sketched in was graphic enough.

The motor-cycle turning into the top of the Rue Mirimar,

suddenly roaring down the street. The child on the pavement looking up, frightened by the noise, watching it approach. Then the realisation coming to Skeet that the machine was out of control. The fellow in the saddle lurching from side to side, laughing drunkenly to himself. The machine swerving across to the far kerb, the handlebar catching the boy on the side of the head, flinging him to the ground. The back of his skull striking the kerb...

"I ran a few yards down the street, shouting to the fellow to stop. He didn't even attempt to slow up. He merely lifted an arm in the air and waved his hand..."

Although at that time Skeet didn't know his name, he'd got the driver's description and he'd gone to the police. But nothing came of it. For weeks after the tragedy he'd rambled round the town, searching the faces of every passer-by, combing the bars and cafés, making enquiries at every garage and filling-station in the neighbourhood. But in the long run he'd given up. Perhaps, after all, the fellow had only been passing through the town.

But eighteen months later, when they'd come face to face in the sun-loggia at Cockfosters, they'd recognised each other at once.

"After our little set-to I guessed he'd nip back across the Channel as fast as he could make it. Well, to cut a long story short... I got his address from Gwenny Marrable—an address here in the Old Town—and the next day I set off after him. He was lodging with a Madame Gonville just off the Cours de Castellar. But I was too late...about twelve hours too late. He'd arrived the day before, packed his things in a hurry and told madame he'd no longer be needing the room.

He'd spoken of a business trip to Italy, but I guessed that was a red-herring. I felt sure he was still in Menton. So I started all over again, trudging around the town, searching for him. Madame Cambremont, too. I'd been down here for about a week, when last Sunday evening in a *bistro* near the harbour I heard a fellow mention the Villa Paradou. I got talking to him over a drink. Evidently the night before he'd seen a man letting himself into the place through the front-door. That's when I first had the idea that Duconte might be skulking out at the villa. So I waited until after dark on Tuesday and walked out to Cap Martin…"

Beyond the dusty window the light had long since faded. Blampignon had already reached out and switched on the brass table-lamp. The hubbub in the bar had died down as, one by one, the majority of the *habitués* had drifted off home—just an intermittent rumble of voices, the clink of glasses, the occasional rattle of the till. Skeet had drawn his cloak closer about him, lying back in his chair, fumbling for a cigarette, his long recital evidently at an end. For a moment it was so quiet in the room that Blampignon could hear some-body in the house on the far side of the yard winding up a clock.

"And that trip up the Rhine…?"

For the first time Skeet's face crinkled into a smile.

"I wired an artist friend of mine in Boulogne to meet me off the boat. I knew he was just off for a holiday in the Black Forest. I'd bought the postcards on a previous visit to the Rhineland. I only had to string together a few of the usual clichés one writes on a postcard and fill in the addresses."

"Your alibi, of course."

"Exactly."

"And Madame Marrable? You've heard—?"

"Yes. I read about it in the papers. Poor old Gwenny! She was a good friend of mine. It's a shocking business...so damned humiliating and undignified to finish up like that... dumped like a sack of coal on the doorstep of her own villa. If Duconte hadn't everything to lose by her death I might have suspected—"

"An old friend, and yet you didn't trouble to turn up at the funeral?"

Skeet shrugged.

"And wreck my alibi?"

A curious chap. One couldn't get to the bottom of him. A moment back, speaking of the child's death, he'd seemed no more than a broken, vulnerable, rather pathetic old man. Now towards the murder of his old friend and benefactress he seemed to display an almost cynical indifference. "Poor old Gwenny." That's all it amounted to. As if he'd just heard that she'd slipped and sprained her ankle. And his vindictiveness towards Duconte—something unbalanced, almost inhuman about it. Yet when Sheila Marrable had found herself in a dilemma it was to Skeet she'd instinctively turned. A contradictory, complex character—shrewd, cynical, sentimental, passionate, unfeeling, turn by turn. Obviously one might live with him for years and never really get him into focus.

"When did you last see Madame Marrable?"

A moment's reflection. An unhurried pull at his cigarette.

"The night before I crossed over to France."

"It was then you persuaded her to add that codicil to her will?"

No attempt this time to conceal his surprise. Snatching the cigarette from his mouth, he said explosively:

"Now how in the name of thunder...!"

So it was true. A word from Skeet and evidently this strong-willed, single-minded woman had meekly fallen in with his demands. And it was the same with Duconte's address. By all accounts Duconte was her lover. She knew Skeet was out for his blood, and yet...

Blampignon said dryly, "You seem to have been very successful in persuading madame to do as you wanted."

The mocking light was in Skeet's eyes again. He winked.

"There's only one way to deal with a domineering woman. Refuse to take her seriously."

Grunting and wheezing, Blampignon heaved himself out of his chair. What was he to do with the fellow? He'd really got nothing against him. That scuffle in the bar? But one couldn't go around arresting every hot-tempered fool who'd started up a café brawl. And out at the Villa Paradou it wasn't Skeet who'd fired that gun. On the contrary, it was he who had nearly been shot!

Blampignon picked up his raincoat and hooked it over his arm. Skeet was watching him intently. In no way apprehensive, but no doubt wondering just where he stood with the police.

"I'll have to get a statement from Simone Berthode. You know where I can find her?"

Skeet nodded.

"When we cleared out of the Rue Mirimar we took a couple of rooms at the Hotel Sirene. It's a little place round the back of the station."

"All right. You'd better come with me. I've a car outside."

II

It was just short of nine o'clock. Thinking of Raunay and Loisel, Blampignon drove first to the Commissariat. As luck would have it, Hamonet had returned to his office to catch up with his desk-work, which had been disorganised by the Marrable case. Blampignon gave him a thumbnail sketch of the evening's events.

Hamonet said, "Raunay and Loisel were relieved at midday. But I'll send somebody up to recall the fellows who took over. Where did you say Skeet and the girl had been hanging out?"

"Hotel Sirene."

"I know it. Rue de Vertais—behind the station."

A narrow, pink-washed building, with faded blue shutters, a gilt and crimson reception-hall, a shaky matchbox of a lift. Skeet knocked on the door of Room 15. Simone Berthode had obviously been in bed. She had the flushed and tousled look of one wakened from a deep sleep. Her soiled petticoat, fringed with a wisp of black lace, left half her thighs uncovered. On seeing the two men in the doorway, she gave a little yelp of alarm, grabbed up the counterpane, and flung it hastily about her shoulders.

Skeet said with a sardonic chuckle:

"We were in such a damned hurry to get out of No. 24 that we never even thought of grabbing up a pair of pyjamas. We've only the clothes we stand up in. Not even a toothbrush between us!"

Blampignon turned to the girl, who was now sitting on the edge of the bed, the bedspread clutched across her bosom.

"It was you who recognised me from the window?"

"Yes. I'd seen your photo in the papers."

"So, after I'd rung the bell, you lay low, waited until I'd gone, then slipped out of the house with M'sieur Skeet?"

"Yes."

"And last Tuesday night out at the Villa Paradou...suppose you tell me..."

A halting statement at first. The girl kept glancing across at Skeet, as if to say, "Should I have told him that? How much does he know? How much have you told him yourself?"

She must have been wondering, too, why Skeet had turned up at the hotel with a detective in tow. But presently, with Blampignon at his most benign, her nervousness wore off and she began to talk without restraint. Nothing really new. Merely a corroboration of what he'd already learnt from Skeet.

Five, ten, fifteen minutes went by...

The sound of footsteps coming quickly up the corridor, a woman's voice saying: "It's that door there, m'sieur—room No. 15."

A rap. Blampignon crossed over and opened up. It was Hamonet. Something tense, grim about his expression. He was breathing hard as if he'd been hurrying.

"Anything wrong?"

Hamonet glanced over Blampignon's shoulder into the bedroom beyond, where Skeet and the girl were sitting silent and unmoving, obviously puzzled by the sudden interruption. Hastily Blampignon closed the door, grabbed Hamonet by the arm, and drew him a few paces down the passage.

"Well?"

"Duconte."

"You've picked him up at last?"

"Not exactly. He's been stabbed."

"Dead?"

"Yes."

"Any witnesses?"

"An old girl of about seventy. She saw Duconte collapse on the pavement and somebody running away towards the promenade. But I doubt if she's going to be much help. She's evidently short-sighted. She can't even tell us whether it was a man or a woman."

"When did this happen?"

"About ten minutes ago."

"Where?"

"Avenue Edouard VII...opposite the tennis courts. We haven't moved the body. I left a man to keep an eye on things. It's only a few hundred yards away. You'll come?"

"At once." Blampignon gave a backward jerk of his head. "I'll let the couple in there know that I've been called away." A thought struck him. "Ten minutes ago, you say?"

"Just about."

"Then that lets out Skeet and the girl."

Hamonet stared at him in surprise.

"Then who the devil...?"

Blampignon lifted his shoulders.

"That's what we've got to find out. Get along and fetch up the lift. I'll join you in a minute."

17

It hadn't taken Hamonet ten minutes to fetch Blampignon from the Hotel Sirene, yet already a little knot of rubbernecks had drifted up round the body, gawking at it, muttering among themselves, trying to find out what had happened. A chair had been brought out for the old woman from a café across the road. She was sitting there, gazing vacantly ahead of her, muttering to herself, fumbling with the crucifix at her breast. The uniformed constable was standing with folded arms, almost straddling the body. The light from the nearby lamp-post glistened darkly on the pool of blood that was slowly seeping outwards from under the dead man's head.

As the two inspectors stepped out of the Vedette, the onlookers fell back a little, suddenly falling silent. Going down on one knee, Blampignon peered closely at the twisted features. It was Duconte all right. Strange to think that only a few hours before he'd been sitting opposite the fellow in the Café de la Mairie. He'd been stabbed in the side of the neck, the point of the knife evidently severing the carotid artery. A violent, vicious blow that seemed to rule out the possibility that his assailant had been a woman. He lay on his left side, legs drawn up, his left arm bent beneath his body. Clutched in his right hand, a slip of paper.

Gingerly Blampignon eased it from between his fingers. It was the torn half of a ten-thousand-franc note. The inspector straightened up and turned to Hamonet.

"You've sent for the ambulance?"

"That's it coming up the street now by the look of it. The police surgeon's making his examination at the mortuary."

"All right. I'll question the old woman, then we'll get along to the Commissariat."

But it was uphill work. The old woman was not only short-sighted and, more or less, stone deaf, but clearly a bit simple in the head. Moreover, when the attack had occurred, she'd been on the far side of the road. A figure running away up the street, a body jerking on the pavement. . .that was the sum total of her evidence. Paralysed with fright, she'd stood there moaning and muttering to herself until a waiter had slipped out of the Café Moderne and asked her what was wrong. Too late for the fellow to do anything, of course, except dash back into the café and ring the police.

Pressing a folded note into the old woman's hand, Blampignon drove Hamonet back to the Commissariat. Once in the latter's office, he asked:

"What made you so sure it was Duconte? You'd only his description to go on."

Hamonet groped in a pocket and pulled out a black leather wallet.

"I found this lying on the pavement near the body. There was a photo in it. . ."

A snapshot taken on the terrace of the Villa Paradou.

Duconte and Madame Marrable seated at a table, smiling at each other over their lifted glasses, between them a magnum of champagne cooling in an ice-bucket.

"Anything else of interest?"

"I can't say. Once I'd decided it was Duconte, I shoved the wallet back in my pocket, and got round to the Hotel Sirene as fast as I could."

"In that case…"

Blampignon emptied the wallet, spreading out the contents on the desk. A couple of letters, a few lottery tickets, a driving licence, a bulky wad of notes. He opened the letters first. Both from Madame Marrable, written in French, but posted in England. Addressed, Poste Restante, Menton. Date-stamped Saturday, April 16th and Tuesday, April 19th respectively. Sent off from Wendhurst, Kent. The letters of a middle-aged mistress to her lover—coy, gushing, sentimental, amorous, turn by turn.

> *My darling André,*
>
> *The house seems empty now that you have gone. I've never felt so lonely and depressed. When I got home after driving you to the station I felt like creeping up to my room and having a good long howl. Even now, my dear, I don't think you fully realise…*

There was more in this vein. A lot more. Two closely-written sheets, in fact. But nothing of interest to Blampignon. He turned to the last page.

It's no good being angry with me about giving Harry your Menton address. I was forced to do it. I daren't refuse. Don't ask me why. Harry could ruin me if he wanted to, bring my whole life crashing to the ground. It's an ugly fact, but it's true. But now that I've given you the key of the villa, you've somewhere to sleep, and you'll be safe for the time being. But take great care of yourself. Take no undue risks, my darling. Harry's in a vicious mood. Why wouldn't you tell me what the trouble is between you? I wish you'd be frank with me, André. I'm terrified something dreadful's going to happen. You may think this stupid, fanciful. . .but I have a premonition. It hangs over me all day like a black cloud. And at night I can't sleep because all the time I'm thinking of you. . .wondering if you're all right. . .

Hamonet was now thumbing through the wad of notes, counting them under his breath. Somewhere outside the window a loose shutter was banging in the wind. A taxi pulled away with a quick whine of gears from the rank across the road. Blampignon picked up the second letter.

Five days now since I waved good-bye to you on the station. I've made up my mind, chéri. I'm shutting up the house here and joining you at the villa. It's more than I can stand. . . the boredom and restlessness, this cruel longing to be with you again. Just two days in which to arrange everything and I shall be on my way south. I shall cross by car-ferry on Friday morning and I should be with you, André, late on Sunday night. If only I wasn't so wretchedly upset by air-travel, I would have taken the

plane to Nice. Anything, anything, to hasten forward
the moment of our meeting. I'm racked with impatience.
How thankful and relieved I was to get your letter. At
first, when I didn't hear, I was frantic with worry. But
Harry will never suspect that you're sleeping at the villa.
As you're keeping away from the house during the day,
I haven't bothered to tell the Fougères that you have a
key. We can't trust them not to talk. You know what a
damned gossip that woman is! And if word got around
the town...

And this was the woman who'd wired the Fougères from
Lyons:

DELAYED—DON'T EXPECT ME UNTIL TUESDAY
AFTERNOON.

Delayed!...when she was jealous of every minute that kept
her from her lover. Would she have allowed anything, anybody,
to impede their reunion? No, when that telegram was sent the
widow was already dead. Blampignon no longer doubted it.

"Fifty-three thousand francs!" Hamonet slapped down
the bundle of notes on the desk and tilted back his chair.
"*Alors!* is that why he was knifed?"

Blampignon took a leisurely puff at his cigarette.

"Motive...robbery?" He shook his head decisively. "If that
were the case, why was the wallet left lying on the pavement?
Plenty of time for the chap to snatch it up and stuff it in his
pocket. There was nobody about...only the old woman on
the far side of the street. And he wouldn't have been scared

of her. No. What I want to know is this...why was the wallet lying on the pavement anyway? Why was Duconte clutching the torn half of a ten-thousand-franc note in his right hand?"

"What's your idea?"

Blampignon smiled.

"The wallet was in Duconte's hand when the fellow drew the knife on him."

"But why had he taken it from his pocket?"

"Two possible explanations. Either Duconte was handing over money to his attacker or *vice versa*."

"And of the two?"

"The latter's more probable. The wallet in his left hand, in his right the money he'd just received from the man who knifed him. Duconte, in fact, was about to slip the notes into his wallet when the fellow struck. The wallet dropped from his hand, but the murderer snatched at the notes he'd just paid over to Duconte, leaving just a torn ten-thousand note clutched in his victim's fingers."

Hamonet objected.

"But the wallet...why didn't he trouble to pick it up?"

Blampignon lifted his shoulders.

"How was he to know that it held fifty-three thousand francs?"

Silence for a moment. Blampignon had gathered up the letters and notes to replace them in the wallet. Hamonet had a pencil in his hand, doodling on the message-pad beside the telephone. At length, throwing down the pencil, he looked up and said:

"So this wasn't a chance attack. You think they'd arranged to meet in the Avenue Edouard VII?"

Blampignon yawned, nodded. He didn't want to talk

about the case. Not yet. He wanted time to churn the facts over in his mind. His heavy-lidded eyes were almost closed, his great bulk sagging with tiredness in his chair. For days now he'd been on the go, here, there, rushing around, asking questions, at concert pitch, never letting up. Now the strain was beginning to tell. A long night's sleep. That's what he needed. And the hands of the wall-clock already stood at twenty-past eleven. With a little grunt of effort he got to his feet.

"Duconte's fingerprints…see that you get them over to Variot as soon as you can."

"Very well."

"And the report for the examining magistrate?"

"I'll deal with that to-night."

"Good. And if you get on to anything…"

"I'll let you know at once."

II

A tricky drive back along the Moyenne Corniche to Nice, his aching eyes narrowed against the constant glare of headlights, confused by the shifting shadows on the mist, stung by the rising smoke of his cigarette. Yet his mind on its toes, as it were, as sharp and shrewd as ever.

He was thinking back to the night before, to the lamplit square, to Gammon breasting the terraced steps that led up from the quayside, to his meeting with the unknown man on the steps of the Chapel des Pénitents-Blancs. Gammon had not asked for that meeting. It had been forced on him. No question about that. Something had passed between them. Money, perhaps, a sheaf of notes. And the slight, rather dandified figure that had slipped away down through the Old Town could have been Duconte.

A whiff of blackmail in the air. Duconte having some sort of hold over Gammon, ringing him up at the villa, ticketing his silence with a price, fixing these clandestine meetings. Last night, the Pénitents-Blancs. To-night, the Avenue Edouard VII.

Which meant, of course, that Gammon was now wanted for murder...

There were facts to support this theory. The fifty-odd thousand francs, for instance, found in the dead man's wallet—it could well have been the silence money he'd lifted from Gammon by the chapel steps. And that night opposite the tennis courts, everything happening more or less as Blampignon had imagined. Gammon taking the wad of notes from his pocket with his left hand, the right grasping the knife. Duconte pulling out his wallet to put the notes away. The knife gleaming in the lamplight, descending. And as Duconte sagged to the pavement, Gammon snatching back the notes and running away up the street.

An act of desperation, of a man afraid. But of what? What had Duconte found out? Why was he in a position to put the screw on Gammon? Was there, after all, some link between the stabbing and the Marrable murder?

Other pictures forming in Blampignon's mind...

The Villa Paradou on Sunday night, five days ago. Duconte letting himself into the house after dark, sneaking upstairs to the guest-room, eventually falling asleep. But presently jerked awake, hearing somebody moving in the hall below, thinking, no doubt, that it was Madame Marrable. Duconte creeping down the stairs to investigate, seeing the front-door open, the silhouette of an outsized cabin-trunk dumped at the far end of the hall, a figure hurrying down the steps to the big grey saloon parked in the drive. And, as the car moved off, catching a glimpse of the man at the wheel in the reflected glow of the headlamps, aware, in that instant, that it was Gammon!

And later, opening up the trunk, sick, horrified, in a panic, knowing Gammon for what he was, gathering up his few belongings from the room upstairs, clearing post-haste out of the villa.

Blampignon sighed and eased his cramped limbs in the driving-seat. The lights of Nice were already spread out below him, stretching away into the haze. Another ten minutes and he'd be garaging the Vedette, turning the handle of his own front-door, calling up to his wife to let her know that he was home.

But before that ten minutes was up he knew that he'd run his head into a blank wall. Gammon might have stabbed Duconte, but he couldn't have murdered Madame Marrable. January, nearly four months ago—that was when he'd last set foot in France. At least, until he'd stepped off the plane at Nice two days ago. His passport proved that. And from the moment he'd left Cockfosters, the day before Madame Marrable had crossed to Boulogne, he'd been staying with Mam'selle Gaye. Not only his word for that, but hers.

So if he'd killed Duconte, it was not to ensure his silence over the Marrable affair, but for some other reason. But what reason? *Merdre!* the answer to that one could wait. Blampignon had had enough of it. His mouth gaped open in a long shuddering yawn. He was almost asleep at the wheel.

Little had he realised when he first stepped in through the doorway of the Villa Paradou...

18

NINE HOURS OF UNBROKEN SLEEP, HIS *PETIT DÉJEUNER* in bed, a shave, a cold shower. It was well past ten o'clock before Blampignon sauntered into the *Sûreté Nationale,* but his eye was full of zest, his step jaunty. Emile was in the outer office, sorting the inspector's morning mail.

"Anything turned up?"

"No, but Variot's rung through three times from the laboratory to know if you were in."

"Tell him to come up at once."

Overnight the dismal weather had cleared. There was a sparkle in the air, an unaccustomed freshness after the rain, but already the thermometer was rising, the sun blazing down from a cloudless sky. Cocking an eye from his bedroom window, Blampignon had put on a nylon shirt, a cream tussore suit. He looked cool enough, but he hadn't been two minutes in his office when the sweat was mottling his forehead, trickling into his eyebrows, darkening his shirt-front.

A knock on the door. It was Variot.

"I've been trying to get you on the telephone. Hamonet sent over a motor-cyclist this morning with a specimen of Duconte's fingerprints."

"And you've matched them up with the second set on the cabin-trunk?"

"Yes"

"Well?"

"Identical."

A supposition proved, a loose end tied up. Nothing more. It didn't help one jot in furthering the progress of the Marrable case. More than ever it looked as if Blampignon would have to shift the focus of his interest further north—to the first three hundred miles of Madame Marrable's journey south. Little question now that it was somewhere along this stretch of her route that she'd been set on and smothered. A section of the *Police Mobile* had already been checking up on every garage and filling-station along the main roads in the area, but so far without success. The trouble was that after passing through Abbeville there were at least three major routes to the Riviera. No mention of the road she intended to take in those letters to Duconte. Just the fact that she would be arriving at the villa late on Sunday evening.

The letters to Duconte…

Blampignon flicked back the clasp of his brief-case and took out the black leather wallet. A faint perfume was still clinging to the expensive deckle-edged notepaper. Now that he was reading them for the second time the widow's passionate effusions seemed curiously naïve and insincere. She was evidently one of those women who, strongly emotional, have little talent for putting their feelings into words. One phrase, at any rate, gripped his attention.

Harry could ruin me if he wanted to, bring my whole life crashing to the ground...

What had she meant by that? A skeleton in her cupboard to which Skeet held the key. And evidently it had been like that for years...Skeet calling the tune, she dancing to it. The annuity she'd settled on the painter shortly after her marriage, the presumptuous way in which he treated her, his high-handed demands to which she so meekly yielded—they all stemmed from the same root. Something had happened in the past—in Canada, perhaps—that had put Skeet in a position to blackmail the woman.

And Sheila Marrable was in the know. Either she'd found out or Skeet had confided in her. Blampignon remembered asking the girl, "He had a great deal of influence over your aunt?"

And at once she'd appeared confused, uneasy, evasive. If only it were possible to establish the real relationship between Skeet and the widow, between Skeet and the girl herself. So far he'd handled the young woman with velvet gloves. Now it was high time to alter his tactics. Somehow or other he'd got to frighten her into talking. And if he were going north, the sooner the better.

Snatching up his beret, he went through to the outer office. Emile was sitting at the typewriter, his jacket off, his sleeves rolled up.

"I'm driving over to the Villa Paradou at once. So if anything new comes in—"

"A moment, Commissaire."

The telephone was ringing. Emile lifted the receiver, listened, clapped a hand over the mouthpiece and turned to Blampignon.

"It's for you…the *gendarmerie* at Le Touquet."

It was the inspector who'd driven him from the airfield when he'd flown north to examine the abandoned car. An apologetic note in his voice.

"About that telegram you asked us to trace."

"Well?"

"As you know, at the time of your enquiry we didn't have any luck. But about ten minutes ago a girl walked in here…"

A *guichet* clerk in the head post-office at Le Touquet. On the Friday that the telegram was supposed to have been handed in she'd suddenly been taken ill. As it turned out, a slight case of food poisoning, but it had kept the girl away for a week and she'd only returned to work that morning. Somebody had mentioned the telegram, the police enquiry concerning it, and at once the girl had remembered.

The inspector went on.

"It was handed in sometime between one and one-thirty on Friday, April 22nd, as you suspected. Evidently by a chap of about thirty—an Englishman all right. Big, muscular young fellow with fair curly hair, dressed in grey flannel trousers and blue high-necked jersey…a long white scar running diagonally across the back of his right hand. Just bad luck that the girl was taken ill about three o'clock that same afternoon…"

An observant young woman. Easy to picture the fellow. But who was he? A casual passer-by who Madame Marrable had waylaid in the street, recognising him as a fellow-countryman, perhaps, getting him to dispatch the telegram for her. But why should she do that? It wouldn't have taken her five minutes to slip into the post-office herself. She spoke fluent French. No reason for her to conceal the fact that she'd sent the telegram. A simple, straightforward invitation to Nigel Derry to join her at the Villa Paradou.

One other possibility, of course. It was the murderer who'd walked into that post-office, stepping out of a grey Panther saloon, on the back seat of which, perhaps, was a big black shiny cabin-trunk containing the body of his victim. Which meant that the widow had been strangled somewhere between Boulogne and Le Touquet. No hitchhiker to whom she'd given a lift. No casual acquaintance picked up on the boat. But somebody who knew her well. Somebody who knew a great deal about her friends, her movements, her affairs in general.

And he'd sent that telegram to fetch Derry down to the Riviera, to swing suspicion on to him. In the same way that he'd planted Derry's lighter and the sheet of paper bearing his handwriting in the abandoned car.

A close, even intimate friend of Madame Marrable's… and yet nobody at the villa had thought to mention him. Neither had Derry, nor Skeet. Why this exasperating reticence?

Blampignon's temper was rising. As he stamped out of the building to his car, his jaw was thrust forward aggressively. There was a flinty light in his eye. For a moment it had seemed that the fog was about to lift. Now it had come down again.

II

There was a car parked in the villa drive—a big American limousine. The front-door was wide open. For a moment Blampignon hesitated, his finger on the bell-push, then, taking off his sunglasses, he stepped quietly into the cool and shadowy hall. A murmur of voices coming from an upstairs room, of footsteps bustling about somewhere above his head, the gush of water running into a basin. Then, from somewhere near at hand, a clink of glass, the sibilant hiss of a siphon, a creak of chair springs. Evidently there was somebody in the lounge, the door of which, like the front-door, was wide open. Blampignon took a few stealthy paces down the hall and glanced in.

It was Gammon. He was sitting bolt upright in his chair, a big porcelain-bowled pipe in one hand, a tumbler in the other. His bulbous eyes were fixed in a kind of vacant stare on the wall before him. Something tense in his attitude. At first Blampignon was puzzled by his immobility, his air of concentration. Then he got it. Gammon was listening to the sounds coming from that upstairs room. And not out of idle curiosity. That was obvious. He was listening intently, apprehensively, almost holding his breath.

A discreet cough. Gammon started violently, jerked round in his chair and glared, open-mouthed, at the massive figure standing in the doorway.

"What the hell!"

"I hope I'm not intruding. That car on the drive…I wondered, perhaps…"

As Gammon got unsteadily to his feet, setting down his

glass, Blampignon saw that his hand was shaking. There was a guarded look in his glazed eyes. He said thickly, "It's the doctor. He's upstairs now. We had to call him in. It's Deborah...Miss Gaye...she's been taken ill."

"When did this happen?"

"Not half an hour ago. I found her in a dead faint at the foot of the stairs. With Madame Fougère's help I managed to bring her round and somehow we got her up to her bed. Luckily the doctor was able to come right away. He's been up there a good ten minutes already. Madame Fougère's with him."

"And Mam'selle Sheila?"

"Somebody rang her up soon after breakfast. Young Derry, I suppose. Unfortunately she left the house only five minutes before Deborah collapsed." All the time he'd been talking Gammon had been edging back towards the table. Now he took up his glass. "Just having a snifter to steady my nerves. You'll join me, Inspector?"

"Thank you...a cognac." When they were seated, Blampignon went on casually, "By the way, where were you last night?"

"In Menton."

No hesitation. He didn't even look up from his pipe, which he was filling from a large pigskin pouch.

"Another meeting with that elusive friend of yours, perhaps?"

He still didn't turn a hair. He merely gazed at Blampignon with a reproachful air, as if to say: "Now why the devil drag *that* up?" and began to pat his pockets, searching for his matches.

"As a matter of fact I had to go to the chemist's. Deborah

had a splitting headache—the first symptoms, I suppose, of to-day's collapse—and as there wasn't an aspirin or anything of that sort in the house…"

"Which chemist's?"

"The English chemist on the corner of the Avenue Boyer, near the casino gardens. It was the only one open at that time of the evening."

"What time exactly?"

"Eh?" His attention had evidently been caught by the sound of footsteps coming down the stairs. He was looking anxiously out into the hall. But it wasn't the doctor. Only Madame Fougère bustling down the passage towards the kitchen. Blampignon repeated his question. Gammon shrugged, struck a match and held it to the bowl of his pipe. "Oh, somewhere between nine and nine-thirty. I can't be sure. But if you're so anxious to check up on my movements last night, why not ask the chemist?"

His complacency was exasperating. He certainly wasn't the sort of chap to be tricked into giving himself away. He'd got his story all right. And the devil of it was, his story was probably true. Mam'selle Gaye's headache had given him a perfectly innocent reason for going into the town. He *had* gone to the chemist's. And it wasn't more than a few hundred yards from the Avenue Boyer to the Avenue Edouard VII. He could have slipped in and bought those aspirins, and ten minutes later, opposite the tennis courts…

Footsteps on the stairs. This time it was the doctor. With a muttered excuse, Gammon sprang up and blundered towards the door, almost knocking over the table in his haste.

"Well, doctor, what's your opinion? How is she? It's nothing serious, is it?"

Blampignon's smile was sardonic. The fellow seemed half off his head with anxiety. And no wonder! A fine lookout for him, when he was all set to marry the woman's money, if at the eleventh hour she slipped through his fingers.

"Serious? Don't you believe it! Forty-eight hours in bed and she'll be as right as rain. It's the strain of these last few days, of course...the tragic death of her sister, the hurried journey down, the emotional upset of the funeral. You know how it is, m'sieur. Nerves at full stretch, then...phut!...the inevitable reaction. No, no...as long as she takes it easily... I'll send her along some sleeping tablets..."

The reassuring voice died away to a murmur as the couple went down the terrace steps to the car. Without waiting for Gammon to return, Blampignon finished his cognac and, with his usual lumbering gait, made a bee-line for the kitchen.

III

Madame Fougère said acidly, "Don't ask me where he was last night. At the bottle, I daresay. He's not going to last long if he goes on at this rate. No, m'sieur...me and Fougère were out of the house by seven. So what he got up to after that..."

It wasn't very satisfactory. He couldn't question Mam'selle Gaye—at least, not at the moment. And earlier that morning the girl had gone into Menton. He could check up with the chemist, of course, and, later, when he could make contact with Sheila Marrable...

"By the way...Mam'selle Sheila...do you know who rang

her this morning?"

"Yes—it was a M'sieur Skeet."

Skeet! So now that Duconte was dead and Skeet was no longer worrying about his alibi, he'd evidently decided to get in touch with the girl. Eager, no doubt, to find out how things were going at the villa.

"She was meeting him this morning in Menton?"

"So I believe."

"Where?"

"The Hotel Sirene. I heard mam'selle say on the telephone 'The Hotel Sirene in the Rue de Vertais.'"

"What time did she leave the villa?"

"Less than an hour ago."

"She caught the bus?"

"Yes."

So if he drove direct to the hotel he might well be in time to question the girl there. Nothing to gain by prolonging his interview with Gammon. For the moment, through lack of evidence, it looked as if the Duconte case were at a standstill. Anyway, there was no sign of the fellow in the lounge. Doubtless, greatly enheartened by the doctor's news, he'd hurried upstairs to see how the invalid was getting along.

IV

"M'sieur Skeet?"

The genial full-bodied woman behind the reception desk didn't even have to refer to her books.

She said at once, "No. 18...on the third floor."

"He's in?"

"Yes. But I'm not sure if he'll be all that pleased to see you."

"Why not?"

"He's got a young woman up in his room. Of course, it's nothing to do with me, but—"

"How long has she been with him?"

"About ten minutes."

The first thing Blampignon heard when he stepped out of the lift was the whine of a vacuum-cleaner. Nobody in the corridor, but a broom and a mop were leaning against the wall outside the open door of No. 19. As he came to a stop outside No. 18 the vacuum-cleaner was suddenly switched off. In the silence that ensued he could hear the sound of furniture being moved, of brisk footsteps thudding about the room, a girl's voice singing.

Then, unexpectedly clear from behind the door of No. 18, Skeet's voice saying:

"But, damn it all, my dear, what's the point? You've nothing to gain and everything to lose if you insist on taking up this high-minded attitude. Now that poor old Gwenny's no longer with us—"

Then the girl's voice, taut with distress, blurting out:

"But the money's not ours, Harry! We haven't a legal or moral right to a penny of it. Nor had Aunt Gwenny. That's what's so awful! Ever since you told me the truth that afternoon at the studio, I've been almost off my head with worry... trying to make up my mind what I ought to do. Then when this other dreadful business happened—"

"But in heaven's name!... Why do anything?"

"Because we can't go on living a lie."

"We? I don't follow. You're not involved in this."

"Not at present, perhaps. But the moment I spend a penny of the money that's been left to me, knowing that Aunt Gwenny and Humphrey Marrable—"

Then the vacuum-cleaner started up again, its high drone echoing in the empty corridor, blotting out the conversation. For an instant, cursing under his breath, Blampignon waited, his ear pressed close to the door. Hopeless. The clang of the lift-gates. He swung round. An elderly carpenter, a bag of tools slung over his shoulder, was hovering uncertainly at the end of the passage.

Noticing Blampignon he approached and shouted above the noise of the machine, "*Pardon*, m'sieur...the room where the lock has jammed?"

"I can't say. You'd better ask the maid in No. 19."

"No. 19?"

Blampignon pointed to the open door, hesitated a moment, then, as if coming to a decision, went rapidly towards the lift.

The woman was still behind her desk, totting up columns of figures in a massive ledger. Glancing up, she enquired politely, "You saw your friend, m'sieur?"

"No, madame. I thought, after all, it would be indiscreet to break in on his little *tête à tête.*"

"Can I take a message? You won't catch M'sieur Skeet here much longer. He's leaving directly after lunch."

"No—the matter can wait. I'd rather you said nothing of my visit, madame."

"As you wish. *Au revoir*, m'sieur."

"*Au revoir*, madame."

A bow, a smile, and he was out in the burning sunlight,

fumbling in his pocket for the keys of his car. Five minutes later he was stumping up the steps of the Commissariat, puffing and wheezing, in a furore of impatience. One thing in mind and one thing only—to get to a telephone as fast as his ungainly legs would carry him!

19

A TELEPHONE CALL TO THE INTERNATIONAL POLICE Commission in Paris, a machine set in motion, a radio call going out to the headquarters of the Canadian C.I.D. in Ottawa. By the time Blampignon was questioning the chemist on the corner of the Avenue Boyer, a police inspector, some three thousand miles away, was phoning the Registrar-General's office in Toronto.

The chemist's assistant, who'd been on duty the previous night, remembered Gammon coming into the shop. He thought the time was a few minutes before nine-thirty. He'd bought a bottle of aspirins and a stick of shaving soap.

From the chemist's to the Hotel Mimosa, where Derry had just gone up to his room before lunching at the restaurant. He was leaving Menton that afternoon by the five o'clock train.

"You're returning to London?"

"Only for one night. I have to get back to the school where I teach on Monday. The new term starts the day after."

"And the address?" Blampignon made a note of it, then

turned to the real reason for his visit. "We've managed to trace the person who sent off that telegram from Le Touquet."

"You mean—?"

"It may have originated with Madame Marrable. It may not. That's a point over which I haven't yet made up my mind. But the man who actually walked into the post-office…"

Blampignon gave his description, but it obviously didn't ring a bell where Derry was concerned.

"It's certainly nobody I ever met at Cockfosters. Perhaps Sheila or George Gammon may know him. After all, they were actually living in the house. I only slipped down for an occasional visit."

And yet if Derry's lighter and that specimen of his handwriting had been planted in the abandoned car, how had the fellow obtained possession of them? How had he known Derry's London address—the address to which the telegram had been sent? Yet the young man wasn't to be shifted.

"Hang it all! it's less than three weeks ago since I first missed that lighter. If I'd met the chap during that time I'd certainly have remembered him."

It was a point, of course. And, in any case, why should he want to lie? If he could have identified the fellow, it would have finally cleared him of suspicion concerning the Marrable affair.

"You're certain the lighter was missing before you arrived at Cockfosters?"

"Yes."

"Those notes you jotted down about the route to Ely… they might have been in one of the dashboard pockets of your car?"

"It's possible, of course."

"And your lighter might have been there, too?"

"No, I rather doubt if..."

And then he remembered! A couple of days before he'd left London to stay at Cockfosters, he'd been driving along Piccadilly. A brief hold-up at the traffic lights. He'd stuck a cigarette in his mouth, taken the lighter from his pocket and was just about to flick it on when the lights had turned green.

"I was a bit slow off the mark, because I'd forgotten to change down. One or two cars started hooting behind me. You know how damned impatient some drivers are! So I chucked the lighter into the left-hand pocket of the dashboard to leave both my hands free." Adding with a hangdog look: "Though why the devil I didn't think of it before...!"

But there was really nothing surprising in that. The gesture had been instinctive, carried out when his mind had been concentrating on making a quick getaway, distracted by the hooting cars, the desire, no doubt, to avoid making a fool of himself.

"A lot of junk in the pocket—dusters, gloves, maps, that sort of thing. Easy for the lighter to have slipped down among all the odds and ends..."

Blampignon was pacing restlessly up and down the little bedroom, the smoke from his cigarette trailing out behind him, a glitter of excitement in his heavy-lidded eyes. A critical moment. Just one question to be answered and, perhaps...

"While you were down at Cockfosters was your car kept in a locked garage?"

"Yes. The stables there have been converted into a row of lock-ups."

"And you alone had the key?"

"Yes."

"During your stay, did you take anybody out in the car?"

"Sheila, of course. But apart from her…"

"Nobody?"

"As far as I can remember—no."

Blampignon's voice was flat with disappointment.

"Think carefully. Somebody, perhaps, to whom you gave a casual lift…one of the staff…"

A little exclamation. Something seemed to have clicked in Derry's mind. Taut with expectation, Blampignon waited.

"The day before I left, at breakfast, George Gammon asked me to drive him to the station."

"Which station?"

"Canterbury."

"And you did?"

Derry hesitated, then admitted with a little chuckle:

"Well…no. I was only just clear of the drive-gates when George asked me to drop him at the cross-roads about a mile up the lane."

"Why had he changed his mind?"

"He hadn't. He'd never intended to catch the train at Canterbury. That was for Mrs. Marrable's benefit. He didn't want her to know that he was going back to Honeypot Cottage with Deborah Gaye."

"And later, no doubt, she picked him up at the cross-roads and drove him to the cottage?"

"Well, that's my guess. I went on to Canterbury to collect a new fan-belt for my car, but by the time I arrived back at Cockfosters Deborah had left, and there was no sign of George at the spot where I'd dumped him."

"How far is it from Cockfosters to Honeypot Cottage?"

"About twenty-five miles."

Blampignon had drifted to the window, staring down between the slats in the shutters at the shadowy courtyard below, digesting the information he'd just obtained. A reflective silence. He didn't quite know as yet what to make of this fresh evidence. It certainly blackened the case against Gammon, because it looked now as if he'd taken the lighter and that slip of paper from the pocket of Derry's car. Who else would have had the opportunity? And surely it was the murderer who'd planted these articles in Madame Marrable's car? On the other hand, how was one to dismiss the fact that, before this recent visit, Gammon hadn't entered the country since January?

The pros and the cons, this conjecture, that... What the devil was he to make of it?

"One last point—did Mam'selle Gaye know that in the event of her sister's death she would be inheriting half her fortune?"

"Yes—I'm sure she did."

"She spoke of it to you?"

"No. But Mrs. Marrable had mentioned the matter to Sheila. More than once, in fact."

"You'll be seeing Mam'selle Sheila before you leave?"

"Yes. We haven't had much time together and there's so much to talk about. I'm going out to the villa directly after lunch."

II

Dropping into the first likely-looking restaurant, Blampignon had a hasty meal, a half-bottle of wine, and drove round to the Commissariat. Hamonet, in a somewhat mellow mood, his *képi* pushed well back on his head, his tunic unbuttoned, had just returned from the Café Floreal. The moment he saw Blampignon, he jumped up from behind his desk and thrust a message-pad impetuously under the inspector's nose.

"Interpol came through from Paris on the telephone not five minutes ago. I've jotted down the details. You're dead right in your suspicions. But it beats me how you got on to this in the first place. After all, when you come to..."

But Blampignon was no longer listening. He was tearing off the top sheet of the message-pad, a flicker of triumph in his eyes, his monumental face wreathed in smiles.

"So that's one little matter..." In his impatience he was already moving towards the door. Then, suddenly, a thought struck him and he swung round. "By the way, a few minutes before nine-thirty last night Gammon was in the English chemist's on the corner of the Avenue Boyer."

"*Tiens!* only a few hundred yards from the spot where Duconte—"

"Exactly. And since the stabbing occurred about that time, Gammon must have gone direct from the chemist's to the Avenue Edouard VII."

"Along the Avenue Thiers?"

Blampignon nodded.

"Where somebody may have spotted him. There are flats over the shops, one or two hotels and cafés... You'd better get on to it at once—a door-to-door enquiry."

"And you?"

Blampignon flipped a forefinger at the sheet of paper torn from the message-pad and winked.

"The Hotel Sirene…and if he's left there, to the Rue Mirimar."

III

But Skeet was still at the hotel. He was sitting over a *café-cognac* at one of the little iron tables on the pavement, diligently picking his teeth, a preoccupied expression on his lined, sardonic face. Parking the car on the far side of the street, Blampignon strolled over and tapped the painter lightly on the shoulder.

"Well, *mon ami*…"

Recognising the voice, Skeet gave a start of surprise and glanced up sharply.

"Hullo! What brings you here? Have a drink? Or are you in a hurry? If it's poor little Simone you're after…"

"It isn't. I want a word with you."

Skeet's eyebrows lifted enquiringly.

"Something unsavoury in the wind, eh? Well, we can't talk here." He gulped down the dregs of his drink and got to his feet. "You'd better come up to my room." Adding as they walked down the hall towards the lift, "Twenty minutes later and you'd have missed me. I'm returning this afternoon to the Rue Mirimar."

A kind of siesta-hush seemed to have settled over the upper part of the hotel. The domestics, no doubt, were down in the basement having lunch. No sign of the carpenter who'd come to mend the lock. The corridor smelt of dust and carpeting and stale tobacco smoke. From the open bathroom door, a whiff of scented soap and rubber floor mats…

They went into No. 18. A replica of the room in which

Blampignon had questioned Simone Berthode. A brass-railed bed, a *bidet* and washbasin half-hidden by a threefold screen, a couple of chairs, a marble-topped chamber-cupboard, a wardrobe and chest-of-drawers in bird's-eye maple. No personal belongings to enliven the drabness of the room. No suitcase on the baggage-rack. Not even a shaving-brush on the glass shelf above the basin.

The sun, which had evidently been shining directly into the room during the morning, had now moved round. Crossing to the window, Skeet flung open the shutters. A little gust of warm air flowed into the room, stirring the curtains, tatting out the smoke of Blampignon's cigarette.

Skeet said, "Well, what's the trouble? What do you want to see me about?"

Obvious questions to set the ball rolling, but wasn't there a hint of anxiety in his voice?

"I've picked up some information that may prove of interest to you."

"Information...from where?"

"Toronto."

He saw Skeet stiffen, the sudden sharpening of his interest. "But how—?"

"To be more exact, from the Registrar-General's office in Toronto." Blampignon consulted the sheet of paper torn from the message-pad. "A record, in fact, of your marriage on the 27th of August, 1934, to Gwendoline Mary Gaye, and the subsequent birth of your daughter, Sheila Elizabeth Skeet, on the 16th April, 1935."

For a moment Skeet said nothing, did nothing. With his back to the dazzling light beyond the window it was difficult to see his expression. But Blampignon could imagine it. The defeated, dumbfounded look of a man who realises that he's cornered. But it didn't take him five seconds to recover himself. A hollow chuckle, a philosophical shrug, and he was saying with a sarcastic edge to his voice:

"So the cat's out of the bag, is it? Well, sooner or later, I suppose…" He shrugged again. "What am I expected to do now? Go into the confessional? But how can I do that when I've nothing on my conscience? You're thinking of Humphrey Marrable, perhaps. But what the devil had *he* got to grumble about? The old boy never suspected that he was living with another man's wife. Those last two years of his life…good God! he'd never been happier…looked after… pampered…fussed over by a good-looking woman young enough to be his daughter. What more could he have asked for…at his age? He was grateful to Gwenny. Of course he was! She saw to that all right. Gwenny was ambitious, one of the long-headed brigade, with an eye always to the main chance. That's why our marriage went on the rocks. She knew what she wanted, made a bee-line for it, and grabbed it with both hands. Old Marrable's money, for instance. D'you think she would have lived with the bald-headed old bore if she hadn't known that he was well breeched? Not that she had to keep him sweet for long. She knew damn well that his heart was in a bad way…that she'd only got a few years to wait…"

He was no longer standing by the window, but prowling jerkily about the room, his voice edged with sarcasm. Blampignon made no attempt to interrupt. He knew well enough that he'd only got to keep quiet and, little by little, carried away by his own eloquence, Skeet would tell him all he wanted to know.

"Long before the kid was born we'd agreed to go our own ways. Her fault, my fault? God knows. A bit of both, I suppose...oil and water. No grounds for a divorce, of course. Just a separation by mutual consent. She hung on in Toronto until Sheila turned up, then, without a word to me, cleared off back to England, taking the kid with her. She never told me how or where she first met Humphrey Marrable, but when I turned up in London about a year later, she was already living with him as his wife. A house in Lowndes Square, a country-house in Surrey, servants, chauffeur...the whole bag of tricks. A photo in *The Tatler*...that's how I first found out that Gwenny had committed bigamy. I got hold of her telephone number and rang her up. You can imagine what a panic that put her in..."

She'd agreed to meet him. A dingy little pub in a back-street near Victoria. Easy to picture the meeting. Skeet at his most sardonic, revelling in the situation, playing the devil with her nerves. She, curbing her temper, swallowing her pride, ready to do anything he wanted, provided he'd lie low and hold his tongue. A situation that must have appealed to Skeet's warped and cynical sense of humour.

He'd walked back with her through the wet February streets, and they'd finally struck a bargain. When old Marrable "passed on"—that was Gwenny's expression—she was to settle an annuity on Skeet of seven hundred a year. In the meantime he'd accept a cheque for five hundred, to be paid over within a week from the generous personal income already made over to her by the old man.

"I never set eyes on Gwenny again until we met in the solicitor's office about four months after the old boy had kicked the bucket. That, of course, was to arrange about the settlement. God knows! I had to take my hat off to her. She was so damned businesslike about it all. We sat in that office—just off St. James Street, if I remember—smiling at each other, tickled to death, ready at the drop of a hat to fly at each other's throats. And that's the way it's been with us ever since. Armed neutrality…grinning at each other and sticking out our tongues! Even after Gwenny had got her hands on the old man's fortune she could never be sure of me. Point is this—in his will Humphrey Marrable had naturally named her as his wife—which, of course, in the eyes of the law, she wasn't. So even after his death the money wasn't legally hers. She'd got hold of it by fraud, by false pretences. And since there were other members of his family still living…"

On the other hand, she must have guessed that Skeet would never talk. Not unless he were prepared to lose his seven hundred a year. He was as much up to the neck in it as she was. And for fifteen years he'd held his tongue. Until that afternoon, in fact, about three weeks ago, when Sheila had walked over from Cockfosters to seek his advice about Nigel Derry.

"You never get anything in this life without paying for it. That's trite enough, but true. There's always a balance sheet to reckon with. You've money to burn and cirrhosis of the liver. A constitution like an ox and nothing in your pocket. Freedom from want, eh? Well, I'd got that and a bit over, but I never knew what it was to be a father to my own daughter. My own damned fault, of course. No need to tell me that. But don't forget, if I'd blown the gaff about Gwenny's little bit of bigamy, we'd have all felt the draught—Sheila included. And, after all, we wanted her to have the best possible start in life. But you see the fix I was in, how tricky the situation was?"

Blampignon nodded. He'd been wondering when Skeet was going to bring the girl into the picture. Breaking in for the first time, he asked, "Your daughter...was she ever in South Africa?"

Skeet ran a hand round his two days' growth of beard and winked.

"The Isle of Man—that's as far as she ever got from England. Gwenny got a nurse to take charge of the kid a few months before she set up house with Marrable. The nurse thought that Gwenny was trying to hush up a little indiscretion, and naturally Gwenny didn't trouble to disillusion her."

"And after Marrable's death?"

"She wanted the child back, of course. She'd always had that in mind. So she put out a story about the child's parents being killed in a car crash near Jo'burg and took Sheila to live with her at Cockfosters as her adopted daughter. Ironic, eh? We both adored the child, but neither of us dared tell her the truth. I've seen her grow up from a kiddie to a young woman. We met and talked and got to know each other, but never as father and daughter. An affectionate niece, a privileged uncle—that's the sort of relationship it had to be. And then, about three weeks ago, she slipped over to see me in my studio..."

She'd been desperate, in tears, hurt and bewildered by her "Aunt Gwenny's" intractability about Nigel Derry. So she'd turned to Skeet for advice and Skeet had understood at once.

If Sheila were to marry then Gwenny would have to produce either the child's birth certificate or the document showing that she'd been legally adopted. The first she couldn't do, and the document didn't exist. A contingency that she'd long foreseen, of course, that she'd attempted to postpone by that inhuman clause in her will.

And in the face of his daughter's unhappiness, Skeet had at last come out into the open and told her the truth about her parentage.

"I didn't realise then the terrible predicament in which I was placing the child. I never stopped to think. I'd lived so long without a conscience, it never struck me that she might consider it her duty to go to the police. On the other hand, she knew that if she did she'd probably land me in court. After all, I'd connived with my wife to commit a fraud. Sheila wasn't slow in getting on to that. And this morning, in this very room…" Skeet made a curious indeterminate gesture and sat down on the edge of the bed, his head clasped in his hands. "What the hell does it matter anyway? You've taken the decision out of her hands. It's your pidgin now."

But it wasn't here, in this dingy little hotel bedroom, that the law would catch up with him. If the legality of Marrable's will were to be disputed it would be in the English courts, perhaps months hence, even years. A summary of Skeet's statement would have to be handed on to Scotland Yard, and there, from Blampignon's point of view, the matter would end.

He said, "Before I go…there's just one other little matter."

Skeet glanced up wearily. He didn't even trouble to look interested.

"Well?"

"Among your wife's circle of acquaintances was there a young chap…?"

Blampignon described the fellow who'd sent off the telegram from Le Touquet. Skeet shook his head.

"Not as far as I know. But I never saw half the toady-boys who came sniffing around after her money. A scar on the back of his hand—was that it?"

"His right hand…big, broad-shouldered…fair, curly hair…"

Skeet said musingly:

"A scar on the back of his right hand…" Then, suddenly, he clapped a hand to his thigh. "Good God! yes. I know the chap you mean. Anyway, that description fits him like a glove. I've never spoken to him, but I've seen him around the pubs in Folkestone."

"With your wife?"

"No. Pubs were never Gwenny's line of country. But I tell you who I did see talking to him on one occasion in the Billington Arms."

"Yes."

"That wall-eyed old soak—George Gammon!"

20

"No—I can't say I remember the chap. But you know how it is, a pub's like a *bistro*...you get hobnobbing with a fellow over a couple of drinks, and unless he's a regular at that particular house you never set eyes on him again."

"Skeet said it was only about three months ago when he saw you talking with the young man in the Billington Arms."

Gammon said triumphantly:

"Folkestone! The Billington Arms! That just bears out what I was saying. I doubt if I've set foot in the place twice in my life. Now if it had been the Talbot or the Dog and Bear... my usual stamping-grounds..."

They were lounging in a couple of wicker *chaises-longues* in the villa garden. Blampignon had found Gammon dozing there in the shade of the magnolia, his panama pulled down over his red and raddled face, his lips blowing in and out, his hands crossed on his paunch. More relaxed than he had been in the morning, less uneasy. Yet there was still something about him that got under Blampignon's skin. You couldn't pin him down—that was the trouble. He was so damned plausible that you didn't know what to believe. Over this meeting in the Billington Arms, for instance. It was quite possible that he *didn't* recall the fellow. On the other hand he was such an old hand at prevarication that he made even the truth sound like a lie.

"So you can't help us in tracing this young chap?"

"I'm sorry, old man...but there it is."

Even his affability was galling. One felt all the time that he was grinning up his sleeve, having one on a string. But over what? That was the point. The stabbing of André Duconte? The murder of Madame Marrable?

Nothing to be gained by hanging about the villa. Blampignon decided he'd return at once to Nice—a jerky and irritating drive along the Moyenne Corniche. The return of the fine weather had brought the traffic back on to the roads. To make matters worse it was Saturday, and from all round the district, and even further afield, the weekenders were converging on the coast.

Only a skeleton staff were at work in the offices of the *Sûreté Nationale*. Emile was off duty. No message on Blampignon's desk. Just an accumulation of routine paper work that he felt like kicking into the wastepaper basket. He wasn't really depressed, but on edge, frustrated. Five days had gone by since he'd been called to the Villa Paradou. He'd picked up a lot of information, got to know something of the dead woman's background, seen and questioned a number of her intimates, solved the relationship between her and Harry Skeet, between her and the girl. But how much further had he got where the actual murder was concerned? Derry, Skeet,

Gammon, Duconte—they'd all come under suspicion. And, one by one, in the face of the available evidence, he'd been forced to drop them off his list of suspects.

And now this big, curly-haired young fellow with the scar on his hand had come into the picture…

Blampignon picked up the telephone and got through to the girl on the internal switchboard.

"Put me through a call to Scotland Yard, will you? Superintendent Meredith, if you can get hold of him. If there's any delay, see that the call's kept in hand. I'll be hanging on here in my office."

Blampignon took up a report of a local shopbreaking incident and began to read it. The heat of the afternoon was rising to its peak. There wasn't a breath of air in the room. Even the flies circling under the ceiling seemed almost too listless to keep themselves on the wing. Drops of moisture were sliding off Blampignon's jowl and splashing on to his desk. Five, ten, fifteen minutes went by. Then the jarring note of the telephone.

A voice he recognised at the other end. The brisk voice of a man he'd worked with about four years before—a case involving an English forger, who'd been flooding the Côte d'Azur with spurious French banknotes. At that time Inspector, now Superintendent Meredith.

"Blampignon, by all that's wonderful! How are you? Run off your feet, I imagine. Anyway, it's good to hear your voice again. What's the weather like down there?"

Blampignon aired his opinion of it in no uncertain terms. It was raining cats and dogs in London. The temperature was in the lower fifties. And how was Madame Blampignon? For a moment the friendly exchanges went on, then Meredith enquired:

"Well, what's the trouble?"

"The Marrable murder."

"I thought as much. Something you want us to follow up over here?"

"Yes. I'm anxious to get a line on a young fellow who may be tied up with the case. I got some information from the *gendarmerie* at Le Touquet early this morning..."

The details followed. Presently Meredith was saying, "I can't promise to get back to you to-day with the result of our efforts. We'll get the Folkestone police on to it at once, of course. What about to-morrow? Where can I get in touch with you? It's Sunday, remember."

"I'll be at home all day, pottering around in the garden, seeing something of my wife for a change. Unless, of course, anything dramatic turns up. But by the look of things at the moment..."

"Good enough. If you'll let me have the number, I'll ring you there."

II

It was late on Sunday afternoon when Madame Blampignon appeared in the french windows and called her husband in to the telephone. He'd been drowsing in a deckchair, a newspaper over his face, his feet up on a hassock. Still half-drugged with sleep, he swallowed a prodigious yawn, staggered into the house, and took up the receiver.

"Hullo. Blampignon speaking."

"Meredith here. Well, we've found out what you wanted to know, and a good deal more. We've traced that young fellow all right."

"Excellent, *mon ami*...and the details?"

"William Harold Loftus, aged 31, of 14 Albion Crescent, Folkestone...that's in the Old Town not far from the harbour. The local inspector picked him up this morning, after a talk with the publican of the Billington Arms, and took him back to the station for questioning. He admitted to having met Gammon at the Billington. Not just on one occasion, as Gammon suggested, but regularly over a period of months."

"*Tiens!* So he knows Gammon well?"

"Too well for his present comfort, by the look of it. But I'll come to that in a moment. The point is that he flatly denied having been in Le Touquet on April 22nd. He swore he knew nothing about that telegram to Derry. At first, that is. But the inspector wasn't satisfied with Loftus's statement. Nothing he could put his finger on. Just a feeling that the chap was holding out on him...something in his manner. You know how it is?"

So he'd got in touch with Meredith and Meredith had driven down to Folkestone to interrogate Loftus himself.

"We grilled him for two solid hours without a break. We didn't get tough with him. Nothing of that sort. You know how we do this kind of thing over here. For a long time we didn't get anywhere. He'd got a passport all right. But he'd only made use of it once since its date of issue, and that was for a trip to Holland last year. But the local chaps knew the way he made a living, and that set me thinking. I was convinced from the start that if we could only get through his guard..."

The line wasn't too good, and several times Blampignon had to ask Meredith to repeat a phrase. But as the report came in, he knew, without any shadow of doubt, that this was the evidence he'd been waiting to hear. Curious how this one phone-call brought the whole of the Marrable case into focus, how all the little unrelated clues, like the coloured scraps in a kaleidoscope, suddenly coagulated into a clear and satisfying pattern. He was no longer asking himself where this fact and that fitted into the picture of the crime. Now it was obvious. So obvious that, ready to kick himself, he marvelled at his previous lack of perception.

A check-up here, a recapitulation there, a question answered, a further fact brought to light, and Blampignon was saying:

"No—that covers everything! I'll get on to the *gendarmerie* at Le Touquet without delay. No reason why they shouldn't get started on the enquiry before I join them to-night. And the alibi angle... I can leave you to deal with that, *mon ami*?"

"Of course."

Five minutes later Blampignon was in telephone touch with the director of the *Sûreté Nationale*. Ten minutes later he was ringing the airport at Nice. And a few minutes after that he was saying:

"Le Touquet? *Sûreté Nationale*, Nice...Blampignon speaking. Can you put me in touch with Inspector Bernard? At once, if possible. The matter's urgent."

III

Monday, Tuesday. A night flight from Le Touquet back to

Nice, and early on Wednesday morning Blampignon was once more in his office at the *Sûreté Nationale*. There was a report on his desk from Meredith. Blampignon read it through, smiling broadly to himself, grunting with satisfaction. No doubt about it now. The last pieces of the puzzle had slipped into place. He was on the brink of the final interrogation.

A cough. He glanced up. Emile was dithering in the doorway of the outer office.

"Eh bien?"

"Inspector Hamonet's on the telephone from the Commissariat at Menton. He rang earlier this morning, hoping you'd be in."

"All right—put him through."

A note of elation in Hamonet's voice.

"Well, that enquiry along the Avenue Thiers has paid off. I've picked up two witnesses there who have something to tell us. I won't bother you with the details, but it boils down to this. Gammon was seen in the Avenue Thiers a few minutes before nine-thirty, making for the Avenue Edouard VII. A few minutes later he was seen again opposite the church, running down the avenue towards the promenade."

"No doubt that it was Gammon?"

"No. We'd a full description to go on, remember. Both my witnesses would be prepared to swear in a court of law—"

"So that settles that, eh? Not that we need bother with the Duconte affair at the moment. Since we were last in touch things have been moving fast in the Marrable case. I've just returned from Le Touquet. You'd better let me bring you up to date…" Five minutes later Blampignon was saying, "Well, that's how things stand at the moment. I'm driving over with Emile directly after lunch."

"To the Villa Paradou?"

"Yes. I want you to meet us there—two o'clock sharp."

IV

There was nobody on the terrace. The garden was deserted. The foliage of the trees and shrubs hung flaccid and unstirring in the somnolent heat of the early afternoon. An automatic sprinkler was spinning slowly over a sere patch of lawn. The villa itself was silent, shuttered, like a house from which the occupants had fled at the rumour of an advancing enemy.

Unspeaking, keyed up with anticipation, the three men mounted the terrace steps. On this occasion the front-door was shut. At a nod from Blampignon, Emile rang the bell. A brief wait, then the sound of footsteps coming down the hall, the door opening, and Madame Fougère standing there, blinking in the brilliant sunlight, a startled look in her eyes. Blampignon snatched off his beret.

"M'sieur Gammon?"

"He's upstairs with Mam'selle Gaye."

"Anybody in the lounge?"

"No, M'sieur le Commissaire. Mam'selle Sheila's spending the day in Monte Carlo."

"Then we'll see him in there."

They didn't have long to wait. Emile was just handing Blampignon a clip of typewritten statements and reports, when Gammon sauntered in, his hands in his pockets, his ridiculous porcelain pipe sagging from a corner of his mouth.

There was something studied and insolent about his entry. Even when he realised that Blampignon wasn't alone he didn't seem put out. Gazing slowly round the room he observed derisively, "Quite a reception committee. I understand you wanted to see me, Inspector."

"Yes." Blampignon stumped over to the windows and, one by one, pushed open the shutters. "Sit down, will you."

Gammon dropped into an armchair, sprawling back with his legs crossed, puffing stolidly at his pipe. Behind him Emile had quietly slipped a notebook from his pocket. Hamonet was leaning against the door, his arms folded, his eyes fixed on the ceiling. Silence for a moment, save for the drowsy hum of a bee that had wandered in through the open window, the cool swish of the revolving sprinkler on the lawn outside. Blampignon, lighting his cigarette, seemed lost in thought.

Suddenly his heavy-lidded gaze shifted to Gammon.

"The night before Madame Marrable crossed to France—where were you, m'sieur?"

"Damn it! I've already told you. I returned with Miss Gaye to her cottage."

"She drove you there from Cockfosters in her car?"

"Yes."

"Arriving at the cottage?"

Gammon ran the stem of his pipe through his thinning hair.

"Sometime during the early afternoon. Three…three-thirty…somewhere about then."

"That evening—Thursday evening—did either of you leave the house?"

A split second hesitation, a wary light in his eye, a hint of uneasiness.

"No. We never set foot outside the cottage."

"Not even to visit a friend of yours in Folkestone?"

Gammon said sharply:

"A friend? What friend?"

Blampignon glanced down at the typewritten notes of Meredith's report.

"A young man by the name of William Harold Loftus."

The change in Gammon's expression was almost comical. His face seemed to crumple as if from the impact of a vicious and unexpected blow. He stared at Blampignon dumbfounded, his jaw hanging loose, his bleary eyes almost starting from their sockets. Nothing jaunty about him now. For a moment he seemed unable to find his voice.

Then he croaked out, "So you've...you've...?"

But he couldn't go on. All the fight had gone out of him. He was cornered and he knew it.

Blampignon nodded.

"Yes, we've found out a great deal from your friend Loftus. How you met him, for instance, on the evening of Wednesday, April 20th—that is, two days before Madame Marrable was due to leave for Cap Martin. How you sat in the car and discussed with him your little plan to murder madame. How, with his assistance, you intended to..." Blampignon broke off and flipped a finger against the sheaf of papers in his hand. "But it's all set out here in his official statement. Perhaps you'd care to read it—just to make sure how much we *do* happen to know."

Gammon shook his head. He seemed to sag there in his

chair, a glazed look in his eyes, twisting his pipe round and round between his stubby fingers.

Suddenly Blampignon tossed the wad of papers across to Emile and, moving away to the window, gazed out into the sun-drenched garden. A moment's silence. The tension was almost unbearable. Then flicking the butt of his cigarette out on to the terrace, Blampignon swung round and looked Gammon squarely in the face.

"It's not for me to advise you. It's up to you, of course—but if you wish to make a statement..."

Gammon lifted a hand and let it fall.

"Why not? It's all the same to me. I know when I'm beaten. I'll talk if you want me to." He got unsteadily to his feet, lurched towards the table and took up the decanter. "But before I do, for God's sake let me have a drink. There's a hell of a lot to remember and I want to get things straight. Give me a bit of time...just a couple of drinks. It's not going to be easy..."

21

He stood at the Varley cross-roads, watching Derry's car as it pulled away and swung out of sight round a corner. He glanced at his watch. It was ten-past eleven. If all went as arranged, in a few minutes Deborah would be along to drive him to Honeypot Cottage.

He lit his pipe, sat down gingerly on one of his battered suitcases, and began to run once more over the details of the job that lay ahead of him. First, the key—the spare key to the west door at Cockfosters that Gwenny always kept in the drawer of her bureau. Well, he hadn't forgotten that. It was in his pocket. So was Derry's lighter and the slip of paper bearing his handwriting that he'd managed to sneak from the pocket of the fellow's car.

He didn't know exactly what he was going to do with these articles, except that, somehow or other, they might be used to incriminate Derry. It was this idea, at any rate, that had fostered his impulse to drop the things in his pocket. Time enough to work over this angle and make something of it. About a quarter to nine that evening—that was when the wheels would really begin to turn.

With a sudden uprush of anger, he thought: By God! she's pushed me a bit too far this time. She's asked for it all right... throwing me out on my ear just because that bloody little gigolo of a Frenchman has caught her fancy...calling me a "disgusting old soak"...slapping my face...

But it was no good getting worked up. That was a mistake. Once you let your feelings run amok in your head, you were done for. He'd got to keep his wits about him, move with absolute assurance through the hazards of the days ahead, wary and cunning as a fox.

He eased a flask from his hip-pocket, uncapped it and took a generous nip of whisky. He felt better after that, more relaxed. It was warm and pleasant in the April sunshine. The air was as soft as silk, the sky cloudless. A little wave of optimism swept through him. He felt absolutely sure of himself. This point, that point...everything was accounted for. In his head he carried a strict time-table of events. As far as he could see, he'd left nothing to chance.

II

"What is it, dear? What's the matter?"

"My diary! I've just remembered. I left it on the table beside my bed at Cockfosters. Of all the damned stupid things to do! I've got to get hold of it. At once if possible... before anybody gets their hands on it. If Gwenny ever stuck her nose into it...then heaven help us!"

Deborah spoke anxiously.

"You mean you've written something in it about… about *us*?"

"Pretty well everything that's ever happened between us, my dear."

"Not about you coming to stay here at the cottage?"

He nodded. She looked at him, aghast.

"But what are we going to do? Even if it hasn't been noticed already, Gwenny's bound to see it when she comes back from her stay at the villa."

"I've got to get hold of it at once…to-night."

"You mean, drive over to Cockfosters in the car?"

"Why not? It's only twenty-five miles. I could be over there before ten."

She said with a bewildered expression: "But what are you going to do, dear? Gwenny thinks you're in London. You can't just turn up and tell her that you've—"

He tapped his pocket.

"I've got the key of the west door in my pocket. I forgot to leave it behind when I left this morning. I can sneak up the back-stairs to my bedroom, and with any luck—" He broke off and added: "You'll come with me? You could wait in the car. I'll get out and walk up the drive, so you needn't worry about anybody seeing us together."

"You'd like me to come?"

He smiled, slipped an arm about her waist and gave her a little hug.

"Of course." There was a blissful, foolish expression on her face. She was like clay in his hands, wanting only to please him, to fall in with his every wish. He kissed her lightly on the cheek. "Now slip upstairs, my dear, and put on your hat and coat, while I run the car out of the garage."

He picked up his own hat and overcoat in the hall, flicked on his pocket-torch, and went out to the garage. A clear, star-lit night, with only a breath of wind soughing through the elms that ringed the cottage. A scent of violets on the air. He unbolted the doors, slipped into the driving-seat of the car and pressed the starter-button.

He was smiling to himself. Not without reason. He'd never kept a diary in his life!

III

The car was there all right. Drawn up at the foot of the wide curving steps, ready for Gwenny's departure in the early morning. On the back-seat, just as he'd anticipated, her enormous black cabin-trunk. It was always left ready like that. That's where he had the advantage. He knew how everything ticked in the place, the rules that Gwenny had laid down, the things she did and the things she didn't do, the way she ordered her life. No light in the window of Gwenny's bedroom. Sheila's room, at the other end of the house, was also in darkness. No doubt, thinking of the exhausting day ahead, they'd gone up to bed early. The servants' rooms were in a wing at the back. Nothing to worry about there. After the beds had been turned down during dinner, they never entered the front part of the house.

As he turned the key in the lock of the west door, the clock in the copper-domed turret above the stables chimed ten. He switched on his pocket-torch, closed the door so that it wouldn't slam, and stood listening. The tick of the grandfather clock at the end of the passage, the faint stirring of the night breeze. No other sound. He went up the back stairs, along a short passage, and came to the main landing. Gwenny's door was the first on the left. Going down on one knee, he peered through the keyhole. The room was still in darkness. No scroop as he turned the handle. Slowly the rays of his torch travelled over the floor and came to rest on the bed.

No movement. Her breathing was regular, unhurried. The rays of his torch went on travelling, this way and that, searching for the brief-case in which Gwenny always placed the documents she'd need on her journey—passport, *carnet*, insurance papers, maps. She always collected them overnight and locked them away in the case. It was there all right—on her writing-table. He picked up the brief-case and tucked it under his arm.

Her key-ring next—the key of the brief-case, the car keys, the key of the cabin-trunk, the villa—each, as he knew, neatly labelled with ivory tags. Her handbag was on the bedside table. He took up the bag, made sure the keys were in it, and went out on to the landing.

A moment or so later he was out on the drive unlocking the door of the grey saloon, aware that it had been parked a couple of yards from the crest of the long rise that mounted to the house. Slipping the brief-case and the handbag into one of the wide dashboard pockets, he took off the handbrake, made sure the engine was out of gear, and moved round to the back of the car. At first he couldn't budge it. Then, little by little, it began to inch forward, its tyres crackling faintly over the gravel. When he felt the car gathering momentum, he ran forward and jammed on the brake. Then he climbed into the driving-seat, took off the brake for an instant, and made sure that the car would move off down the slope without having to start up the engine.

He took the bunch of keys from the handbag and unlocked the brief-case. Then, replacing the keys in the handbag, he gently closed the car door and went back upstairs to Gwenny's bedroom.

Again the rays of his torch swept searchingly around the room. He noticed the cup and vacuum flask on the table beside the bed. He picked them up, went over to the washbasin, swilled a little coffee round the bottom of the cup, emptied the flask, and dribbled a little water into the basin to clean it. Then he took the dirty cup and the flask and replaced them on the table.

The rays of his torch began to travel again...

There was a big silk cushion in the armchair by the window. His memory hadn't let him down over that. So far his memory hadn't let him down over anything. Whenever he and Gwenny had set off for the villa, the preparations for departure had always been the same. The overnight farewells, the car left ready on the drive, the cabin-trunk on the back-seat because it was too cumbersome to go into the boot, the brief-case in her bedroom, the keys in her bag, the flask of coffee on the bedside table—everything organised, teed up for the early morning run to the dockside.

He laid the torch on the table, shining it directly on to the bed, crossed to the chair and picked up the cushion...

Curious how little Gwenny struggled. A spasmodic jerking of her body beneath the green eiderdown, her hands rising above the coverlet, groping for the cushion, her jewelled rings sparkling in the cone of light. Then her fingers opening, contracting, once, twice, her body shuddering for a moment, then going limp.

He waited for a time, still thrusting down on the cushion to make quite sure that she was dead. Then slowly he straightened up. Beyond the window he could hear the night breeze hissing through the creepers, the clock above the stables chiming the first quarter of the hour. Nobody moving in the house. He stayed a moment to get his breath, wiping his sleeve across his forehead, then, averting his eyes from Gwenny's face, he replaced the cushion in the armchair, gathered up her clothes that were laid out ready for the morning and tied them into a bundle. Then he pulled down the bedclothes, stripped off her nightdress, and wrapped the body in a car-rug that he'd noticed on a chair beside the dressing-table.

Somehow, with the torch gripped in his right hand, he managed to work his arms under the body and lift it from the bed, together with the bundle of clothes. He crossed to the door and, hooking it closed with his foot, went down the landing, turned along the passage and came to the head of the stairs. He took the stairs one tread at a time, circumspectly, without haste, knowing that a single slip might spell disaster.

A moment or so later he was stumbling over the uneven flagstones of the courtyard. In an angle of the house, a few yards from the west door, there was a big galvanised rainwater tank. He eased the body on to this, locked the door and slipped the key in his pocket. A hasty pull at his hip-flask. A moment to work the cramp from his limbs, then, shouldering the body in a fireman's lift, the knotted bundle of clothes hooked over his arm, he moved round to the front of the house and set off down the drive.

IV

Twenty yards short of where Deborah was waiting in the car, just inside the entrance gates to the park, he lowered the body and the bundle of clothes on to the grass bank under the lime trees. So far he'd bungled nothing, but he wasn't fooled into believing that he was yet out of the wood. This was the critical phase. Up to that moment everything had been more or less foreseeable. He'd been able to anticipate, to plan ahead, with only himself to blame if anything went wrong. Now he was staking everything on the reactions of another, taking a chance, uncertain which way the cat was going to jump.

The moon was now rising. A faint wash of light filtered down between the interlocking branches of the avenue. He began to lumber towards the car, the breath rasping in his throat, his heart thudding behind his ribs. Hearing his hurried footsteps on the gravel, Deborah got out of the car and came a few paces down the drive to meet him. There was a note of anxiety in her voice.

"Is it all right, dear? Did you find it?"

"Find it?"

"Your diary."

In the turmoil of the moment he'd forgotten the excuse he'd thought up for the drive over to Cockfosters. He said breathlessly, "There's been an accident."

"What do you mean?"

"It's Gwenny."

"She's…she's hurt?"

He shook his head.

"It's worse than that. Even now I can't understand how it happened. I was up in the bedroom looking for that diary. I didn't think anybody had heard me enter the house. Perhaps Gwenny just happened to catch sight of me as I went into the room. Anyway, she suddenly appeared in the doorway…"

His voice went grating on, giving Deborah no time to interrupt, to question him, slowly, graphically, building up a picture in her mind. Gwenny entering the room, knowing why he was there, referring to the diary, in a white-hot temper, because he'd dared to deceive her by sneaking off with Deborah to Honeypot Cottage. Her scathing innuendoes whipping up his anger, goading him to answer back. Then, shrilling like a fishwife, she'd called Deborah a name that had made him see red. He'd taken a threatening step towards her, so that she'd recoiled, stumbled against a chair and lost her balance. And in falling back she'd hit her head against the sharp corner of the bedpost…

"For a moment I thought she was just unconscious. Then I realised that she was no longer breathing, that her heart had stopped beating. Nobody seemed to have heard anything of the dust-up. They'd gone up early to bed, I suppose, and were fast asleep. At first I thought of rousing Sheila, calling the servants…to tell them what had happened. Then I realised the ghastly fix I was in. Suppose they wouldn't take my word for it that it was an accident? Suppose they were suspicious of my story and got in touch with the police? God knows! I wouldn't have a leg to stand on. Sheila knew that I hated Gwenny for the damnable way she'd treated me…"

A note of self-pity, of desperation, was creeping into his voice. He was acting now as he'd never acted before, straining every nerve to rouse her sympathy, to enlist her help, to drive home to her the terrible situation in which he was placed.

"I stood there for a moment, trying to make up my mind what to do. Clear out of the house as quickly as I could? But what was the use? You know how the police get to work on these things. A clue here, a clue there…and in the long run they always catch up with you. Suppose they found out that I'd been to the house to-night. You can see what they'd want to know. Why had I left Gwenny lying there and made myself scarce? If it was an accident, why hadn't I roused the others? Only a man with a guilty conscience would have acted like that. And if they charged me with murder…"

Rigid with terror, she uttered a stifled cry.

"But if it happened as you said…if you never touched Gwenny…?"

"Do you think they'd take my word for that?"

"But if it were the truth…?"

"The truth!" He grasped her suddenly by the wrists. "Listen, Deborah—do you think they'd believe my story about sneaking into the place to get hold of that diary? Of course they wouldn't! And how had I got into the house anyhow? That's another thing they'd want to know. Suppose I told the police that I'd walked out of Cockfosters this morning with the key of the west door in my pocket? That's true enough, but in the circumstances…good heavens! don't you see?… I'd never be able to convince them I hadn't crept into the place to-night *meaning* to kill Gwenny." His voice grew more urgent, more persuasive. "Listen, my dear—you've got to help me. If you're ready to do that, then I think I can see a way out of this mess."

"Help you?...of course...but how? What do you want me to do?"

He drew in a deep breath. This was the crucial moment.

"To drive Gwenny's car to the ferry and cross with it to Boulogne...to travel on her passport."

She stared at him, dumbfounded.

"To impersonate my sister?"

"Why not? Nobody's going to suspect. Why should they? You'll be driving Gwenny's car. All the official documents will be signed in her name. You're the same height, with the same coloured eyes and hair. As for the photo in her passport...I've always said it was more like you than Gwenny."

The clearance papers for the car, of course, would have to be signed at the Customs office. But their handwriting was remarkably alike. Easy for her to dash off a passable replica of Gwenny's signature. The car was ready at the front-door. All she had to do was to slip into the driving-seat, take off the handbrake, and coast as far as she could down the drive. Once she was well clear of the house, of course, she could start up the engine. Just before it grew light—that would be the safest time for her to leave. Too big a risk to drive the car away during the night in case anybody should wake and notice that it had gone.

"You won't understand what all this is about, but don't ask me to explain anything now, my dear. I daren't waste time going into details. But once you've landed at Boulogne, take the coast road that runs through Étaples and Le Touquet to Abbeville. There's a map in the car...it shows the route clearly enough on that. Unless anything goes wrong—and there's no reason why it should—I'll be waiting for you somewhere along the road, a mile or so north of Étaples. If the boat docks on time, you should be there about half-past twelve."

She said in a bewildered voice:

"But Gwenny?… Suppose Sheila or any of the staff look into the bedroom to-morrow before they leave…?"

"I wrapped her body in a rug and carried it from the house. Don't you see, if you'll do as I say, nobody's going to suspect that she didn't drive off to the boat as arranged. She always slips away without waking anybody." He placed his hands on her shoulders. "You'll do this for me, Deborah. It's my only chance. You won't let me down?"

She shook her head mutely, clinging to him for a moment, no longer troubling to hold back her tears, caught up in a sudden nightmare of events that had brought her to the brink of hysteria. He held her close, waiting until the storm had passed, curbing his impatience. Gradually she got her feelings under control. He said:

"The summer-house in the shrubbery…you'll be all right there until it's time to leave for the boat?"

"Yes! Yes! You're not to worry about me. You've got to think only of yourself. You must get away from here as quickly as you can."

She pressed his hand, too overwrought to speak again, and, turning away, walked off slowly up the drive. As she did so he heard the stable-clock in the distance chime the third quarter of the hour.

Ten forty-five! A flicker of a smile hovered about his lips. Everything was still running to schedule.

22

ALBION CRESCENT, FOLKESTONE—AN ILL-LIT STREET of mean and grimy houses sloping down towards the harbour. Outside No. 14 he pulled up the car and took a cautious look up and down the road. There was nobody in sight. The body lay doubled up under the rug on the floor at the back of Deborah's roomy pre-war saloon. He hadn't forgotten to arrange the limbs before rigor mortis set in so that, later, the body would fit into the trunk.

He didn't trouble to get out of the car. He knew Bill Loftus would be watching for him from one of the darkened windows on the ground-floor—11.30 he'd arranged to be there. It was just two minutes after the half-hour. He wasn't wrong in his surmise. Almost at once the door opened and, without a word, Bill got into the car and dropped into the bucket-seat beside him. As he let in the clutch, Gammon said:

"Well, is everything fixed up?"

"Yes—everything's O.K. And the little business...?"

Gammon gave a backward jerk of his head.

"Under the rug... It went off without a hitch."

"And the sister?"

"She's playing all right."

It took them twenty minutes to drive to Soundings Cove, mostly through empty and twisting lanes, with only an occasional cottage to break the monotony of the upland pastures. They didn't speak much on the way. There wasn't much to talk about. Only the previous evening, after a quick drink at the Billington, they'd parked the car in a deserted side-street and sat there discussing every detail of this trip.

And now it was all going as they'd planned. Earlier that evening, just after dusk, Loftus had run the *Mirabel* from her moorings at Folkestone along to Soundings Cove. Nothing much in that to arouse attention, because, out of the holiday season when his two pleasure launches were always kept busy, he often took a line and a jar of clams and went night-fishing. From Soundings Cove he'd trudged up the cliff-path, prospecting for a suitable spot in which to conceal Deborah's car, and eventually hitch-hiked his way back into the town.

Suddenly Loftus rapped out:

"O.K. Sharp left here. And watch out for your springs. It's a hell of a road."

Little more than a cart-track, bordered by a hedge of wind-bitten thorn. Two hundred yards of this, then the lane dipped suddenly and came to a sudden stop.

Loftus observed:

"A disused chalk-pit. You can run the car in among that clump of elder. Not that anybody's likely to stooge around this time of the year. The cliff-path's farther to the right. I've a torch in my pocket, in case you forgot."

Fifteen minutes later they'd manhandled the body and the bundle of clothes down the cliff-path and placed them in the launch.

II

Nodding towards the *Mirabel* which had been hauled above the high-water line, Loftus said, "Well, she can lie up here all day under the overhang of the cliffs without anybody spotting her."

He'd run the boat into a sandy cove some miles north of Étaples. Not by chance. He knew this stretch of the coast like the back of his hand. Based on Le Touquet just after the war, he'd spent a couple of months as a sergeant in the Engineers clearing the beaches round about of mines. It was just growing light. Swathes of filmy mist hung over the water. The breeze had freshened with the dawn and the air had grown chilly. Despite his heavy overcoat and the several nips he'd taken from his flask during the night, Gammon was shivering. He asked:

"Where's this path you were talking about?"

"Round the next bluff."

"Then we'd better get moving before the sun gets up."

They lifted the body from the boat, still shrouded in the rug, and soon, stumbling and sweating, they were carrying it, together with the bundle of clothes, up the shallow gully that mounted to the cliff-top. A flat landscape still half-wrapped in darkness. A little way off to their right, a tangle of stunted trees and undergrowth in a bowl-shaped hollow. Between them and this hollow, a rutted farm-track, scoring a dead straight line into the grey and hazy distance.

Thinking of the rough map Loftus had sketched on the back of an envelope the previous night, Gammon nodded towards the trees.

"Is that the spot where you thought we might lie up?"

"That's it. A good six hours before we need get out on the main road. Might be an idea for you to catch up on your sleep. You've a hell of a long drive in front of you."

They dropped down into the hollow, the rug slung between them like a sagging stretcher, and hid the body and the clothes in the undergrowth. Gammon's eyelids were already drooping. He barely had the strength to keep on his feet. Loftus said:

"You get your head down while you can. I've a basket of grub in the launch. I'll slip down and get it."

For a moment Gammon sat there, sucking at his empty pipe. He was thinking of the telegram he was going to send to Derry, wondering how best to word it. Somewhere in mid-Channel the idea had come to him how best to swing suspicion on to Derry. He'd get Loftus to send a telegram from Le Touquet. Better than sending it himself, in case the police checked back. It was a lucky break running into Loftus again a couple of months ago in the Billington. Four years since he'd last set eyes on him. Luckier still what he'd happened to find out about Loftus and Connie Thorne. She'd been picked up in a Soho side-street in the small hours with a knife wound in her back. Not that she'd died of the wound, but his knowledge of the affair had put Loftus in the right frame of mind to co-operate when he'd first broached the subject of this little trip across the Channel.

He looked at his watch. It was ten-past six. By now

Deborah should be well away from Cockfosters, heading for Canterbury and the Dover road. Terrified, no doubt, with her nerves stretched to breaking point, thinking of the ordeal that lay ahead of her. But she wouldn't let him down. He was convinced of that.

His mouth opened in a long shuddering yawn. Loftus was right. A hell of a drive in front of him. He ought to get some sleep.

Turning up his coat collar, he stretched himself full length on his back, pillowing his head on his hands, seeing the sky above him growing light, the first low-slanting rays of the sun gilding the high branches of the trees.

A few minutes later he was dead to the world...

III

Shortly after midnight, about a hundred and fifty miles south of Paris, he pulled the car on to the verge a little way up a side road, and shut off the engine. Save for a couple of stops for a drink and a snack, he'd been driving without a break since one o'clock. He hadn't had his meals at a restaurant on the *Route Nationale*. He'd turned aside to one of the many villages lying just off the highway. It was here, too, that he'd had the tank of the car refilled.

Now as he lounged there behind the wheel, easing the cramp from his limbs, he was thinking back to the day's events. It had been about noon when he and Loftus had left their hideout in the hollow and walked down the cart-track to the main road. Twenty minutes later the grey saloon had come in sight, braking to a stop as, waving their arms, they stepped out from the bushes in which they'd been lurking. A hug, a kiss for Deborah, a discreet but ardent reunion, a hurried and sketchy explanation, putting her *au fait* with the situation, as with Loftus at the wheel they'd driven back to the hollow. There, keeping Deborah discreetly out of the way, they'd emptied the contents of the cabin-trunk on the floor of the car, added to it the bundle of clothes taken from Gwenny's bedroom, and substituted the body.

Then, leaving Deborah to get some sleep, warning her to keep out of sight until Loftus returned, he'd driven him the mile or so into Le Touquet to send off the telegram to Derry. That was the last he'd seen of Loftus. For the rest of the day Loftus and Deborah were to lie low, crossing back to Soundings Cove in the launch after dark. From there Deborah was to drive back to the cottage.

A few hours' sleep, that's what he needed now. He switched off the side-lights, the dashboard light, slumped yet further back in his seat, legs extended, eyes closed, and slid away into unconsciousness…

It was seven hours later when he awoke, cramped, chilled, a sour taste in his mouth. It was already broad daylight. Cursing under his breath, he started up the engine, swung the car on to the road, turned back on to the *Route Nationale*, put his foot down hard on the accelerator and kept it there. He'd planned to reach the villa sometime after dark on Sunday. Five hundred and fifty miles still to do. It wasn't by any means impossible, but he'd have to keep moving, step up the pace a bit.

By midday he was in Lyons. From the post-office on the Quai Gailleton he sent off the telegram to the Fougères.

DELAYED—DON'T EXPECT ME UNTIL TUESDAY
AFTERNOON—MARRABLE.

Leaving the locked car parked a little off the quayside, he
dropped into a back-street café and had a hurried lunch. Forty
minutes later he was on his way again.

Vienne, Valence…somewhere short of Montelimar he
again turned off the highway to a nearby village and had a
meal at the local *hostellerie.* That night he slept a good eight
hours with the car parked a few hundred yards up an unfre-
quented lane ten miles north of Orange.

A little over two hundred miles still to go. He was no
longer worried. Barring accidents, he should make it with
time to spare.

IV

At exactly twenty-past ten on Sunday night he swung the car
through the open gates of the Villa Paradou. Everything as
he'd anticipated. The house shuttered, in darkness. Nobody
about. His telegram to the Fougères had obviously taken care
of that.

He took the keys from Gwenny's handbag, opened the
front-door, and stood in the hall for a moment, listening. Not
a sound. Not even the ticking of a clock.

He went out to the car, dragged the cabin-trunk from the
back-seat, hauled it up the terrace steps and in through the
door. Then, dropping to his knees, he unlocked the trunk,
pulled the car-duster from his pocket and vigorously polished
away all possible trace of his fingerprints. His thoughts at that

moment running on to the discovery of the body, picturing the scene. The Fougères on Tuesday morning, no doubt, making ready for their mistress's return, unlocking the door, stepping into the hall and...

His reflections came to an abrupt stop. He sprang up, every nerve in his body taut and tingling with apprehension. Somewhere upstairs a door had been opened. There were footsteps padding along the landing, coming stealthily down the stairs...

The next instant he was stumbling down the steps, groping for the handle of the car door, fumbling for the starter-button. Anticipating the possibility of a quick getaway he'd had the sense to turn the car before shutting off the engine. A flood of light streamed suddenly from the hall. But by the time the shadowy, gesticulating figure appeared on the terrace the saloon was already moving forward...

V

Up on the Grand Corniche he rid himself of the contents of the trunk. The brief-case and handbag he later threw into a ravine.

Nice, Cannes, Aix-en-Provence, Avignon—the road back. Nearly eight hundred miles of it. He drove like an automaton, sleeping, eating when he felt like it, willing himself to go on when every muscle in his body was cramped and aching, talking crazily to himself to keep awake.

Lyons again, Mâcon, Chalon-sur-Saône...

By Tuesday afternoon he was north of Paris and the tension in him began to unwind. Midnight, Tuesday, at the little cove north of Étaples…that was the deadline he'd fixed with Loftus.

By sundown he was running through Le Touquet. A few miles beyond Étaples he pulled up, waited until the road was clear, and backed the car in among the bushes bordering the dunes. He switched off the engine for the last time, felt in his pocket for Derry's lighter, the paper bearing his handwriting, and dropped them on the floor of the car. After that he took up the duster and began diligently to polish every surface that might have taken the impress of his fingerprints.

Then, moving out on to the road, he trudged off through the gathering darkness, making his way wearily to the cove.

23

"BUT, FOR GOD'S SAKE, GET THIS STRAIGHT!" GAMMON
jerked his head towards the ceiling. "She never suspected that
I hadn't told her the truth. An accident, that's what I said,
and she still believes that was how it happened. You've got
me in a corner all right, but you can't bring anything against
Deborah. She's innocent. You've got to believe that. She did
what she did to get me out of trouble. When we drove over to
Cockfosters that night, she never thought for a moment that
I had everything worked out beforehand…that I was going
there because I'd made up my mind to put an end to Gwenny."
He paused for a moment, breathing heavily, a hand pressed
to his ribs. Then, taking a gulp from the tumbler beside him,
he went on: "God knows, I've never had much respect for
women. I suppose I've been mixing too long with the wrong
sort. But these last few weeks—perhaps for the first time
in my life—I've known what it meant to live with someone
who really cared for me. Right from the start, once Gwenny
was out of the way, I'd made up my mind to ask Deborah to

marry me. No need to tell me what you're thinking. That I'd be on easy street for the rest of my life once she'd cleaned up on her inheritance...that this was one of the reasons why I decided to get rid of Gwenny. Well, there's a lot in that. No point in denying it. But these last few days I've begun to look at Deborah in a different light. I've wanted to marry her, not merely for her money, but for herself. That's damned funny when you come to think of it, because as things are..." He lifted his shoulders, heaved himself slowly from his chair and moved unsteadily to the table. With a shaky hand he slopped himself another drink and turned to Blampignon. "As a matter of fact, you may as well know...yesterday morning...I proposed to her. She agreed to marry me. Not at once...in three months' time. But if she'd known the truth about that night...about Gwenny... Damn it all! you see what I'm getting at? Do you think she'd have been ready to tie herself up with a man who'd murdered her own sister? Ever since we arrived down here at the villa...can't you imagine how she's felt? Wondering if, at any moment, you'd hit on the truth...sick with worry on my account, terrified...thinking that perhaps...every time you walked into the place...that you'd...you'd..."

His voice suddenly slurred into incoherence. He staggered back against the table, gasping for breath, a hand to his forehead, the sweat breaking out on his face. Even as Blampignon moved forward to help him to a chair, the glass slipped from his fingers, and he slid heavily to the floor.

Hamonet came quickly across the room. Blampignon was already kneeling, his arm under Gammon's shoulders, loosening his collar.

"What is it?"

"Heart attack by the look of it." He said over his shoulder to Emile, "Get hold of Madame Fougère. Tell her to ring the nearest doctor. And tell her to hurry."

Gammon's lips were still moving. He was evidently struggling to say something. Blampignon bent lower.

"What is it, *mon ami*?"

He whispered.

"You've got to believe…she…she still thinks…an accident…you've got to…"

But he couldn't say any more. There was an empty look in his eyes. Beneath the gentle pressure of his fingers, Blampignon felt the pulse flutter unevenly for a moment, then cease. Slowly he slipped his arm from under Gammon's shoulders and got to his feet. Hamonet looked at him enquiringly. Blampignon nodded. Outside in the hall he could hear Madame Fougère shrilling over the telephone:

"Yes…yes…the Villa Paradou…Madame Marrable's place…on the right about half-way up the hill…"

Emile came in, made ready to say something, then, glancing down at the body, held his tongue. Out in the garden old Fougère had turned off the sprinkler and was busy winding in the hose. A faint breeze stirred the fronds of the palm trees. The heady scent of carnations drifted in through the open window…

With a preoccupied air, Blampignon fished for his packet of *Bastos*, stuck a cigarette in the corner of his mouth and fumbled for his matches. He was thinking to himself how Gammon had nearly got away with it. Just one little slip. That was all. He looked across at Hamonet and lifted his massive shoulders.

"*Eh bien*, a curious case."

"In what way?"

"Well, hasn't it occurred to you? The telegram. If it hadn't been for that we might never have broken the fellow's alibi. We'd never have tumbled to the fact that Madame Marrable was murdered on the other side of the Channel."

"Telegram? I don't quite...what telegram?"

Narrowing his eyes, Blampignon drew slowly on his cigarette and watched the smoke rise and fan out under the ceiling.

"The one he got Loftus to send to Derry," he said. "The telegram from Le Touquet."

If you've enjoyed
A Telegram from Le Touquet,
you won't want to miss

the most recent BRITISH LIBRARY CRIME CLASSIC
published by Poisoned Pen Press,
an imprint of Sourcebooks.

poisonedpenpress.com

Don't miss these favorite British Library Crime Classics available from Poisoned Pen Press!

Mysteries written during the Golden Age of Detective Fiction, beloved by readers and reviewers

Antidote to Venom
by Freeman Wills Crofts

Bats in the Belfry
by E. C. R. Lorac

Blood on the Tracks:
Railway Mysteries
edited by Martin Edwards

Calamity in Kent
by John Rowland

Christmas Card Crime
and Other Stories
edited by Martin Edwards

Cornish Coast Murder
by John Bude

Continental Crimes
edited by Martin Edwards

Crimson Snow: Winter Mysteries
edited by Martin Edwards

Death in the Tunnel
by Miles Burton

Death of a Busybody
by George Bellairs

Death on the Riviera
by John Bude

Fell Murder
by E. C. R. Lorac

Incredible Crime
by Lois Austen-Leigh

Miraculous Mysteries
edited by Martin Edwards

Murder at the Manor
edited by Martin Edwards

Murder in the Museum
by John Rowland

Murder of a Lady
by Anthony Wynne

Praise for the
British Library Crime Classics

★"Carr is at the top of his game in this taut whodunit... The British Library Crime Classics series has unearthed another worthy golden age puzzle."

—*Publishers Weekly*, STARRED Review,
for *The Lost Gallows*

★"A wonderful rediscovery."
—*Booklist*, STARRED Review, for *The Sussex Downs Murder*

★"First-rate mystery and an engrossing view into a vanished world."
—*Booklist*, STARRED Review, for *Death of an Airman*

★"A cunningly concocted locked-room mystery, a staple of Golden Age detective fiction."
—*Booklist*, STARRED Review, for *Murder of a Lady*

"The book is both utterly of its time and utterly ahead of it."
—*New York Times Book Review* for *The Notting Hill Mystery*

★ "As with the best of such compilations, readers of classic mysteries will relish discovering unfamiliar authors, along with old favorites such as Arthur Conan Doyle and G.K. Chesterton."
—*Publishers Weekly*, STARRED Review, for *Continental Crimes*

"In this imaginative anthology, Edwards—president of Britain's Detection Club—has gathered together overlooked criminous gems."
—*Washington Post* for *Crimson Snow*

★"The degree of suspense Crofts achieves by showing the growing obsession and planning is worthy of Hitchcock. Another first-rate reissue from the British Library Crime Classics series."
—*Booklist*, STARRED Review, for *The 12.30 from Croydon*

★"Not only is this a first-rate puzzler, but Crofts's outrage over the financial firm's betrayal of the public trust should resonate with today's readers."
—*Booklist*, STARRED Review, for *Mystery in the Channel*

★"This reissue exemplifies the mission of the British Library Crime Classics series in making an outstanding and original mystery accessible to a modern audience."
—*Publishers Weekly*, STARRED Review, for *Excellent Intentions*

"A book to delight every puzzle-suspense enthusiast"
—*New York Times* for *The Colour of Murder*

★"Edwards's outstanding third winter-themed anthology showcases 11 uniformly clever and entertaining stories, mostly from lesser known authors, providing further evidence of the editor's expertise... This entry in the British Library Crime Classics series will be a welcome holiday gift for fans of the golden age of detection."
—*Publishers Weekly*, STARRED Review, for *The Christmas Card Crime and Other Stories*

Poisoned Pen
PRESS

poisonedpenpress.com